Chalice of the Rainbow

VICTORIA OSBORNE-BROAD

Book one of the Jewels of the Rainbow trilogy

Victoria Osborne - Broad

Paperback ISBN: 978-1-9999772-6-9
Ebook ISBN: 978-1-9999772-7-6
First published in 2018
Publication support
TJ INK
tjink.co.uk
Printed and bound in Great Britain by
TJ International, Padstow, Cornwall

In memory of
Allan Morley Butler
With thanks

Contents list

Chapter One

Thursday 26th June 2014

The shaft of blue light blazed out as the sun caught the centre of the stone. The force of that beam should have struck everyone in the street, yet as Gerry stared, dazzled, people just walked past her as though nothing had happened. It was as if she alone had seen that flash of sudden glory coming from the tray on the stall. As the glowing colour began to fade, Gerry gazed around, bewildered, then saw she was being watched.

The woman standing behind the bric-a-brac stall was wearing a long green dress and had dark eyes and rippling black hair, tied back loosely. She was staring at Gerry as if the young woman in front of her was the only person in the street, or even in all Penzance. The stallholder's gaze was so intense that Gerry wondered if the woman had mistaken her for someone else. No-one could care that much about a trinket. Gerry meant to step back and turn away, but found instead that she'd picked up the stone from the tray.

Even without the flare of light that had caught at her, the depth of the blue was enchanting. The colour was so like sapphire that Gerry was sure the stone must be way out of her range. She looked at the tray she'd picked it up from. A handwritten card lay on it: "Everything on this tray £1.50". She looked up, startled, and met the eyes of the stallholder. The woman had moved nearer, and again Gerry's instinct was to retreat - but she was still holding the blue stone.

The stone was set in battered gold-coloured metal. Gerry tore her eyes away, needing to say something to break the unnerving silence.

'It's beautiful,' she said. 'But what would I do with it?'

The stallholder leaned over to take the stone. Gerry felt a small shock as it left her fingers.

'Look,' the woman said, turning the stone over. Her voice was deep, and carried the same urgency as her eyes had. 'Look,' she repeated, 'you see these two loops on the back? You could wear it on your gold chain.'

Gerry didn't like being pushed into anything, and wanted to say no, but she couldn't help taking a closer look. The stallholder was right; the chain Gerry always wore would fit through the metal loops as if they'd been made for each other. It seemed only right that this beautiful thing should go with her most treasured possession.

'All right, I'll take it,' Gerry said, and thought she saw a flash of triumph in those dark, intense eyes. What, she wondered, would this woman have done if she'd refused, had put the stone back on the tray and turned away? It was an uncomfortable idea.

She handed over the £1.50, and left with the stranger's eyes following her. Eager to get away, Gerry hurried down Causewayhead through the lunchtime shoppers thronging the pedestrianised street. She passed shops selling everything from flowers and pet foods to stationery or furniture, and stopped outside a small art gallery. Her straight red-gold hair had come

2

loose and was falling across her face. Pushing it back behind her ears, Gerry looked carefully at the stone clutched in her hand. The setting was badly scratched, but that didn't matter; she was only interested in the stone itself. If it had been a real sapphire, Gerry guessed that such a large one would cost more than she earned in a year.

The next shop window had a display of watches, rings, pendants and small silver ornaments. Gerry had gone into this shop one day during her lunch break, asking the price of some earrings in the window. Mr. Trewartha, the elderly owner, had probably guessed she couldn't afford them, but he'd been patient and courteous. Through the glass door Gerry could see his thin, slightly stooping figure at the counter, and on impulse she reached for the door handle.

'Hello,' he greeted her with a smile, as she pushed open the door and the bell jangled. 'I remember, you're the young Scots lady. What's caught your eye today?'

'Oh, it's not that this time,' Gerry said. 'It's only –' she hesitated, then plunged on. 'I've just bought this. It cost next to nothing, but, well – could you have a quick look at it?' She put the blue stone down on the counter.

Mr. Trewartha showed only polite interest, but when he picked up the stone, Gerry saw his expression change. He moved a lamp across the counter to shed more light on it, took a jewellers' glass from a shelf behind him, and examined the stone and its setting for a long time. Finally he looked up, raising his eyebrows.

'Could I ask where you got this?' he inquired.

'From that stall at the top, up where the shops end,' Gerry said, disconcerted. She waved her hand in that direction. 'You must know the one, they have books, CDs and DVDs as well as stuff like this. Why, what's the matter? It's not stolen or anything, is it?'

The jeweller looked back at the stone, and shook his head.

'No, it's not stolen, not that I know of. But I do think it might be quite old. The way it's cut, and then the setting - it could even be centuries old, though the condition's surprisingly good.' Mr. Trewartha wrinkled his brow. 'I'm no expert, though. My friend Alastair Fletcher knows a lot about historic objects, but his shop's over to Redruth. If you'd let me keep this for a day or two, I know he'd be interested. I'd give you a receipt, of course.'

'No.' Gerry heard the sharp word as if someone else had said it, and realised how abrupt it sounded. 'I'm sorry,' she went on, 'it's just that, well, I've only just bought it, and -' Gerry ran out of words, and instead picked up one of the shop's business cards and a pen lying on the counter beside them. She checked her phone and wrote the number on the back of the card with her name, Gerry Hamilton. 'Look, this is my number. Call me if your friend's coming over, I'll bring it in and he could have a look at it.'

Gerry gave Mr. Trewartha the card. He looked disappointed and also rather hurt at her refusal. She couldn't explain that sense of panic she'd felt at the prospect of being parted, even for a day, from her new acquisition. She'd simply known that she mustn't leave it behind.

The bell rang again as the shop door opened and a small silver-haired woman came in, taking a watch out of her bag.

'Can you check if this needs a new battery?' she asked, and Gerry seized the opportunity to leave. Once outside on the pavement, she tucked the stone inside the deep pocket of her smock dress. She could feel the weight of it through the thin fabric, and wondered about it as she walked. If it was stolen, that would explain why the stallholder had been so keen to get rid of it. Yet Gerry couldn't believe that was the answer. She'd seen programmes like "Antiques Roadshow" or "Flog it". People brought a vase or a painting they'd bought at a car boot sale for next to nothing to show to the experts, and it turned out to be worth a fortune. Had she done something like that? Mr. Trewartha had seemed more interested in its age than its worth, but if the stone was really old, it might be valuable too. She realised that from the start she'd thought of it as a stone, not a piece of coloured glass or plastic like the others things on that tray. She knew there were semi-precious stones, but didn't know if any came in this shade of blue.

Gerry stopped walking and found she'd automatically gone to the lower end of Causewayhead and turned right towards Morrab Road. She'd crossed two roads without conscious thought, oblivious of the traffic, and had already reached the solid grey stone building of the School of Art, next to the public library where she'd started part-time work a couple of weeks earlier. Beside the art school, a footpath led down to Penlee Park where she spent some of her lunch hours. Following this footpath, Gerry went through a wooden gate and turned left along another path which was thickly lined with shrubs. This path passed a row of tennis courts where a couple of games were in progress, and a walled scented garden, then came out by Penlee House. This was an elegant two-storey cream and white building on the edge of the park, which housed exhibitions of Cornish paintings. It also had a café with tall French windows leading out onto a terrace with tables and chairs.

On this beautiful June day all the outdoor seats were taken, as well as those at the wooden tables and benches on the level below the terrace. Gerry followed a further path with stretches of grass and flowerbeds on either side. It had wooden seats at intervals, but she was too restless to stop and sit down, and continued towards a wide stretch of open grass partly shaded by tall trees.

'Hi, Gerry,' called a familiar voice.

Of course, it was lunchtime, and people from work might be out here. Gerry brought her attention back from what felt like a long way away. It was Debbie, her best friend at the library, sitting on the grass with a celebrity magazine in one hand and a can of Diet Coke in the other.

'Hi, Debs.' Gerry sat down on the grass beside her.

'What are you doing here on your day off?' Debbie asked, putting down her magazine. 'Like your tights,' she added.

'Thanks.' Gerry was wearing peacock blue tights which brought out the main colour in the pattern on her dress. Pleased to find how cheap clothes were in Penzance after London, Gerry had indulged herself, buying three of the currently fashionable short smock dresses, and an array of different coloured tights and leggings to go with them. She enjoyed choosing what to wear each morning, but right now clothes, and work, seemed to belong to a different world. Absently she rested her hand on the stone inside her pocket.

A couple of young mothers with pushchairs walked past, chatting as they headed towards the playground in the lower part of the park. The thud of racquets on balls, and occasional shouts, drifted over from the tennis courts. Conversation and laughter floated down from the terrace where people were eating lunch and drinking coffee. It was all so ordinary, yet Gerry still felt that odd sense of being distanced from it all. Suddenly she gripped her friend's wrist.

'Hey,' Debbie protested, 'watch what you're doing. 'You nearly made me spill my Coke.'

'Look,' Gerry whispered. 'Don't be obvious, but look at those two standing under the trees over there.'

Debbie swivelled round. Ignoring Gerry's first words she stared openly at the couple. Then she sighed.

'Wish I had a figure like that.'

'No, I didn't mean her,' Gerry said, though she couldn't deny that the woman stood out among the people relaxing in the park. Her shining copper hair was cut in layers to set off the fine cheek bones and perfect nose, and her clothes looked too smart for Penzance. 'No,' Gerry said again, 'I meant him. He's really something.'

Debbie shifted her attention to the man for a couple of minutes, then turned back and shook her head.

'Not my type,' she said firmly. 'I like a man to have brown wavy hair and to smile a lot. Like Ryan.' She gave Gerry a meaningful look.

Debbie was convinced that Ryan, who gave computer lessons in the library, wanted to ask Gerry out. Gerry, however, had sworn off men after a recent bad experience in London. But she couldn't help looking back at the man standing in the shadow of the trees.

It was hard to pin down just what it was that had drawn her attention. Perhaps it was the way he stood, casual yet poised for instant action, his lean body controlled like a dancer or a fighter. Or the arrogant turn of his head. He was speaking to his companion, but as Gerry watched, the woman shook her head then abruptly turned her back on him. The man laid his hand on her arm, but she flung it off and walked away. She didn't go far but the meaning was clear enough. She might just as well have put the whole park between them.

'Ouch,' said Debbie, who was still staring, fascinated. 'That was a bit public. He doesn't look too pleased, does he?'

That, Gerry reckoned, was the understatement of the year. The man was furious, though it had only been visible for an instant. His expression became controlled again so fast that she wondered if she'd imagined it. Gerry hoped he hadn't noticed them watching him. But then he turned slightly and looked straight at her. That look seemed to drill right through her head. It was followed by an expression which looked uncomfortably like calculation. That too was gone almost at once, and an equally brief smile replaced it, but the smile was inward, not directed at Gerry. Finally, his face neutral again, he strolled off towards the tennis courts and the exit from the park.

It all happened so quickly that Gerry had hardly had time to draw a breath, but her heart was thudding. The man's features were cool and clean, and the slender body promised a hidden strength. His fair hair had stood out in the shadows under the trees, and even at a distance Gerry had felt an urge to touch it.

Debbie, however, hadn't been looking at him. Instead, she was watching the woman with the copper coloured hair, who'd wandered over to a nearby seat. She sat down and took a couple of sheets of paper out of her bag. Although she held them in front of her in shaking hands, she wasn't looking at them.

'Well, that was exciting,' Debbie said. 'Two-nil to her, I'd say. I've a feeling I ought to know who she is. Just let me think.'

A few minutes passed. Debbie was trying to recall why the woman's face was familiar. The woman herself continued to look, unseeing, at the papers in her hand. Gerry thought about the man with the fair hair. She had an impression of high cheek bones, a straight nose, a firm chin. The source of his magnetism eluded her, yet it had carried half way across the park. And he had looked at her as if he knew exactly what she was thinking. He probably did know; he must have that effect on women all the time. So

8

why had his companion turned away, openly snubbing him? Gerry couldn't imagine. She realised her hand was resting on the stone in her pocket again. Then she saw someone else coming from the direction of the Coach House.

Gerry groaned, and Debbie looked at her. She followed Gerry's gaze and groaned too. A thin woman in a skirt and jacket more suited to an office than a library was marching towards them.

If Debbie was Gerry's favourite person at the library, Monica was definitely the opposite, and Gerry was certain this was mutual. Yet after a quick scan of the park, Monica came straight towards them.

'You're just the person I wanted,' she said to Gerry, ignoring Debbie completely. 'Are you still looking for somewhere to rent?'

Gerry nodded, surprised. She'd mentioned it in the staff room, but didn't expect Monica to even listen to, let alone remember, anything she said. 'Yeah, I am. Why?'

Monica indicated the woman on the bench. 'Well, Claudia there wants a lodger. Would you be interested?'

Completely taken aback, Gerry responded without thinking. 'Well, yeah, I suppose so.'

'Good' Monica said. 'Stay there and I'll go and ask her.'

She hurried off and Debbie gaped after her, as astonished as Gerry was.

'Since when has "Miss" Fraser taken it on herself to do anyone a favour?' Monica was the only unmarried woman on the staff who always insisted on being addressed as Miss, not Ms. 'At least, not for one of us plebs. Still, now I know who she is.' Debbie indicated the bench where Monica was speaking to the stranger. 'She's Claudia Mainwaring, she owns an art gallery in Chapel Street. They had a big event a couple of weeks ago, her picture was in the "Cornishman".' Debbie gave a wicked grin. 'Well, that explains it. Monica always wants to look like she's best buddies with the rich and famous, specially in the art world. Even at the cost of doing you a good turn.'

Claudia Mainwaring seemed an unlikely person to be looking for a lodger, but she and Monica were still talking. Gerry studied Claudia curiously, but couldn't add to her earlier impression. Lovely face, slim figure, expensive clothes and haircut; not like anyone Gerry knew.

Debbie took out her phone, and gave a yelp of dismay.

'I'm on the desk in five minutes,' she gasped, leaping up and grabbing her magazine and Coke can. 'Text me, let me know what happens.'

Gerry nodded. 'Sure.'

'Cool, see you later.'

Debbie hurried off as fast as she could; her plump form wasn't designed for speed. Gerry stood up too, looking at Monica and Claudia, and found they'd both turned towards her. She walked across the grass to join them, very conscious that her bag was old, over-filled and slipping off her shoulder, and her hair was falling loose and untidy around her face. She tucked it back again behind her ears. Close to, Claudia Mainwaring looked about thirty, nearly ten years older than Gerry, though her skin was flawless. Claudia wore pressed linen trousers, a pale blue silk shirt and a tailored cream jacket. Monica, who liked to consider herself well-dressed, looked positively dowdy beside her.

Claudia gave Gerry a quick, searching look that encompassed her outfit and well-worn bag, then rested on her face. She spoke in a business-like manner, but her voice was clear and pleasant.

'Monica tells me you work in the library, and you need a place to live.' The inflection made it a question, neatly cutting Monica out of the conversation.

'Yeah, that's right.' The answer seemed inadequate, and

Gerry explained, 'I've only been in Penzance three weeks, since I left London. I'm staying in a B & B till I can find somewhere.'

'You don't have a London accent,' Claudia commented.

'No,' Gerry told her, 'I'm Scottish. From the Western Highlands.'

Claudia nodded, and turned to Monica.

'Thank you,' she said. It was so plainly a dismissal that Gerry wished Debbie had been there to witness Monica's embarrassment. Gerry had to fight to keep her face straight, certain no-one had ever sent Monica away like that before.

Claudia looked Gerry over again with that appraising glance, and Gerry thought she'd better explain.

'I can't afford much rent,' she said. 'Not yet, anyway. I'm only working part time, though I might get more hours soon.'

Claudia shook her head, the neat layers of her hair moving a little then settling back perfectly into place.

'That doesn't matter,' she said. 'My house is quite isolated, and I often have to go to London. I'd rather have someone there than leave it empty. I'd only expect you to pay your share of the bills. That is, if you don't mind being on your own with no neighbours?'

'No, not at all.' This sounded too good to be true. 'I'm used to places in the middle of nowhere.'

'Of course, your Western Highlands must still have some of those, even in the twenty-first century.' Claudia looked amused now, though her voice remained cool. 'Would you like to come and see the house later? We could talk a bit more, then if I think you'd suit we could give it a trial.'

Gerry agreed at once, hardly daring to believe her luck. There had to be a catch. Whatever Claudia was looking for, it probably wasn't a hard-up ex-student who barely knew her way round Penzance. Would she 'suit'?

11

Claudia gave Gerry directions and suggested arriving about six. Then she left, walking briskly towards Penlee House and the wide gates which led from the driveway onto Morrab Road.

The visit to Claudia's house sounded more like a job interview than a room viewing, Gerry thought, beginning to walk slowly in the opposite direction. There was an exit from the park by the playground at its lower end which would take her towards the B & B and her car. How would she feel about being there alone? Gerry shrugged mentally. She couldn't tell till she'd seen the house and its location. She didn't suppose Claudia was expecting a gang of armed burglars. It was probably more like house-sitting, keeping an eye out for a dripping pipe or blown fuse. Remembering she was supposed to text Debbie, Gerry sent a message saying she was going to see Claudia's house later and she'd let her know what happened.

She decided to get her car and drive to Chapel Carn Brea where she and Debbie had gone three nights earlier. It had been a Midsummer's Eve celebration with a beacon fire, an annual ritual on the top of a hill near the little town of St. Just. There had been musicians, people singing Cornish songs and Christian hymns, the Mayor in his chain of office and a van selling pasties. The hilltop had been full of people of all ages, and quite a few dogs too. Gerry had caught glimpses of the sea, visible in almost every direction from that height, but the place was too crowded for her to be able to see the view properly. Gerry had resolved there and then to go back when she had the chance. Now would be perfect; there was plenty of time to spare before going to see Claudia.

She walked down Alexandra Road almost as far as the Promenade where the brightly-coloured flags along the sea-front hardly moved in the still air. The Angoves' house was in a small

12

side road here. They were a retired Cornish couple who enjoyed supplementing their pensions by taking B & B guests. Although the room was officially "Bed and Breakfast", they didn't mind if Gerry came back during the day. They also let her use the kitchen, which was cheaper than getting take-aways.

Gerry's car was parked outside the Angoves' house, but she decided to go in first and leave some of the things from her bag in her room. The Angoves were in their living room when Gerry came in, and she called out hello as she ran up the stairs. Before doing anything else she took the blue stone from her pocket, put it down on the table and undid the catch on the gold chain she always wore. It had been a gift from her beloved great-aunt Seona, doubly precious because Seona had died within weeks of giving it to her. The chain fitted perfectly through the loops on the back of the stone, creating a strikingly beautiful pendant. Gerry took it over to the big south-facing window, recalling the flare of light which had first drawn her to it. She held the stone in the sunlight, tilting it at different angles, but there was no dazzling flash of blue this time, though the sun brought out the warmth and depth of the sapphire-like colour. As she raised the chain to fasten it round her neck again, her hand slipped and the pendant slid from her fingers down into the laundry bag under the table. It only took a minute for Gerry to rescue it from among her clothes, but in that brief time her heart began to pound and her breath caught in her throat. It was like how she'd felt when Mr. Trewartha had asked to keep the stone for a day or two. As soon as she found and picked up the gold links with the Celtic pattern on the clasp, she felt normal again.

Gerry looked at the stone in her hand, frowning. She was beginning to wonder just what it was that she had bought.

Chapter Two

Wasn't this just typical. When Gerry arrived at the car park at Chapel Carn Brea, she hardly recognised the place. On Monday evening the road leading there had been filled end to end with a wide range of cars and vans, and the paths were chock-a-block. Today there wasn't a person or vehicle in sight, but Gerry had still been thwarted. She'd driven here through the same bright sunshine that she'd left in Penzance, only to find that the hill itself was wrapped in mist. The view from the top with the sea on three sides, which she'd come to see, would be completely hidden.

Then Gerry remembered one morning when she'd stood on the sea front at Penzance looking out at Mounts Bay. The tiny island of St. Michael's Mount, outlined against the curve of the Lizard, had been wreathed in a circle of mist like fluffy grey cotton wool, but this had only been sitting on the lower half of the Mount's sloping sides. The upper part, with the jutting shape of the castle rising above its gardens, had been sharp and clear in the morning light. Perhaps it would be the same here.

Gerry cheered up and got out of the Volvo estate, taking a hooded top from the back seat and pulling it over her dress. She turned the key to lock the car door; the Volvo was much too old to have an electronic key or other mod cons. The car had been Seona's, and she had given it to her great-niece when she could no longer drive. Gerry had passed her driving test, but there was no way she could afford to buy a car. In Cornwall, as in Scotland, having her own transport made all the difference.

Gerry walked to the wide gate at the beginning of the footpath, stopping to glance at a plaque attached to a slab of stone standing at the side of the path. This listed several things about the site, mentioning a Bronze Age burial site at the summit of the hill, a former medieval chapel which gave Chapel Carn Brea its name, and the beacon which was lit every midsummer eve. The five bar gate itself was padlocked, but beside it there was a narrower gate with a sliding metal catch. Gerry undid this, walked through, and set off up the gently sloping path.

When she'd come with Debbie they'd been chatting as they walked, and Gerry hadn't paid much attention to her surroundings. This time she was more concerned about the swirling mist. The path, although stony, was quite even, with grass on each side. She could make out bracken and cow parsley growing beside the grass but the mist came so far in that she could see nothing beyond it. As Gerry climbed further she passed a solid granite bench where presumably on a clear day people would sit to enjoy the view. What view, she muttered to herself, glancing at the impenetrable greyness and wishing she was in jeans. Her tights, though colourful, were thin. The mist-filled air was damp and chilly and she pulled the hood of her top over her head. During her three years in London Gerry had missed the hills around her home village of Lochallaig, but there too the mist could come in and obscure the view without warning.

Suddenly Gerry found herself in bright sunshine again, with blue sky above. She'd reached the top of the hill, and it was flat and empty. There was no trace of the tall metal stand on its pole which had contained the beacon fire on Monday night. Gerry walked over to the further side of the open space, where there had been a waist-high stone oblong with a flat piece of metal on top. This had arrows etched into it which pointed in all directions, naming many places of interest visible from this high spot. Gerry was sorry not to see it, but also puzzled. She was certain it had stood about here where she was now. She supposed that like the beacon it might have only been there for the evening, to be helpful for visitors. Yet it had looked solid, permanent.

Gerry was beginning to feel uneasy, and found her left hand was resting on the blue stone, which was now held securely on Seona's gold chain. Everywhere was too quiet. She tried to look at the vista, which was what she'd come for, but found that whichever side of the hilltop she went to, the mist was swirling below so that the near view was completely obscured. It was impossible to see the farms with their cattle, or the small airport close to the road leading to the Brea. Gerry could easily imagine herself cut off from civilisation here: there were no roads in sight, no cars or planes; nor, for that matter, any ships. For she could at least see the sea, far beyond the mist, blue and flat, straight-edged along the horizon. Gerry could make out some of the land close to the coast, but no buildings. The distance had to be deceiving her eyes.

The sea, as she had remembered, could be seen in three directions from this point, looking towards St. Just on the right and Land's End on the left. Then Gerry turned round and looked the opposite way. In this direction she could see right across to Mount's Bay, edged by the long shape of the Lizard but that didn't look right either. St. Michael's Mount appeared flatter on top, as

16

if the distinctive shape of the castle was lost in perspective across so many miles.

Much more of this and she'd be thinking she needed glasses. Gerry turned round again and walked to the far side. The path continued downward on the other side of the hill. A little way down some massive grey boulders stood beside the path as if a giant's hand had grouped them, stacked in twos and threes. Then, though she hadn't seen anyone, Gerry heard voices, surprisingly near to where she was standing.

The voices sounded angry or upset, or both, but she couldn't make out any words. Gerry decided to get out of sight, not wanting to get caught in a row. There were no trees or even shrubs on the hilltop, let alone hedges. She sprinted to the closest of the giant boulders and darted behind it.

Gerry peered cautiously round the edge of her hiding-place. The angry voices belonged to three women who appeared as suddenly as if they'd emerged directly from the huge granite stones. They wore ankle length green robes belted with cords like girdles round their waists, and their long dark hair fell in braids down their backs. Their ankles were bare, and they all wore sandals fastened with thongs. Gerry wondered if they were in costume and if this was another local tradition like the lighting of the beacon. She saw that each girdle had a sheath attached with a bone-coloured knife hilt protruding from it. She was glad she was out of sight, but kept watching.

Gerry could hear the voices clearly now but still couldn't make out what they were saying. Her fingertips strayed to Seona's gold chain and rested on the blue stone again. As they did, the words she was hearing began to make sense. The woman in the centre lifted something in her hands, and held it out to show the other two. As it was raised Gerry would have sworn that the

17

stone at her neck gave a throb in response, but she had no time to wonder at this because the woman's words gripped her as the beam of blue light had done earlier.

The speaker addressed the woman on her left. Her voice was deep and solemn as she turned what she held to display one side of it.

'Well, Morvoren, and do you believe me now? Do you accept that our sacred Chalice has been violated? And you, Ysella?'

She showed what she was holding to the third woman who merely nodded. Ysella was the most striking of the three, with a face that was more than pretty though less than beautiful. It was spoiled, however, by her self-satisfied smile, the arrogant set of her shoulders and the swing of her hips.

The other woman, Morvoren, cried 'Yes, I see it with my own eyes or I would still not believe it possible.' Her features, plainer and grimmer than Ysella's, were eclipsed by the rage on her face. She gripped the handle of the knife in her belt. 'In the name of the Goddess, I swear I will hunt down whoever has done this. But tell me, Baranwen -'

The woman addressed as Baranwen was holding what must be the chalice they were talking about, though it was blocked from Gerry's view by Baranwen's body. Baranwen held up her hand to interrupt Morvoren.

'Not yet. First we must seek out Delenyk, for this has happened during her time of care. When I was last here, all was as it should be.'

'I find it hard to believe Delenyk would fail in her vigilance,' Morvoren said sombrely. 'Yet the evidence is here before us. We will do what we must.' She raised both her hands to the base of her throat where there was a dark bruise mark, or perhaps a tattoo.

Gerry couldn't see the shape from where she stood. There was a curious formality to the gesture, as if it were part of a ritual.

Gerry felt her skin crawl. From Morvoren's tone, this Delenyk was in deep shit. She couldn't imagine what was going on here. Talk of a chalice, robed women carrying knives; it didn't sound like a midsummer festival. Maybe they were rehearsing a play? Perhaps there was going to be an open air performance here.

There had been no sound or movement other than from the three green-robed women, yet something made Gerry glance to her right. A little further down the slope, beyond two of the largest granite boulders, someone was standing, motionless, perhaps another actor waiting for a cue. This person wore dark brown leggings and tunic, topped by a hooded jerkin. The hood was up, covering their hair and shadowing the face.

Whether Gerry moved and disturbed a stone underfoot, or made some involuntary sound at the sight of this new individual, suddenly Ysella turned and caught sight of her. She yelled to the others, 'There is a boy there, watching, spying on us. A boy has dared come here!'

Gerry didn't know why they should think she was a boy, but all three women turned towards her, their expressions so furious that she stopped wondering and backed off as fast as she could. Ysella shouted again, this time so shrill it was more like a scream. As Gerry began to retreat her hood had fallen back, revealing both her face, and the stone at her neck.

'That is no boy,' Ysella called, 'she is a woman dressed in man's clothing.'

Morvoren was nearer, but had stopped dead. She was staring at Gerry, appalled.

'Baranwen – she is wearing the very stone, the sapphire missing from the Tegennow. And the thief dares come *here*, flaunting her prize before us, the Guardians of the Stones? Or was she hoping to find them unattended and maybe take another?'

'Then, Morvoren, you may fulfil your vow,' said Ysella, her tone full of menace, but an oddly satisfied look on her face.

'No, wait,' Baranwen cried, moving forward too. 'Do not kill her yet, there are things we need to know.'

But Morvoren had already begun to sprint towards Gerry, moving at a remarkable speed for one hampered by long garments. Gerry seemed to be rooted to the spot, watching Morvoren racing towards her, the knife blade flashing in her hand. Then as she stood there, mesmerised, Gerry heard an urgent shout from the watcher on the hillside.

'Run, you fool – run for your life!'

The spell holding her was broken. Gerry began racing across the hilltop, trying to avoid Morvoren. Morvoren swerved, aiming to cut across Gerry's path, and came at her from the side. She was now near enough to lean forward and aim a vicious stroke at Gerry's throat, either hoping to cut the fastening that held the stone, or to wound her, fatally if possible, ignoring Baranwen's orders. But the solid gold chain foiled the attempt and the knife slipped across it, drawing blood as the blade cut across the skin below the collar bone.

The Guardian hadn't expected to be thwarted and almost lost her grip on the knife. The other two Guardians were running up, but the brief pause as Morvoren grasped her weapon again gave Gerry a head start. She ran as she had never run in her life, her bag banging against her side, her throat burning from the effort of breathing. Beyond the point where the path began to slope down from the flat top of the Brea, she plunged back into the mist, the chill air welcome on her heated face.

Gerry didn't dare slow down to watch for obstacles. She had to trust that nothing would be lying on the path to trip her up, or she was dead. The ground had been easy going on the upward journey, but now the track seemed to go on and on. Surely it hadn't been this long before? She dreaded hearing running feet or cries behind her, but couldn't risk looking round. It seemed like for ever before at last she saw the granite gate posts rising out of the mist. She banged open the catch of the side gate and scrambled through faster than she would have believed possible.

The sun was shining over the car park, and as Gerry turned at last to look back the mist was starting to burn away and disappear. No vengeful figures pursued her. There were two other vehicles in the car park now. A man was letting a black labrador out of the rear of a small dusty van. The dog ran around barking, ready for a good long walk. A middle-aged couple dressed for serious hiking in cargo shorts, walking boots and thick, knee high socks, stood beside their car, consulting a map. Gerry caught a few words in a language that sounded like German. The scene looked completely ordinary.

Gerry was shaking so much that she couldn't even get her car key out of her bag. She just leaned against the side of the Volvo, trying to get her breath back, and staring at the gates. The minutes went by and still no-one came down from the hill. The German couple put away their map, then strode off purposefully across the car park. They stopped at the main gate, checked by the padlock, then went through the side gate and off up the gentle slope, now completely clear of mist. The dog raced to the gate; he obviously knew the way well. His owner called out to him to stay, then locked up the van and followed. Gerry wanted to shout 'Don't leave me'; she was afraid to be there on her own. She forced her trembling

21

hands to extract the car key which had sunk to the bottom of the overcrowded bag as usual, and unlocked the door of the Volvo.

Gerry virtually fell inside, slammed the door, then reversed in a squeal of tyres. She drove out of the parking area much too fast for the uneven surface, heedless of possible damage to the car. She turned left then right and followed the route automatically, not noticing any of the places she passed, desperate to put a good distance between herself and the self-proclaimed 'Guardians of the Stones'. Gerry only slowed down when at last the road came to a T-junction. A sign opposite the junction pointed right towards Penzance, and on the left to the small town of St. Just. She turned left and pulled in at the side of the road.

Gerry switched off the engine and locked the doors from the inside, something she'd not done since leaving London. Then at last she let herself think. She looked down, trying to get a proper view of the cut across her breastbone. Her dress had stuck to it and there was blood across the fabric. It might have been a little, or quite a lot; it was hard to judge from this angle. Gerry didn't try to pull the material away, guessing the wound would start bleeding again if she did. Looking at the dress, she saw again the image of the man who had called out. By chance her hoodie, thigh length dress and tights mirrored his tunic, hooded jerkin and leggings. 'Man's clothing', Ysella had called it. That had to be why.

Gerry touched Seona's chain gently; it had probably saved her life. Sitting there in Seona's car, she wished passionately that she could talk to her great-aunt. She was certain Seona alone would be able to explain what had just happened.

Gerry had been understandably terrified when a total stranger had run at her, waving a knife and threatening to kill her. She couldn't begin to understand why these "Guardians of the Stones" thought she'd stolen something that belonged to them,

22

but they hadn't given her a chance to speak. But what was scaring Gerry now, even more than the violence of Morvoren's attack, was the memory of the moment when the stranger had shouted at her to run.

Now that she was away from the scene, Gerry knew she couldn't possibly have heard the man's voice so clearly at that distance. For it had definitely been a man. When he lifted his head and cried his warning his hood had slid down onto his shoulders. And as the sunlight fell on the shining fair hair, Gerry knew who he was. He was the man she'd seen in Penlee Park, the one Claudia had turned her back on. The man who had looked at Gerry as if he were reading her mind.

He had somehow called to her, helped her to escape, for which Gerry was duly grateful. True, he hadn't come forward to intervene – well, most men might hesitate before confronting three armed and furious women. Yet somehow Gerry didn't think that was why. He hadn't been afraid. There had been an undertone of – yes, it had been amusement – in that call of "Run, you fool".

And though Gerry couldn't begin to imagine what his connection was with the Guardians, one thing was apparent to her now as it had not been in that moment of blind panic. Nothing that had taken place on the hillside just now had made any sense to Gerry; yet it had not surprised the man in the slightest.

Chapter Three

The car clock showed Gerry it was later than she'd realised. A detached part of her brain said she needed to go back to the Angoves' house and get changed. She really wanted to get the room at Claudia's, and turning up with blood on her clothes was so not a good idea. Gerry started the Volvo and did a U-turn on the empty road. It went to Penzance, so she only had to keep following it. Which was just as well, because all her thoughts were on the man on the hillside.

Gerry should have been astounded when she recognised him. It looked like an unbelievable coincidence, but there had always been coincidences in her life. A song would cross her mind and she would turn on the radio to hear it playing. She would think of someone and get a text, call or email from them within minutes. Sometimes she would be about to speak when another person would come out with precisely what she'd been going to say herself. Or she would decide on a whim to take a different way home and find afterwards there had been major hold-ups on her usual route.

Seona was the one Gerry had finally talked to about it. Her

mother was constantly busy, with six people needing meals and clean clothes, as well as a large house to look after. Besides, her mother, who believed only in what she could see, would never take these "coincidences" seriously. Her father was equally down-to-earth, as well as working long hours so he was rarely around when Gerry had questions to ask. Her three older brothers were at the age when they were only interested in girls, football, and cars. Gerry's great-aunt, on the other hand, always had time for her, accepted what she said at face value, and treated the schoolgirl like an equal.

'It's no' coincidence,' she said when Gerry gave her some examples. 'It's more a sort of telepathy; you're picking up other people's thoughts.'

'But no-one can do that in real life,' Gerry protested. 'Only in sci-fi stuff.'

'Of course they can,' her great-aunt answered calmly. They were sitting in Seona's cottage, in the peaceful front room. It had shelves full of books on either side of the fireplace, the spinning wheel Seona could no longer use standing in a corner, flowers from her garden in a pottery jug on the table, and the scent of the herb bed outside drifting in through the open window.

Seona continued, 'The people in some parts of Scotland are descended from the Celts, and they understood things which nowadays would be thought of as magic or witchcraft.' She smiled at Gerry. 'I believe one day it will be understood and be thought as normal as any of these wonders of modern technology you young people all take for granted. Telephones you can carry in your pocket and take photographs with – when I was a lass who would have dreamt of such a thing?'

Seona made it sound as if telepathy was as everyday as a smartphone, but Gerry couldn't see her parents or brothers agreeing. Yet other odd things happened to her too. Gerry would often know if someone was coming to the house and who it was, even if no-one had told her. The title of a book or film would cross her mind out of nowhere, and someone would mention it within a day or two. And after spending a week at home this Easter, something had prompted her to attempt the long drive from Lochallaig to London instead of going by train from Oban as she usually did. It was nearly 600 miles and Gerry took two days over it, spending the night at a B & B near Manchester, but she'd been determined. As a result, she had the car to take her and her belongings when she fled from London to Penzance. And now – well, without the car she couldn't have gone to Chapel Carn Brea.

Gerry was still thinking over this chain of events when she reached the B & B. She made it up to her room without meeting anyone, and rummaged through her clothes. She found a tunic-style dress with a round neck which would hide the pendant. She couldn't bear to take it off, but didn't want it on show after what had just happened. Morvoren had spoken of a missing sapphire, but it was totally impossible that this stone and the Guardians' lost jewel could be one and the same, however alike they might look. That would be a coincidence beyond belief, even for her.

Gerry took the clean clothes to the bathroom along with a box of plasters, and gently peeled off her bloodstained smock. As she'd guessed, the cut started bleeding again as soon as she pulled the fabric away. She felt sick when she looked in the big mirror over the sink at the slash which Morvoren's knife had made across the skin, biting into her flesh. But she didn't have time for self-pity. Gerry washed the cut carefully, dried it and covered it end to end with plasters. Blood began to seep into them at once, and she shoved the box of plasters into her bag so she could put fresh ones on if she got the chance. She changed, then looked in the mirror again to make sure the blood hadn't got onto her clean dress. Her face looked almost as usual: fair skin with a light dusting of freckles, straight nose, eyes which were sea-green in sunlight. They looked anxious, but if Claudia noticed that she could put it down to concern about getting this rent-free room.

Gerry left the Angove's house and drove off up Alexandra Road towards the Penzance bypass and the road to St. Just. She'd decided to go and see Mr. Trewartha in the morning. She wasn't starting work till 12, so she'd have plenty of time. He could at least confirm that the stone wasn't a real sapphire, and set her mind at rest. Gerry also considered going back to speak to the stall holder, but shied away from that idea. In the meantime she had to stop thinking about it all, which wasn't easy with the cut beginning to throb painfully. For now she had to concentrate on finding the house and talking to Claudia Mainwaring. Afterwards she could start worrying again about all the things that were nagging in the background. Even the small ones like how had those four people already been at Chapel Carn Brea? The car park had been empty when she arrived and the place seemed to be miles from any buses.

She had to concentrate on Claudia's directions. With a strength of mind Gerry hadn't known she possessed, she shut off the memory of the events on the hilltop and started watching for the road to the village of Pendeen. She had to take a right turn followed by a left, negotiate a bumpy bridle path then follow the private lane down to the house, which was called Windhaven.

As Gerry came down this lane rabbits scampered away on all sides, and she caught her breath. Ahead was a wide view of the coast far below, the broad sea beyond it sharply edged along the horizon. Between the hill and the sea stretched miles of fields, farms and moorland. Claudia hadn't exaggerated; the house really was isolated. Back at the road there was one house opposite the start of the bridle path, and that was invisible from here, hidden by a row of trees. Some of the trees were bent and battered by years of winter storms, but there was scarcely a breath of wind now.

There were two cars parked outside, a large saloon and a neat little hatchback. Gerry hoped Claudia wasn't interviewing anyone else. Getting out of the Volvo, she was met by such silence that the bang of the car door seemed like an intrusion. The town of Penzance was like a teeming city compared to this.

As Gerry shut the car door, Claudia emerged from the house. She crossed a small courtyard with a white gate, and came over to where Gerry was standing.

'This place is awesome,' Gerry said, staring around as she spoke. 'Do you do all the gardening?'

The old granite house, with its grey slate roofs and white window frames, seemed to be surrounded by flowering shrubs on every side. Below the parking area there were bushes of rhododendrons with the last flowers on them fading to brown. A path led off to a green space lower down which was more or less hidden behind granite hedges, tall bamboos and a clump of pampas grass. A long conservatory jutted out from the end of the house into another small garden with large crimson mob-cap hydrangeas and stems of dark pink mallows like wild hollyhocks, while tall spikes of foxgloves rose from the hedges in all directions. Beside the cars, hebe bushes bloomed in white and purple, while near the courtyard gate stood a tree covered with red flowers hanging like small globes.

Claudia followed Gerry's gaze, and smiled.

'No, I don't do any of it. I've got a gardener, Peter, who usually comes three days a week. Oh, and he sometimes brings a gun for the rabbits, because they eat his vegetables. So don't worry if you see a man turn up in a blue 4 x 4, then going around carrying a shotgun.'

Claudia explained this as if it was already settled that Gerry was moving in. She led the way across the courtyard, past ceramic pots of red and pink geraniums.

'It's awesome,' Gerry said again, looking out at the horizon of the deep blue sea, then back to the tree with the hanging red flowers. 'I love that tree.'

'Yes, that's my favourite too,' Claudia agreed. 'It's a lantern tree. And the place is beautiful on a day like this.' She opened the door on the far side of the courtyard. 'But the winds get vicious in the winter, and when the mists come in the entire view disappears. What's it like where you come from?'

'Well, I grew up in a village called Lochallaig,' Gerry said. 'It's surrounded by trees and mountains, rivers and burns – you'd call them streams,' she added, seeing Claudia look puzzled. 'There's the loch of course, Loch Allaig, but I only saw the sea if we went to Oban, and that's really a sea loch. I'm well used to winds, and rain and mist. You get a lot of that in Scotland.'

Claudia turned towards the house. 'Come in and I'll show you round,' she said. 'Then we can talk. Did you say you'd only been in Penzance for three weeks?'

'Yes,' Gerry replied uncomfortably. Of course her prospective landlady would ask about that. 'I was at Uni in London, till,' she hesitated, 'I left.'

Claudia raised her eyebrows but didn't ask any more for the moment. She gestured for Gerry to follow her inside. The doorway led straight into a long, light, well-equipped kitchen with wooden cupboards, marble style work surfaces, and a pale tiled floor. At the far end was the conservatory Gerry had seen from outside. All three sides of it looked out to the sea and the gardens.

'This is the lounge.' Claudia took Gerry through a door on the right. Like the kitchen, the lounge was a long room, having deep-set windows on both sides. There was a leather-covered sofa and armchair, thick patterned rugs on the carpeted floor, a large screen tv in the corner, and modern paintings on the walls. A tall bookcase on the end wall was full of books on art and artists. Three doors led out of the lounge, including the one they had just come through. Claudia waved a hand towards the door at the far end.

'That leads to the stairs up to my bedroom and bathroom. Yours is at the other end of the house. Officially it's the guest bedroom, but I'm not planning on having any guests.' Again she spoke as if Gerry had already agreed to take the room.

Claudia took Gerry from the lounge by the third door and crossed a room set up as an office, with a desk and computer looking out onto the back garden. A bookcase here covered half the wall at the lounge end. A staircase in the corner led up to a bedroom which had windows on three sides, making it very light. The window at the top of the stairs gave a view of the sea, two opposite overlooked the back garden, and a side one faced a vegetable plot. The room was furnished with a double bed, wardrobe, chest of drawers and dressing table, all in light wood. On the wall hung another painting, a view of a harbour.

'Your bathroom's through there,' Claudia said, waving towards a door at the end. Gerry took a quick glance inside. The room had a large deep window overlooking the back garden, and a bookcase against one wall. The bath looked huge, and even in here there were a couple of paintings. Gerry knew little about art, but it looked like all the pictures were originals.

'Right, that's everything,' Claudia said briskly. 'Come down to the conservatory and we can discuss practicalities.'

Rather dazed, Gerry followed her back down the stairs, through the office and the end of the lounge and along the kitchen into the conservatory. The house felt like a maze, but Gerry supposed she'd get used to it if she was living here. There was a table in the conservatory with three chairs, positioned so that anyone sitting there would be looking out across the gardens to the vista of the sea.

'Take a seat,' Claudia said, waving Gerry towards the chairs. 'Will you have some coffee?' She flicked a switch on the kettle, and when it boiled poured water into a cafetière waiting beside it. It smelled as if the beans had just been ground. Gerry found her voice.

'Yes, thanks. Milk, no sugar, please.'

Claudia left the coffee to brew while she disappeared round a corner and returned with milk in a delicate pale blue jug. She put it on the table and went back to push down the plunger on the cafetière. 'That's the utility room in there,' she added, indicating the door she'd come from. 'Washing machine, tumble-dryer, fridge and freezer.' She poured the coffee into two cups with a light, abstract pattern, and brought them over. Gerry was glad Claudia hadn't offered cake or biscuits. Her stomach was so tight with apprehension she didn't think she could eat anything. Instead, Gerry added milk to her coffee and stirred it, returning the spoon very gently to the saucer. She raised the cup to her lips. The coffee tasted wonderful in this fine china, but the cup and saucer looked so fragile she was afraid she'd break them if she breathed too hard.

Something else had occurred to Gerry during the whirlwind tour of the house.

'Aren't you going to want references and things?' she asked doubtfully.

Claudia shook her head.

'Not a lot of point, is there, when you've only been here for three weeks. I assume your manager at the library could confirm you turn up for work each day. Your landlady at the B & B can tell me you haven't trashed the furniture or thrown noisy parties. And I don't suppose you left London because you were behind with your rent.'

'No,' Gerry agreed, 'but I thought -'

Claudia interrupted her.

'This house belongs to my father, who's a London banker. Property down here's a fraction of Kensington prices, and he probably bought it with his annual bonus. Anyway, he taught me how to assess people when I was still in my teens. He said a woman with money will always have the wrong men hanging around. I've followed his guidelines all my life and there's only ever been one person it didn't work for.'

She drank some of her coffee, and gave Gerry a quizzical look.

'If you agree, I'd suggest a trial period of three months. As far as I'm concerned, you could move in tomorrow evening. That would suit me as I have to go to London on Saturday and I'd want you here before I left. There would be conditions, though. I'll tell you what they are and if you don't feel you can agree to them then just tell me now and we'll forget the whole idea.'

'No loud music?' Gerry hazarded. 'No drugs?'

Claudia dismissed that.

'I'd assume that was understood. And common courtesy, like replacing anything you used from the cupboards.'

She gave Gerry a very straight look.

'There are two things that matter. One, I wouldn't want you asking your friends up here. I can trust you, but I don't know them.'

That was unexpected, but Gerry could live with it. She wasn't expecting much of a social life anyway.

'Okay,' she said, 'I can agree to that.'

'The second one,' Claudia paused and drank some more coffee. She replaced the cup on the saucer and appeared to choose her words with care. 'You were in the park earlier, so I assume you saw the man I was with. It felt like half Penzance saw us.'

Her mouth twisted and she looked down at her hands for a moment. Claudia Mainwaring, daughter of a wealthy banker, didn't do scenes in public. She didn't look like she did scenes at all.

Gerry sympathised, but there was nothing she could say. She remembered the strange look the man had given her, as if he could see right through her.

'Yes,' she said slowly, 'Yes, I saw him.' *And I saw him again afterwards; but that's not something I can talk about.*

Something in Gerry's voice made Claudia look at her sharply.

'Oh my God,' she said, then elaborated. 'It happens to nine women out of every ten. I was rather hoping you might be the tenth.'

No, Debbie was the one who'd been immune to that magnetism which Gerry had felt from her first sight of the man on the other side of the park.

'Well, that's the other condition of your living here. If he comes round when I'm out, or away, you do not let him in the door. I am not having Justin Chancellor set foot in my house.'

She said it in the most matter-of-fact way, yet if she'd screamed with rage it couldn't have been more forceful.

'And that's your second condition? You'd want me to try and keep him out?' Gerry didn't think she'd be strong enough to push a man off the doorstep if he was determined to get in.

Claudia guessed her thoughts and smiled grimly. 'Don't worry, he wouldn't try to force his way in. He'd think that was beneath him. But he'd do his best to talk you into it. That would amuse him. And he can be very persuasive, believe me.'

This was even more unexpected than her first condition, and it gave Gerry pause. Should she agree to it or not? For all she knew, Justin Chancellor had saved her life this afternoon. She wondered what Claudia would have made of that. Gerry realised she'd been silent for too long, and, looking up, met the other woman's gaze squarely. Claudia had revealed something personal to her. It seemed only fair that Gerry should do the same, even if it hurt.

'I'm not good at judging people like you are,' she replied slowly, 'specially not men. That was why I left London. I found out Martin, my so-called boyfriend, had only been seeing me while his girlfriend was away for a few weeks. Once she came back, he dropped me overnight. I just couldn't face people who knew what a fool I'd made of myself. Finals were over, I'd no need to stay.' She'd felt totally humiliated, even if it was Martin who'd behaved badly. 'I didn't go back to Scotland – everyone there had tried to talk me out of going to London in the first place.' Her family and teachers had urged her to try Glasgow or Edinburgh instead. Everyone except Seona who had, for some unknown reason, supported Gerry when she stuck to her decision to head for the English capital. 'So when I, well, ran away from London, instead of going back north I headed for Lands End. It seemed as far away as I could get.'

Away from London, and from home. Away from the people who knew what a sucker she'd been. 'Though of course I ended up in Penzance, not Lands End itself. I needed time to recover.' Gerry was wondering for the first time what had been behind Seona's quiet determination that her great-niece should go to London. Was there some kind of foreknowledge there?

'So you're only here till you feel strong enough go back to London? I assumed you were looking for somewhere long term.' Claudia sounded annoyed. Gerry guessed it hadn't been easy for Claudia to be so frank, and now she thought she'd done it for nothing,

'Oh no,' Gerry said at once, 'I'm staying in Cornwall.' Claudia might as well know the rest. 'All the people who said I'd hate London were totally right,' she explained. 'I realised that as soon as I got there. But I didn't want to give up and admit they'd been right. So I stayed on, all through the three years at Uni, until - well, until Martin.'

An unexpected smile lit Claudia's face, turning the cool perfection into something warmer. 'I can understand. That's exactly how I felt when I moved to Cornwall. I didn't fit in, but I wanted to keep going, to prove something to myself perhaps. So, you're going to try and make a life for yourself here?'

'Yes,' Gerry agreed, pleasantly surprised to find that she and Claudia had that in common. 'Though I ought to go home for a couple of weeks and see my family. But that doesn't have to be straight away. I can go when it fits in with you, when you don't need me here.'

Only after she'd said the words did Gerry realise that she'd just agreed to be Claudia's lodger.

Gerry couldn't wait to tell Debbie the news, and pulled in to a layby as soon as she was well away from Claudia's house. She hunted for her phone, which, like her car key, always seemed to work its way down to the bottom of her bag, then called her friend.

'I'm taking the room,' she told her. 'The house is like

something out of a magazine. I'm not sure I'm doing the right thing, though. She's got all this stuff, I feel like I'm bound to break something priceless.'

'You'll get the place rent free and you're "not sure"?' Debbie was incredulous. 'Though I don't think I'd fancy being all by myself in the middle of nowhere.'

'Oh, I don't mind that – actually I'm quite looking forward to it. It was always too crowded at home, and London was even worse. The only thing I'm sorry about is not being able to ask you up there.' Gerry hadn't mentioned Claudia's second condition.

'Oh well, you'll just have to tell me about it at work.' Debbie said with a chuckle. 'That'll annoy Monica. I bet she's already sorry she introduced you to Claudia. Look, I've got to go, my mum's just shouted that my tea's ready.'

'Okay, Debs, see you tomorrow.'

Gerry switched off the phone and drove the few miles back to Penzance. Now she had to tell the Angoves she'd be leaving them the next day.

Gerry found them both at the large kitchen table, finishing their dinner. When she explained she was moving out, Mrs. Angove got up from her chair, came over and gave Gerry a hug.

'I'm glad for you,' she said warmly. 'It's good to see you looking more cheerful. Those first nights you were here, I'd hear you crying and crying all alone in your room.'

Gerry felt her face turn pink. 'I never realised you could hear me,' she said awkwardly.

'You'll be all right, maid,' her husband said in his loud, cheerful voice. 'Where's the house to?'

Gerry translated this correctly as meaning "Where is the house?" By now she'd come to recognise some of his idioms, like exchanging "we" and "they" for "us" and "them".

'It's near a village called Pendeen,' she said, 'up on the north coast. Look, should I pay you up till Saturday – I mean, it's very short notice, just one day.'

But they both insisted there was no need. Not only was it good weather, a weekend, and high summer, but this was the week of Golowan, the Penzance midsummer Festival of St. John.

'We're bound to get someone tomorrow, as it's the fireworks,' Mrs. Angove said with assurance. Gerry looked blank, and she explained, 'Saturday's Mazey Day, with processions and music and things all day. On the Friday night they have fireworks when it gets dark. They set them off near the Jubilee Pool and the funfair, but you can see them from anywhere along the front. You should go, it's always good.'

Gerry had seen the funfair, and the flags along the promenade and up the main shopping streets, but she'd assumed they were for summer visitors. She'd been too wrapped up in herself to pay attention to anything around her, and hadn't even noticed there was a festival on.

Before Gerry could ask any more, there was a small flurry of notes from the radio in the corner. This heralded the half-hourly news on Radio Cornwall, and Mrs. Angove bustled over to turn up the volume.

'Just let me see if there's any more about that poor man,' she said. 'What a thing to happen in Penzance. Seems you're not safe anywhere these days.'

'What happened?' Gerry asked.

'Jeweller attacked on Causewayhead,' Mr. Angove said, putting down his mug of tea. For the first time since Gerry had met him, he sounded angry. 'Just up the road from that library where you work. What was it they said earlier – whoever it was must have come into the shop about the time it was closing. His staff had already gone. They spoke to his assistant on the news, and she was shocked– frail old man, he was.'

Gerry's mouth went dry. 'He "was"?' she asked, alarm gripping her. 'He's not -' she couldn't bring herself to say it.

'He's in hospital,' Mrs. Angove said, 'but they don't know if he'll pull through or not. Someone hit him really hard.' Then she looked at Gerry. 'Are you all right, my love? You look all shaken up. Sit down, can I give you some tea?'

She filled a mug and pushed it towards her guest, along with the sugar bowl. 'I know you don't usually, but it's good for shock, and you look like you've just had one.'

It was easier not to argue, and Gerry put a spoonful of sugar into her drink. It was hard to swallow, as her throat seemed to be trying to close up.

'I've been in that shop a couple of times,' she said by way of explanation. 'The owner, he was really nice. I feel awful about it.'

'Well, it's not as if it's your fault.' Mrs. Angove's voice was comforting, but nothing could reassure her listener. 'We'll just have to hope he recovers all right.'

But Gerry knew that it was her fault; or at least, it was because of her, which came to the same thing. She finished her tea, excused herself on the grounds of having to pack, and escaped up to her room, refusing Mrs. Angove's offer of a hot meal. Gerry knew she ought to eat, but her insides were churning too much. She'd lost weight since leaving London, being too miserable most of the time to be interested in food. She couldn't even face one of Mrs. Angove's home-made pasties, however inviting they looked and smelled.

Gerry didn't pack. She just sat on the bed and tried to think. There was no way it was just chance that Mr. Trewartha had been attacked after she'd gone in to show him the blue stone. And now she couldn't talk to him before work tomorrow as she had hoped. Then she remembered he'd mentioned a friend in Redruth who knew about old objects.

Old objects. Gerry caught her breath. With everything else that had happened, she'd forgotten Mr. Trewartha's suggestion that the stone and its setting might be old; even "centuries old" he'd said. The Guardians had been speaking of a chalice, and surely chalices belonged well in the past. Wasn't there a chalice in the King Arthur stories? Then maybe the stone really was that old – but no, it couldn't be. Anyway, Mr. Trewartha had said the condition was too good.

Gerry stood up, walked to the mirror which hung on the wall, and looked at the blue stone hanging in the centre of Seona's chain. She'd thought earlier about going back to see the stall holder; perhaps it would be best to just give the stone back to her. Gerry laughed rather grimly at the idea. She'd panicked when Mr. Trewartha had asked her to leave it with him for a day or two. Even here, alone in this room, she wasn't prepared to undo the chain holding the stone just to take it off and look at it properly. And she was seriously considering giving it back?

What was the man's name – Flynn? Frith? – no, it was Fletcher. Gerry opened her tablet to look up jewellers' shops in Redruth. There were half a dozen numbers, but none under the name of Fletcher. She'd just have to try them in the morning. Mr. Trewartha's friend must work in one of them. Gerry shut down the tablet, opened the wardrobe door and began putting clothes in her suitcase. She packed automatically, her mind returning to the afternoon and the scene on the hilltop. The women talking, the appearance of Justin, the inexplicable violence. It was so weird that she could easily believe she'd fallen asleep in the car park and dreamed it all – she hadn't slept properly for days – but there was that knife cut across her front. That was no dream. Gerry remembered she needed to change the plasters, and took the packet out of her bag.

Then she realised something else which stopped her dead. She'd been thinking mainly of Morvoren and the fury on her face as she ran at Gerry, wielding her knife. Then there was Ysella, and her strange, satisfied expression. She'd hardly noticed the other woman, Baranwen. Now in her mind's eye Gerry saw Baranwen again: the green robe, the dark hair. She'd only seen the Guardian's face for a moment as she turned towards Morvoren. But now Gerry realised she'd seen Baranwen before. The dark-haired stall holder in the long green dress on Causewayhead who'd sold Gerry the blue stone was the green-robed woman who'd stood on the hilltop and told her fellow Guardians that their sapphire had been stolen.

Chapter Four

Gerry was exhausted and desperately needed to sleep, but her thoughts were still whirling. Then she remembered a yoga class she'd gone to for a while in London. Each class ended with a calming exercise, so peaceful that she'd often found herself drifting on the verge of sleep. Gerry lay down on the bed, still fully clothed and wearing her sandals. She closed her eyes and tried to take herself through the stages, relaxing her toes, feet, ankles, calves and on upwards, ending at the forehead. She had reached the sensation of floating when her eyes suddenly opened wide.

She was on the hilltop at Chapel Carn Brea, so she must be asleep. Gerry had been thinking about this place all evening so it was only natural she should dream of it. The sun was low though not yet setting. The air was mild, and the grass was dry under Gerry's sandals. She was still wearing the same clothes. The blue stone on its chain was hidden under the neckline of the dress, but she could feel it against her skin.

She could hear soft singing, or perhaps chanting. Gerry looked around. The hilltop was as she had last seen it, bare of everything but stones, grass and low shrubs. She walked to where the path should be, the one she'd walked up from the car park. There was no path, or car park. There was no mist obscuring the view either. The landscape was laid out below, sharply clear in the evening light, bare of houses, farms, airport, roads and cars. The coast was free of buildings as it had been before, but now everywhere else was too. There was, however, far more woodland than Gerry was used to seeing in the Cornish landscape. She swivelled round to look at St. Michael's Mount and there, as she had half expected, was the flattened top. This time Gerry knew it wasn't distance or perspective. The medieval castle wasn't there.

Her surroundings, though apparently deserted, weren't silent. The distant bleating of sheep, lowing of cattle and the song of a bird carried clearly in the still air as well as the singing, which seemed to be getting closer. There was no breeze even here on the hilltop. Gerry could smell smoke, though it was the wrong time of year for bonfires. Was it a gorse fire? She'd seen warnings about these on the local news. She moved to the side of the hill where she thought the smoke was coming from, and looked down.

At the foot of the Brea there was a kind of settlement surrounded by a stone wall. There were about a dozen buildings with pointed or sloping roofs, each consisting of individual units grouped round a central courtyard. The roofs seemed flatter because Gerry was seeing them from above. This was where the smoke was coming from; it was rising straight upwards from openings in the thatched roofs. She could see some animals, maybe pigs, running around, but no people.

The sound of voices was very near now. Then Gerry saw a group of women approaching from the direction where the giant boulders stood. Their long hair was braided, and they wore belted green robes. As they reached the open ground she saw they wore soft, low boots. There were about fifteen women, mostly dark-haired, though one was strikingly fair. The singing died away as they reached the open space of the hilltop, but Gerry could hear talking. The words sounded strange at first. Then, with an unconscious memory from the afternoon, Gerry's hand slid to touch the stone on its chain inside the neck of her dress.

Unlike the Guardians she had seen earlier none of the women appeared to be armed. They didn't look threatening, but Gerry felt conspicuous and vulnerable, standing alone in the bare open space. Then two of the singers caught sight of her. The first approached Gerry swiftly, with determination in her face and a swing in her step. Her companion was younger and plumper, with a naturally cheerful countenance looking solemn for this occasion. Each had a dark mark at the base of her throat, which nudged a memory. Then Gerry placed it - the Guardian Morvoren had a similar marking. She was close enough to these two to see it was a tattoo, or else painted on, but she couldn't make out the design.

'Greetings, stranger,' the first woman addressed her. Gerry found she could understand her now. 'May the Goddess be with you.'

'And with you,' Gerry responded. It felt like the right thing to say, and the stranger could apparently understand her too.

'We did not look to see any guests this evening,' the woman went on, 'and, dressed as you are, I took you for a boy and would have sent you away in shame. But now I see you are a woman, and you are indeed welcome. I am Kerenza, and this is Wylmet.'

Gerry guessed that Kerenza was about her own age, and Wylmet still in her teens, but as neither wore make-up they might look younger than they really were. Both were looking at her with curiosity but not suspicion. Gerry's hair – red-gold, straight and shoulder-length – stood out sharply in this company. She realised at these close quarters that none of the group were taller than she was, and many were shorter, although she was only medium height herself.

It seemed only polite to give her own name.

'I am called Gerralda,' Gerry said, surprising herself.

'That is an unusual name,' Wylmet said. 'But a lovely one,' she added hurriedly.

'Thank you,' Gerry replied. 'The name was chosen by my great-aunt. Her name was Seona, which was special too.' She'd never learned how Seona had persuaded Gerry's no-nonsense parents into something so uncharacteristic. She'd never called herself Gerralda in either London or Cornwall, and by now she was so used to being known as Gerry that at times she forgot it wasn't her real name. Here it seemed only right to use it. Gerry had a momentary notion that Seona had chosen the name for that very reason, but of course that was impossible.

While the three were talking, some of the group had gone down the path again and now came back carrying lighted torches, pottery jugs and beakers. Two carried a small table which they put the jugs and beakers on. They had returned so quickly that Gerry wondered if these things had simply been left by the great boulders. Two brought metal holders with spiked ends which they drove into the ground at four points round the open space, then fitted the burning torches into them. The beakers were filled from the jugs and passed round. Wylmet went over to the women holding the jugs and returned clutching three of the beakers. She offered one to Gerry.

'May I give you some mead?' She handed her the beaker. 'It's our own medh, made from the honey from the sacred hives.'

Gerry took a sip of the drink and nearly choked. It was rawer, and stronger, than anything she was used to.

'Have you travelled far to be with us tonight?' Kerenza asked.

'I don't know how far I have come this evening,' Gerry prevaricated. Then she had an inspiration. 'I grew up a long way from here, at a place called Lochallaig, so please excuse me if I'm not familiar with all your customs.' She didn't say Lochallaig was over six hundred miles away.

'Yes, I guessed from your voice as well as your clothes that you do not come from this part of Cornwall,' Wylmet agreed. The name sounded more like "Cornouall" as she spoke it. 'It was good of you to come,' she added as if to reassure Gerry of her welcome.

Both she and Kerenza took it for granted that Gerry knew why they were surprised to have company on whatever this occasion was. Before either of them could say any more, another woman swept up to them. Gerry's heart began to thud as she recognised Ysella. Gerry had last seen Ysella urging Morvoren to attack her. And if she was here, were the other two here also? Gerry wanted to run, but Ysella wasn't even looking at her. She stood confronting Kerenza and Wylmet, frowning at them.

'Be silent,' she snapped. 'This is a sacred evening, yet you stand here chattering like village maids on washing day. I shall have to speak to Hedra tomorrow. I often wonder if you two are fit to even belong to the Gwenen. Now show some decorum.' She swept, or flounced, off. Gerry noticed that Ysella had belted her girdle just below the waist to emphasise the swing of her hips. She caught the look on both Kerenza and Wylmet's faces. The word "Bitch!" hung unspoken in the air.

Kerenza glanced around, then drew them away from the torches and the other women. The three moved a little way down the further side of the hill towards where the great granite

45

boulders stood stacked in tumbled heaps higher than their heads. The chanting voices had resumed, and Gerry trusted that Ysella hadn't noticed their defection. Kerenza seemed to think they were safe to speak here.

'We would not usually be lacking in respect for any of the Guardians,' she apologised, 'but since she was made Guardian, Ysella takes every opportunity to exert her authority. And when I think of Delenyk; everyone admired and loved her. That's why it was so terrible when –' she broke off, and Gerry heard a choking sound to her right. Turning, she saw that Wylmet had begun to weep. Gerry wanted to go and put her arms round Wylmet, and hug her as if she were her little niece. It seemed best not to ask about this Delenyk. She recalled Morvoren's chilling words "We will do what we must". It sounded like Morvoren had acted already.

Gerry looked away towards the great grey stones. Light from the nearest torch washed them with a reddish glow and she shivered. She could see for the first time a rough square opening beside them, framed with a stone lintel. It looked like the entrance to a tunnel, or else to a tomb. It might be an innocent storage place where the women had collected the torches and jugs a few minutes ago. Yet as she looked at the dark space she felt a sense of dread begin to crawl through her, from the back of her throat to her stomach, and down to her feet, leaving her knees shaking.

'What is wrong?' asked Wylmet, rubbing the back of her hand over her eyes to wipe away the tears. 'You look terrified.'

'That place,' Gerry nodded towards the opening. 'I'm afraid of it, it's like something terrible happened there.'

Wylmet gasped, and a look passed between the two. It was Kerenza who spoke for them both.

'Do you have the Sight, Gerralda?'

Gerry paused before answering, choosing her words carefully. She had heard the phrase, but never associated it with herself.

'I suppose I have,' she said slowly. 'All my life, small things have happened. I didn't realise -' she was about to put her hand to Seona's gold chain again, but stopped herself.

'You have never been taught,' Wylmet exclaimed. 'We must tell Hedra, but that will have to wait until the morning.' She turned to Kerenza excitedly. 'Do you think that is why she has come to us? To help us in our search?'

Kerenza looked at Gerry curiously.

'You have never spoken of this, then? No-one has ever known?'

'I never told anyone,' Gerry said candidly. 'My family would have thought I was talking nonsense. Except for Seona, my great-aunt; she must have known. If only she'd told me!' Suddenly, so many of their conversations fitted into a context Gerry had never even thought of. It was weird that in this place where so much was strange the most unlikely thing about her was accepted as quite natural.

'I expect your aunt had her reasons.' Kerenza didn't seem to find anything at all odd in what Gerry had said. 'If you were living among people who view it with suspicion then it would be best to keep silent.'

'But help in what search?' Gerry demanded. Wylmet's excitement was infectious, and a vista was opening in front of her. Perhaps she did have a gift she'd never recognised.

Kerenza looked all round to make sure no-one was within earshot.

'No one is supposed to know of this,' she began, giving Wylmet a warning look. 'Of course everything concerns the Tegennow a'n gammneves.'

47

Gerry caught her breath. She understood that the Cornish phrase meant 'the Jewels of the rainbow', and again had to stop herself from touching the stone at her throat. She would have sworn she had felt that faint throb again, as she had when Baranwen had raised the chalice.

'They were so beautiful,' Wylmet sighed. 'Each one large, and perfect, and valuable in itself, but together... and they were not just beautiful but powerful.'

'Everyone living here knows this,' Kerenza took over again, 'though few have seen them. The garnet, topaz, sapphire and amethyst, set on a gold chalice bearing our symbols, with rock crystals between them. Gold for sunlight and crystal for water. They take the sunlight, and the light of the jewels overlap to form a full rainbow, blazing with its own radiance. No-one ever forgets the sight of it.'

"Bearing our symbols". Both Wylmet and Kerenza wore marks on the left wrist as well as at the base of the throat. She could just make out that the one on the inside of the wrist was a circle with two crossed lines within it. The other shape, at the throat, looked like two capital B's, one reversed, joined at the spine and with tiny lines above and below. It could have been a rough symbol of a bee. She wanted very badly to examine her stone. Those marks on the metal which she'd dismissed as scratches - Gerry wondered now if they were the bee and the crossed circle. The chalice that Kerenza was talking about must be the one that Baranwen had spoken of earlier. But it had been – what was Baranwen's word – "violated".

Kerenza was still speaking.

'The Kelegel, our chalice, was filled when it was made with a magic unknown in this day, and the power of the Jewels, the Tegennow, was extraordinary. For healing of course, and knowledge, but much more, that we beginners would not even know of. Some even believe the trained adept using them could travel to other places and other times. It is the role of the Guardians to protect them as well as learn their skills. It requires long and patient training, self-discipline. She,' Kerenza looked contemptuous, and gestured back towards the group by the bonfire, 'Ysella, will never be able to do that.'

'But,' Kerenza went on, 'the Kelegel was stolen five days ago, perhaps by a greedy thief reckless of trespassing against the Goddess. The Jewels were worth a queen's ransom, even just as jewels. Or worse, they were stolen by someone who coveted the power the Jewels could bestow on the gifted. We can only pray they were kept together. If parted, they might never regain their powers, and simply be a beautiful and useless memory, to torment us for ever.'

Gerry felt something plummet inside her, from the base of her throat to the region of her midriff. The glowing chunk of blue at her neck was large and beautiful, but it could not, totally could not, be one of these 'Tegennow'. The Jewels of the Rainbow. The name seemed to resonate inside her.

Kerenza continued sombrely, 'It was at the summer solstice, one of our most sacred days. Delenyk, who was Guardian on the night they disappeared, could not tell what had happened to the Kelegel.' The Chalice, Gerry translated inwardly. 'As tradition demands she was tortured, put to death and her body burned. Then the ashes were buried down there.' She indicated the dark opening below the huge boulders. 'A cavity was made in the wall inside and the opening blocked up with stone. Only Baranwen knows where. And since then, despite all our efforts we have had no word of the Tegennow.'

In spite of the dread roused by this story, Gerry knew

this wasn't what had scared her. That entrance held some terror personal to herself; danger as yet unknown threatened there. She looked away down the hill, and saw something else; a motionless dark-clad figure standing unobtrusively in the shadow beyond the stacked granite. The others didn't appear to have seen him; they were lost in gloomy contemplation. But even with nothing visible but a shadowy outline, Gerry knew who it was.

'I'm sorry,' she apologised, 'I've got to go,' hoping it sounded as if she needed a pee. She hurried off past the boulders, and the sinister opening leading into the place where the Guardian Delenyk's ashes were hidden.

The man was standing still below the stones, by some trick merging into the growing shadows so effectively that Gerry wondered how she'd seen him at all. Even through the turmoil of dread which the story of Delenyk had raised in her, Gerry couldn't help being physically aware of him. His body was lean and firm, the planes of his face clear even in the gloom. His attitude was wholly relaxed, yet she was sure he could spring into action in seconds if needs be. The gleaming fair hair was covered by his hood.

Gerry had come to speak to this man, certain he could answer some of her questions about what was happening here, but standing in front of him she felt shy and awkward. The gentle chanting from the hilltop was the only sound now, since the birds and animals had all settled for the night.

'Are you Justin?' Gerry asked. It was all she could think of to say.

'Here they would call me Iestyn.' His voice had undertones of amusement as they had earlier. 'I've been waiting for you.'

'That's impossible,' Gerry said. She was dreaming, wasn't she? 'How could you know I was going to be here?'

Justin smiled calmly.

'Because I brought you here,' he said. 'And you're not dreaming. You must really know where you are; you're just refusing to accept it.'

'Of course I'm dreaming,' Gerry retorted, her shyness vanishing in indignation. Then she took in the implications of his words. 'Are you reading my mind?'

He laughed softly.

'You make it very easy. You need to learn to shield yourself or the Guardians will be picking up your thoughts too, and I can't have that.'

Gerry's panic, temporarily in abeyance, returned in force.

'The Guardians? Are they here? They'll kill me! They already tried this afternoon.'

'Don't worry, you're perfectly safe for now. And it wasn't this afternoon. Here, this is five days later.'

'Of course it was this afternoon,' Gerry protested. That was hardly the best thing to say to someone she wanted to impress, but for the moment she no longer cared. 'Can't you just explain instead of talking in riddles?'

'I can't, not now.' He came closer and put his hand briefly over her mouth. The hand was cool and firm and the touch sent shivers right through her. 'I'll tell you tomorrow. This is not the place or the time to talk. What I want to know is this. There's something here that I need but I can't get it by myself. I have to have assistance, and you're just the woman to do it - but it could be dangerous. Will you help me?'

Justin's other hand was on Gerry's shoulder, pulling her nearer to him. She was acutely aware of how close his body was to hers. Suddenly the things she wanted to know seemed unimportant.

'Help you?' she asked, her voice faltering. 'Help you how?'

'I'll tell you tomorrow, at the fireworks.' He breathed the words into her ear. 'Will you be there?'

'Yes, but -' she stopped, confused.

Justin laughed again. The next moment he had stepped back and disappeared into the shadows.

And Gerry found herself back in her room, sitting up on the bed, shaking and alone.

Chapter Five

Once she was undressed and properly in bed, it took Gerry hours to get to sleep. Her brain was reeling with all she'd seen. Naturally she overslept and had to dash around to get her room cleared. Mrs. Angove, all solicitude, urged breakfast on her, and suggested she could leave her belongings to collect after work. Gerry made herself eat and found she was ravenous. Then, after bringing her things down from her bedroom and putting them in the corner of the Angoves' living room, she went to sit in her car with the list of numbers she'd looked up before going to bed. The jewellers' shops should be open by this time.

Gerry got the right one on the third attempt. The man who answered put the call on hold for a moment, then transferred her. A pleasant voice said 'Hello?'

'Is that Mr. Alastair Fletcher?' Gerry asked.

'Yes?'

She plunged in.

'My name's Gerry Hamilton. You won't know me, but I,' how could she phrase this? 'I know Mr. Trewartha, he's got a shop

53

in Penzance.' There was silence from the other end. Gerry went on nervously.

'I took something in to show him yesterday and he said he'd like you to see it. He was going to ring you but he can't now. I suppose you heard about what happened?' She paused, hoping for a response, but got only silence which seemed to go on and on. At last she said 'Hello? Are you there?'

'Miss Hamilton, can you tell me what it was you showed him?'

Gerry nearly corrected him to "Ms." but for once decided against.

'I'd rather not, not over the phone,' she said instead. 'If you tell me where you work, I could bring it in to show you. I could be in Redruth in about half an hour, he said that's where you are.'

There was another silence, then he said, 'I'm more or less retired, but I used to be a partner in a shop off Fore Street, and I still have an interest in it. By chance it happens that I'm here this morning.'

Gerry didn't correct that either, but she doubted very much if chance came into it. Mr. Fletcher gave the address and told her how to find it. She thanked him and was about to ring off, when he added, 'Francis left me a message yesterday afternoon. There was something he wanted to tell me and he sounded unusually excited. I presume it was regarding whatever it is you don't want to talk to me about over the phone. I'm very sorry that I was out when he phoned.'

So am I, Gerry thought. She thanked him and said she'd see him later.

It took less than half an hour to reach the outskirts of Redruth. As she drove, Gerry thought about Mr. Trewartha, lying unconscious in the Penzance hospital, and about the mysterious Baranwen. Gerry had been convinced the night before that the two women – the Guardian and the stall holder - were one and the same. But why should Baranwen sell her the stone then claim it had been stolen? Assuming of course that the stone in the pendant really was a sapphire, and the same sapphire at that. Gerry should have the answer to the first question soon enough.

She didn't expect to be long with Mr. Fletcher; she'd be able to get a coffee somewhere and still be back in Penzance in time for work. She found a parking space in one of the side streets near the station. Gerry was about to get out of the car when she remembered Kerenza and Wylmet, and the signs they wore: the crossed circle and the mark like a bee. She reached for the clasp on the gold chain to take it off and have another look at the scratches or marks on the setting. Then she felt a faint throb at the base of her throat where the stone rested, as she had the day before. She decided to leave it where it was.

Gerry walked down Fore Street, looking for the passageway Mr. Fletcher had described. She'd become irrationally nervous, and her heart was thudding. There seemed no reason for that; she was only going to show a jeweller something which might be old or modern, valuable or worthless.

It was easy enough to find the building. A quick glance in the right hand window showed they had a range of gold items for men: cuff-links, tie pins, watches, and signet or wedding rings. The other window carried a selection of women's jewellery and small knick-knacks.

Gerry pushed the door open and walked into an interior very like Mr. Trewartha's. There were display cabinets on the right filled with clocks, silver cups, and watches, and a counter on the left. Two men stood there, both wearing suits and ties. The younger of the two was tall and neat, with an open smile and pleasant manner. Addressing Gerry as if she were as self-possessed and smart as Claudia, instead of untidy and flustered, he asked, 'Can I help you? Are you looking for a present for someone?'

Gerry made herself smile back. 'No,' she said, 'I'm looking for Mr. Fletcher. My name's Gerry Hamilton and I think he's expecting me.'

No, not what I expected. It was the older man of course, the unsmiling one. He held out his hand and Gerry shook it uncertainly.

'Miss Hamilton? Would you like to come into the office?'

Gerry could feel the other man regarding her curiously. However, all he said was, 'Can I get you a cup of coffee? What about you, Alastair?'

'No, thank you, Simon.' He looked at Gerry.

'I'm good, thanks,' she said quickly. Now she was here she just wanted to get on with it. Mr. Fletcher motioned her to come round the counter and showed her through to the room behind it. There were shelves of items which could be orders or repairs, an old-fashioned filing cabinet, and a desk with the same kind of metal desk lamp on it as Mr. Trewartha had used. Mr. Fletcher closed the door after them, sat down behind the desk and gestured Gerry towards the chair opposite. She wished she could have talked to his colleague Simon instead. Alastair Fletcher was heavily built, and although clean-shaven and smartly dressed there was something in his manner at odds with his appearance.

The jeweller looked at Gerry enquiringly. She ignored the chair and remained standing, her bag swinging from her shoulder. The pendant was concealed inside her top. Now she felt for the clasp on the chain and reluctantly unfastened it. As she took it off, the stone gave again the faint throb that it had in the car.

Alastair Fletcher reached across and took the pendant from her, switching on the desk lamp and holding the stone under the light. Like Mr. Trewartha, he used a cloth to hold it with and took a lens to examine it more closely. He was silent for so long that finally Gerry asked,

'What do you think? Is it really a sapphire?'

'Oh, it's a sapphire all right,' he said, almost absently, as if that were of no importance. 'No, it's the workmanship that's interesting. It's almost like -' then he stopped.

'So,' Gerry pursued, 'what do you think? Could this be really old? Your friend said it was possible.'

'I wouldn't have thought so before I saw it,' he replied. 'Now I'm not sure. I know what it looks like, but even for that era it's unusual.' He was examining the marks on the gold, which Gerry had dismissed as scratches on first seeing them. Leaning forward, she tried to get a closer look herself. From where she stood she couldn't see them properly, but it was certainly possible that some were the signs she had seen on Kerenza and Wylmet. Others looked more like writing, but in no letters that Gerry could decipher.

'If this is what I think it might be,' Mr. Fletcher went on, 'it would be hard to set a price on. And just how do you come to have it?'

Something in his voice alarmed her. People had told Gerry before that she was too trusting, and for the first time she really understood what they meant. She'd brought a possibly precious object to a complete stranger and she was alone with him. Gerry had assumed that Mr. Trewartha's friend would be like he was: kind, gentle, and trustworthy. This man was none of those things.

'I bought it,' she told him firmly.

'And of course you have a receipt?'

'Not with me,' Gerry said, which was true. She didn't have a receipt at all. She reached out to take back the pendant and at once Alastair Fletcher closed his hand over it. There was greed in his eyes, and calculation.

'I wouldn't do that if I were you,' he said smoothly. 'I'm a very respected figure round here. I could call the police and have you arrested for attempted robbery. Which of us,' his eyes swept over Gerry's cheap clothes and plastic hoop earrings, 'do you think they'd believe? Come now, Miss Hamilton, be reasonable. I can offer you a very good sum for this; money I'm sure you'd be glad to have.'

'No way,' Gerry told him, no longer bothering to be polite, 'It's not for sale. Just give it back to me. It's mine.'

Alastair Fletcher looked at her and smiled. It was not a reassuring smile. 'I don't think so,' he said, 'however you came by it. Really this piece should be in a museum.'

Gerry's heart had begun pounding hard. The gloves were off now.

'You don't want to put it in a museum. You want it for yourself, but you've no right to it.' An anger she'd never known she could feel, a strength that was not hers, had begun to flood through her. 'For your own good, I think you should give it back to me.'

He looked startled as well he might; the tone of Gerry's voice had changed. If she didn't want the Guardians to have her stone, she certainly wasn't going to be robbed of it by this man. Then the jeweller smiled again, a cold, satisfied smile.

'Are you threatening me? Then I really think I should call the police.' He reached with his free hand for the phone in front of him. Gerry didn't hesitate; she leapt forward and knocked the receiver away. At once his hand slid under the desk; there must be a panic alarm button there. Gerry lunged further forward across the desk top, pushing his arm away from the button with a force that toppled him over backwards in his chair. Alastair Fletcher was a big man, but Gerry was desperate, and the unfamiliar rage was driving her. In seconds she'd grabbed the sapphire and chain which had dropped from his hand onto the desk top as he fell, and was out of the room, slamming the door behind her. The jeweller was on the far side of the desk, and there was other furniture between him and the door, but Gerry was sure he'd be up and after her in no time. She raced for the shop door, but to her dismay found it didn't open from the inside. There was some time-lapse mechanism attached to it.

'Let me out!' Gerry shouted at Simon, who was standing at the counter. She was terrified in case Mr. Fletcher had already pressed the panic button and would have her accused of theft. How could she prove the sapphire was hers?

The assistant stared in astonishment.

'What's happened?' he asked, turning towards the office door. 'Alastair?' Gerry pulled her mobile out of her bag.

'Let me out,' she repeated, 'or I'll bang on your door and yell for help. He just tried to grope me!'

Gerry was sure she looked frantic and dishevelled enough for this to be true, and she knew Simon had been puzzled when she arrived. It wasn't likely that young women wearing chain store clothes and "fashion" jewellery usually arrived here asking for one of the shop's owners by name. The assistant looked at her doubtfully, but perhaps thinking Gerry would create a scandal for their respectable business, he released the mechanism, just as the office door flew open behind him. Gerry heard a shout, but she was already out through the door. She fled onto Fore Street, up and round the corner into another road.

Gerry kept running, her heart pounding, but knew she had to get somewhere out of sight as fast as possible. She spotted a stone building with a large glass window and an A-board outside. It looked like it was open to the public. She rushed through the door, spotted a sign saying 'Toilets', and made a beeline for the Ladies. Once inside, she dashed into a cubicle, bolted the door and stood gasping, leaning against the wall. The incomprehensible fury which had invaded her body and mind when Alastair Fletcher had tried to seize the pendant had drained away, leaving her weak and shaky.

Gerry was still clutching the stone and the gold chain as if her life depended on it. She sat down on the closed lid of the toilet seat and opened her hand. The chain was threaded securely through the holding loops at the back of the stone. This time Gerry looked properly at the marks on the front of the setting and confirmed what she'd guessed before. They were indeed the circle with the two crossed lines, and the back-to-back capital 'B's with the little lines above and below. There was also the writing, which was in an alphabet she'd never seen.

Gerry fastened the chain back around her neck, remembering the throbbing that had warned her against taking it off. Then she unlocked the cubicle door and went to the sink. She looked in the mirror, surprised to see how normal her reflection appeared. An oval face, with freckles so light few people noticed them. Grey-green eyes, looking more like hazel under the cloakroom lightbulbs. Her hair, falling straight from its centre parting, was swinging round her face as usual. Gerry tucked it behind her ears and slid the sapphire back inside her top, checking in the mirror to make sure that only the chain showed.

Gerry emerged from the Ladies, praying she could get safely back to her car. She couldn't hang around Redruth in case Mr. Fletcher was searching the streets for her. He wanted the sapphire very much, and might easily report her for stealing it as he'd threatened. For all Gerry knew, he might have already given her description to the police. She could stop for coffee later on the way back to Penzance – she really needed some. As Gerry came out from the carpeted corridor which led to the toilets, she saw that the building she was in was some sort of library. There were rows of books on pale wooden shelves, long tables where people sat, apparently studying, half a dozen computers and a row of some sort of old-fashioned viewing screens. The place felt more peaceful than the Penzance library. There was a pale blue carpet, and a set of pictures round the wall which looked like needlework tapestries.

An earnest-looking man with the beginnings of grey in his hair was sitting at a computer behind a low counter made of the same smooth pale wood as the shelves. Gerry hesitated, but couldn't think of any plausible way to ask if anyone had come in looking for someone like her. As she stood there, irresolute, the man at the counter glanced up. He was wearing a Cornwall Council badge which gave his name as Graham.

'Can I help you?' he smiled, then looked at Gerry more closely. She could feel her heart beginning to thump again, but the next moment he said, 'Excuse me asking, but I thought I recognised you. Don't you work in Penzance library? I was there for a meeting last week and I'm sure I saw you there.'

'Yes, that's right.' Gerry was so relieved that she smiled back as warmly as if he was an old friend. 'I'm one of the agency staff.'

Gerry, who'd spent a lot of time in libraries in London, had gone into the town library on her first day in Penzance to ask where the Jobcentre was. Debbie was on the desk, and told her they were short-handed there in the library. She explained about the agency in Truro who could appoint people as temps for the Council more or less straight away, bypassing the lengthy appointment procedure for permanent work. Gerry had called them, gone to their offices the next day and been taken on.

'Ah, the precious agency.' Graham said. 'And as Penzance have been lucky enough to get you, they're hanging on to you?'

Being employed through the staffing agency meant that Gerry could in theory work in any of the Council libraries if they were below quota due to leave and/or sickness, but she hadn't looked beyond Penzance.

'I get four days' work at Penzance most weeks,' Gerry said. 'That's just about enough to live on.' Or rather, approaching other branches would have entailed more effort than she felt up to.

A woman in a t-shirt and jeans came through a door behind the counter and said 'Tea break!' to Graham. Her name badge read 'Lowenna', which sounded Cornish. She was carrying a stack of booklets which she dumped beside the computer.

'Donations,' she grumbled. 'And I've got to check every single one against the catalogue.'

'Don't complain, you're always telling me we need them,' Graham replied. Lowenna pulled a chair over for herself, then noticed Gerry standing there.

'Sorry,' she said, 'can I help at all?'

Graham stood up. 'This is an agency worker - what's your name, by the way?'

'It's Gerry. Gerry Hamilton.'

'She's a refugee from Penzance,' Graham explained to Lowenna, then turned back to Gerry. 'I was just thinking,

I'm on my break now. Would you like to come and have a cup of coffee?'

For a scary moment Gerry imagined a trap. Was she about to confront an irate jeweller or a uniformed officer? Next minute she realised how unlikely that was. And the last place they would expect to find a runaway would be in the staff room of a library, casually drinking coffee.

'Yes, please,' she agreed, 'but I mustn't be long. I've got to start at Penzance at 12.'

Graham disappeared through the door Lowenna had come from, and Gerry wondered if he expected her to follow.

'Tea break's only 15 minutes,' Lowenna said sternly, but her serious face was suddenly lit up with amusement. She turned to Gerry. 'He's only doing this because you're pretty. If it was someone like "Miss Fraser" he wouldn't bother.' Lowenna had given a very good imitation of Monica's voice, and laughed at Gerry's look of surprise. 'Oh, we all know her. I bet she's hacked off at having you around. That one likes to think she's the beauty queen of the library. As if.' She went to the door again and showed Gerry through into a corridor, pointing out an open door opposite. 'There's the staff room, and be warned, Graham makes terrible coffee.'

Was Lowenna joking? Gerry didn't think she was pretty. Bemused, she went into the room and sat down opposite the large window overlooking the street. Graham was standing at an urn which stood on the work surface next to a microwave. He handed Gerry a mug, and poured hot water into another for himself. Lowenna had been teasing; the coffee was instant but not that bad.

Graham sat down on a chair with his back to the window, and started drinking his coffee. Gerry drank some of hers. It wasn't a chocolate-sprinkled cappuccino, which had become her favourite in London, and the milk was cold when she preferred it hot, but she was glad of it all the same.

'I like it here,' she said, feeling she should say something. 'So, is this the Redruth library?'

'No, it's not. This is the Cornish Studies library.' Graham sounded indignant. He explained that they covered anything and everything to do with Cornwall, present and past: old newspapers, maps and pictures, books on every subject from ships to Cornish cooking; leaflets, census and parish records.

'It sounds fascinating,' Gerry said politely. It probably was, but she really wasn't interested right now.

'I've had a brainwave,' Graham said. 'If you're one of the agency staff, perhaps you could put in a couple of days here next time we're short-handed.'

'It's a thought,' Gerry agreed, though she had no intention of taking it up. 'Anyway, I'd better be getting back to Penzance.'

'You could leave your number,' he suggested, returning his mug to the sink and taking hers too. 'Then we could contact you.'

'I'll give the number to Lowenna,' Gerry said firmly. 'Thanks for the coffee, but I really need to go.' If that had been meant as a chat-up line, it was wasted on her. Anyway, Graham was too old. She remembered Justin's hand on her shoulder, pulling her close to him, his voice whispering in her ear. She wondered how old Justin was, but knew that in his case it wouldn't matter.

Gerry gave Lowenna her number on the way out, then walked back down the road without seeing any policemen. She forgot about Graham, Lowenna and the Cornish Studies library before she got back to the car. As soon as she was alone again her thoughts went straight back to the events in the jeweller's shop.

So, the stone really was a sapphire, and almost certainly old, very old. That much was confirmed. Mr. Fletcher had offered her a large sum of money, so it wasn't just old, but special too. She remembered that strange, powerful anger that had overtaken her at the thought of being deprived of the stone. She mustn't show it to anyone else. She wouldn't even take it off again. This was doing her head in. She could only trust that when she saw Justin at the fireworks in the evening he would explain as he'd promised.

Gerry got to Penzance library with time to spare and headed for the staff room where she found Debbie talking to Ryan. Another agency worker, Ernie, was sitting by himself, checking his smartphone. Ryan looked up and gave Gerry a broad grin.

'Missed you yesterday,' he said cheerfully. 'This place isn't the same when you're not here.'

Gerry tucked her hair behind her ears, and smiled back at him. Ryan was always easy to be with.

'You don't need to flatter me,' she told him, 'I'm not one of your paying customers.'

At that moment Monica emerged from the cloakroom, trim and immaculate as always in pressed slacks and a sleeveless blouse. She gave Gerry a critical look, and she felt even more scruffy than she had at the jeweller's shop.

Ryan rose from his seat, looking at his oversize watch, and gave Gerry a conspiratorial wink.

'I'd rather stay here with you girls, but as Gerry reminds me I've got a customer waiting.' He grinned at her again as he went up the half-dozen stairs and out through the door into the main library.

Gerry pulled out the filled roll she'd bought at a baker's, feeling suddenly ravenous again despite Mrs. Angove's breakfast.

She'd eaten little enough the day before. Monica looked at the roll dubiously.

'I think you're very brave, eating those. You never know what goes into them. I always bring my own food; besides, it saves money.' Suiting the action to the word she pulled a plastic tub of neatly chopped, colourful salad from the fridge. Trying to ignore her, Gerry sat down opposite Debbie.

'That's a nice top,' she said. 'Is it new?'

Debbie beamed.

'No, but I haven't been able to get into it for ages. I've finally got from size 16 back to size 14.'

Before Gerry could congratulate her, Monica broke in. 'Really?' she purred, a forkful of lettuce suspended over her plate. 'I've always found size 10 a bit bigger than I want to be.'

Gerry seethed on Debbie's behalf, but couldn't think of a good retort. She was sure Monica wouldn't have been so bitchy if Ryan had still been there.

'I hate that woman,' Gerry muttered to Debbie later. They were in the workroom; Gerry was unpacking the stock that had arrived on the library van, while Debbie sorted out the reserved books, CDs and DVDs. 'But I can never think of a way of getting back at her.'

'You don't need to.' Debbie checked the computer screen, wrote a name and date on a label, tucked it into the next book and added it to the pile. 'She's jealous of you 'cos she likes Ryan but you're the one he fancies. Besides, some of the punters she thinks of as her property would rather talk to you.'

'Right,' Gerry said, doubtful but pleased. She pulled the last items out from the box and took them over to the computer for Debbie to check in, hoping her friend wasn't brooding. She guessed Monica's snide comment would have spoiled Debbie's simple pleasure at losing some weight.

Gerry got through the day without making too many mistakes, as far as she could tell. There was a quiet time in the middle of the afternoon when she was shelving, and Debbie came over to choose some books for a display. Gerry took the opportunity to tell her some more about Claudia's house, and had covered most of it when Monica came marching over to them.

'If you two don't have any work to do I can easily find you some,' she said. Gerry was reminded of Ysella sweeping down on Kerenza and Wylmet, but Ysella at least had some form of authority. Here only Hilary, the library manager, had the right to allocate tasks to the staff.

Gerry couldn't wait for the end of the afternoon. As the force of her scare of the morning receded, she found herself thinking more and more about Justin. What did he want her to help him with? What sort of danger was he referring to? Gerry had encountered more threats in the last two days than in her whole life. And, aside from either of these questions there was another - would Justin put his hand on her shoulder or arm again? Gerry could feel herself quivering just at the memory.

When 5 o'clock came, she said goodbye to Debbie, then walked back through Penlee Park and down Alexandra Road to the B & B for the last time. Mrs. Angove was in the kitchen and Gerry went to have a few words with her before collecting her belongings from the living room. The landlady urged her to come and have tea with them soon. Mr. Angove was watching the West Country evening news. Gerry threw a casual glance across at the screen and was horrified to see a picture of Fore Street.

'A jeweller's shop in Redruth has been targeted in the second incident in two days,' the announcer said. The camera shot moved up the street to the front of Mr. Fletcher's establishment. 'Two men are in hospital following a violent attack on this small shop at lunchtime today. Police are appealing for any witnesses to come forward. In particular they would like to speak to a young woman who was seen leaving the premises shortly before the incident took place. A man is still in hospital, in a critical but stable condition, following a similar assault in Penzance yesterday. It has not yet been established if anything was stolen.'

The newsreader moved on to the next story concerning a village in Devon whose inhabitants were trying to get the speed limit reduced along the road past the village school. Gerry turned away, moved her things into the hallway and began to take them to the car. Her suitcases were heavy, and she banged her shin painfully on the larger one, but she hardly noticed.

Violence had been following her since she bought the sapphire – was it really only yesterday? And why were those men in hospital? She'd only pushed Mr. Fletcher over in his chair, and hadn't touched the young man called Simon. Gerry had no sympathy for Alastair Fletcher but his assistant had done nothing wrong, and nor had Mr. Trewartha. Who had attacked these men?

And was it fair on Claudia to move into her house? Gerry didn't want her new landlady to be the next victim of this unknown thug. Yet if she stayed here, perhaps it would be the Angoves, and they'd been good to her, as well as being older. Claudia looked like she could cope with trouble better than a couple of retired B & B owners. Gerry could only trust that Claudia would be all right. It was time she went to Windhaven.

Chapter Six

Friday 27ᵗʰ June 2014 - evening

This time, as Gerry turned off the bridle path and drove down the private lane to Windhaven, carefully crossing the cattle grid between two granite posts, she was thinking 'Am I really going to live here? Will I get used to coming back here every day?' The same two cars were parked outside the house, and again Claudia had just come out of the door and up to the gate.

'You look puzzled,' Claudia said as Gerry got out of the Volvo.

'It's those cars,' Gerry explained. 'And you must have very good hearing, you seem to know just when I'm arriving.'

'There's a camera up by the cattle grid. You can't see it,' Claudia added as Gerry turned to look back up the drive. 'It sends an alert to my phone if anything over a metre high crosses there. Not foxes or badgers.' She was as matter-of-fact as if everyone had this outside their home. 'The cars are both mine. I use this one,' she indicated a little Skoda hatchback, 'for local trips like to and from work. The Audi's for when I go to London. It's got six gears and cruise control, so it's good on the motorway.'

Gerry thought of what it cost her just to tax and insure Seona's car, not to mention MOTs and servicing. She couldn't think of any answer.

'Shall I help you bring your things in?' Claudia went on in the same brisk tone. 'Is this all you've got?'

'Yeah,' Gerry said, eyeing the two suitcases of clothes, her laptop, and three cardboard boxes. One of these held bread, tins, milk, coffee and tea, two mugs and some fruit. A second box had personal possessions: books, jewellery, toiletries and make-up. Lastly there was the cardboard box with things from her course at Uni. Gerry took out the bigger suitcase and wheeled it with some difficulty across the gravel to the paved courtyard. Claudia hefted one of the boxes and set off with it. Gerry was worried that Claudia would get dust on her smart clothes, but she carried the box in effortlessly and returned, undaunted, for the next.

When everything was indoors, Claudia showed Gerry space in a kitchen cupboard for her food, and some room in the fridge. Gerry, feeling that none of her possessions seemed to belong in this sophisticated setting and wondering again if she was making a mistake in coming here, had to remind herself it was rent-free. She left the box of food in the kitchen and started moving the rest of the luggage up to her room.

Once the cases and other boxes were upstairs Claudia made them both coffee. Gerry had a momentary vision of moving into a small untidy flat in Penzance with Debbie. She could picture them laughing as they investigated the fixtures and fittings, and wondered if Claudia ever laughed.

'I'll show you the alarm,' Claudia told her, adding milk to her own coffee and stirring it. 'You'll need to know how to set it if you're the last one out, and how to cancel it if you're in before me. If you've any problems you can always ring me.' She passed

Gerry a square of paper with her number on it. 'Now, what else might I need to tell you about? My cleaner comes mid-morning on Tuesdays and Fridays, but I expect you'll be at work then. I told you about the gardener, didn't I? You might see him working anywhere outdoors. He sometimes leaves a bag of vegetables by the back door; feel free to help yourself to them.'

Gerry hadn't done much proper cooking when she was living in London. She thought perhaps she ought to make an effort here, but was nervous about damaging things in this kitchen. Remembering their conversation in the park, Gerry asked, 'So, you're happy that I'm not local?'

Claudia's brows drew together briefly.

'Like I told you, I'm glad you're not' she said. 'I've lived here six years, but it's a very closed circle, the art world at least. There's some very exciting artists here, and I enjoy taking their work to new markets, but I've never felt I belonged. It's the same in the village only more so. You can't say anything about anyone, because you're bound to be talking to their neighbour or sister or someone their son works with. Still,' she looked out through the conservatory windows, across her gardens and along towards the coast, 'when I'm in London, I can't wait to get back here. London feels so dirty, crowded and noisy when you're used to this. Did you find that when you went there from Scotland?'

Gerry nodded. 'I grew up in a small village, a few miles from even the next village in any direction. And the air was so much cleaner there. Even after three years I never got used to London.'

'No, I can imagine,' Claudia agreed. 'Now, I've always lived with a house alarm and wouldn't feel comfortable without it, but this is a very safe location. I checked on a website where you can see how many burglaries, drug-related or anti-social behaviour incidents and so on you get in an area. I looked up some places I knew in London, where the stats varied from a dozen to over 50 in a week. Then I tried this postcode. It scored zero on almost every count, and single figures on the rest. I don't expect you'll have any trouble.'

Gerry thanked her, and as she'd finished her coffee, she stood up, then realised she ought to mention her plans for the evening. She hoped Claudia would put her obvious embarrassment down to the fact that this was her first night at the house. What would Claudia say if she knew who Gerry was going with? Her new landlady had said specifically that she didn't want Justin coming into the house. Yet Gerry was sure Claudia wouldn't like the idea of her seeing him. This wasn't a date; Justin had asked Gerry if she would help him. But she still felt guilty as she explained.

'I'm not often out late, but the Angoves – that's the couple who run the B & B – told me there's a very good fireworks display on the front at Penzance tonight, and I thought I'd go. I don't know what time it finishes, but I expect it'll be after dark.' That would be pretty late, given it was midsummer. 'I'll come in quietly,' she added.

Claudia's eyebrows rose but she only said, 'There's a security light outside; it should come on when you park. There's an automatic light in the courtyard too, so you'll be able to see your way to the front door. Just bolt the door once you're inside.'

There were no street lights here nearer than the village at the bottom of the hill. This was more remote than her family home in the village of Lochallaig. Gerry nodded, and went off upstairs to put her things away, wondering what Claudia was really thinking. Would she have preferred someone like Monica who could at least talk to her about art? Gerry recalled her cool dismissal of Monica

72

in the park, and smiled to herself. No, she decided, Claudia would rather have her than Miss Fraser.

It didn't take long to unpack. Gerry's few belongings seemed to rattle around in the spacious bedroom and bathroom. She looked out of the windows, seeing rabbits in the garden at the back, and, at the side, the allotment section where the rabbits annoyed the gardener by eating his vegetables. The window at the top of the stairs looked out towards the sea, though the view was partly blocked by the kitchen roof. When Gerry went downstairs she found Claudia in the lounge, sitting on the sofa with her laptop on a small table in front of her. Gerry said she was just off out.

'I'm working in the morning, though I don't start till ten,' she added. 'I'd better be away by half nine. Will I see you?'

'Oh, yes,' Claudia replied, looking up. Gerry noticed the wide screen tv was showing a wildlife programme in what looked like the latest high definition, but she didn't think Claudia was watching it. 'I'll be gone to London before you get back from work tomorrow, though. Let me show you the alarms now, in case you're in a rush in the morning. Oh, and I'll give you your key. Remember, call me straight away if there's any problems. Any time.'

Half an hour later Gerry was back in Penzance. She parked at the top of Alexandra Road and walked down to the front. There seemed to be hundreds, no, thousands, of people out and about, exchanging shouts and greetings all round. The streets were packed; the pubs were heaving, and cars inched their way along the road as people spilled off the pavements. Gerry could hear the music of the funfair from the other end of the front. Gazing at the crowds of people she couldn't imagine how it would be possible to locate one individual. Even if they knew each other's numbers it would be impossible to hear a phone ring. Yet Justin had seemed certain they would meet up. She would just have to leave it to him.

Gerry began to work her way foot by foot between the solid mass of bodies, forcing her way to the other side of the road to have the sea on her right creating an illusion of space. Behind her, towards the fishing village of Newlyn, part of the sea wall was still fenced off by metal barriers where the damage from the winter storms hadn't yet been mended. Even in London Gerry had heard about the storms: the flooding of the Somerset Levels, and the railway line to the West Country cut off at Dawlish in Devon. Working here in Penzance she'd been told how the prom had been closed as the sea had burst over the wall and the full width of the front, gale-whipped breakers storming over the tops of the lamp-posts. The force of the waves had even ripped up paving stones and hurled them across the road. The footpaths at the Newlyn end, beloved of dog walkers, had been sealed off for safety for weeks and even now in midsummer not all the destruction had been mended.

It was hard to imagine it now, with the sea barely rippling beyond the painted railings. There was just enough breeze for the long row of banners along the front to wave gently. They had cheerful seaside holiday motifs: jolly mermaids, fish, ice cream cornets, buckets and spades, and octopuses. The colours in the evening sunlight were still bright as a child's poster paints: red and yellow, blue and green, orange and violet. The colours of the rainbow. Gerry felt a catch in her throat as she remembered Kerenza's words. The young woman had spoken of a chalice with jewels, the light of sun and water, the glowing colours of the rainbow making a sight never to be forgotten. The description had woken a hunger in Gerry, a longing to see this wonder for herself. But then she'd seen Justin and everything else had somehow taken second place.

A rumble from her stomach brought Gerry back to earth. There would probably be hot dogs at the funfair, and guessing what Monica would say about them added spice to the idea. Gerry started to push towards the coloured lights of the helter-skelter and the big wheel. When she finally reached it, there was indeed a stall selling hot dogs. These were made with proper Cornish sausages and real onions, unlike the pale imitations Gerry had sometimes tried in London. She ate her way through a generous portion and was just licking the last of the ketchup off her fingers and wondering whether to have a coke or a mug of tea, when all at once she felt herself go still. Gerry couldn't tell how she knew, but she was certain that Justin was somewhere close by.

She looked round in all directions, into the heart of the funfair on the left with its stalls and music and noise, and towards the crowds on the promenade on the right. Lastly she turned to stare behind her, beyond the sleekly curving white walls of the Yacht Inn to the pavement at the foot of Chapel Street where St. Mary's Church towered above all the other buildings. The fair-haired figure Gerry would have known anywhere was there on the far pavement. He was wearing stone coloured chinos and a pale blue short sleeved shirt. Gerry tried and failed to picture him in jeans and trainers, and a t-shirt with a heavy metal band slogan.

She pushed her way across the road and towards the other side, but before she reached Justin he turned and walked towards a stone arch set in the wall. As he turned he looked over at Gerry and smiled. That smile, like the one in the park, seemed to indicate inward amusement rather than to be directed towards her. Despite that, just to be near him again was enough to set Gerry's insides fluttering. Next moment he stepped through the archway and set off up a flight of stone stairs leading into St. Mary's churchyard. Gerry knew a moment's resentment; a word of greeting would have been welcome, an acknowledgement that she'd succeeded in finding him in the massed crowd. Gerry sighed, and made for the wall herself.

When she got there and passed through the archway, Justin was already crossing a flagged path higher up. He climbed more stone steps, and Gerry followed. Apart from the two of them, the churchyard was deserted, though as it got dark lovers, or drunks, might find their way here. At the top of the second set of stairs there was a bench on each side. More steps led to the upper part of the churchyard. Justin was sitting on the bench on the left, so Gerry walked over to sit there too. This close to him, she had trouble breathing normally. The slanting light emphasised the planes and angles of his face with its high cheekbones and unusually dark grey eyes. As Gerry sat down, Justin touched her lightly on the arm, and she shivered. As had happened earlier on the hillside, all the questions she wanted to ask seemed to have slid away. The fact that she was here, sitting next to him, was enough. Finally Justin spoke.

'You said that you would help me. Are you still prepared to? It won't be easy.'

Gerry nodded and sat up straighter, her eyes fixed on his face. 'Yes, of course.'

'Good,' he said, and seemed to relax a little. 'Then I'll explain.' However he didn't start his explanation at once, but sat looking out across the bay into the middle distance. The bench where the two of them were sitting was high up, far above the packed roads, looking across to the darkening waters. At last Justin seemed to come back from a distance and began to speak.

'You heard those women earlier on, speaking of a chalice. They were talking about the Kelegel a'n gammneves, the Chalice of the Rainbow. They keep it hidden on the hilltop and no man

76

is allowed there. I have to have it, or at least borrow it for a while, but it isn't possible for me to go near it.'

Immediately Gerry was full of questions. Why did Justin want the chalice? How did he think she could get it for him? Could she dare risk going near the Guardians again? In the few seconds while she hesitated, trying to decide what to ask first, Justin raised his hand a little.

'Wait,' he said, 'let me finish. I'll answer your questions then, if you still have any.'

Was Gerry really so transparent? Apparently so, at least to him. He had said she needed to learn to guard her thoughts. Again Gerry briefly felt resentment, but Justin's hand brushed lightly against the side of her knee as he lowered it again, and silenced her. Gerry could feel her throat beginning to go dry. She was growing afraid, and it didn't help to be sitting, as it grew dark, in a graveyard, with the carved grey stones scattered seemingly at random, lying among the grass.

Justin looked straight ahead again, his face set.

'I need the Kelegel,' he said, 'to prove that I'm innocent. The chalice was stolen, and I was accused of stealing it. The charge still hangs over me, and always will unless I can show that I'm blameless.'

The long, sensitive fingers were tapping his knee. Gerry wanted to reach over and take his hand, promise that of course she'd help him. The idea of Justin Chancellor as a common thief was ludicrous.

The noise of the people on the streets below, and even the throb of the music of the funfair, seemed diminished and far away. From her seat Gerry could see, way below them, the string of lights looped from one lamp post to the next, part of a linked line swinging along the length of the front. The flags fluttered beyond them. She risked a sidelong glance at Justin and the urge to touch him grew stronger. She looked down at her knees instead.

'The chalice is an heirloom of my family,' Justin went on. 'They have many old things, although nothing else like the Kelegel. For generations they have collected objects which are rare, old, and beautiful, but there also has to be something special about them. The world is full of items which meet one or all of the first three criteria, but very few fall into the fourth category too. And even among these the Chalice of the Rainbow is unique. There has never been another like it in any place or time.'

Gerry wondered how he could be so certain but didn't want to interrupt. Justin went on.

'It disappeared from the collection and Gregory, my younger brother, accused me stealing it. It is more likely that he has it himself, but he convinced them all that I was to blame. It would suit him well to have me out of the way and branded a criminal; then he could have the lands and wealth that should be mine. It was well known that I was fascinated by the Chalice, and Gregory made full use of that.'

Gerry couldn't help noticing that Justin's speech was surprisingly formal; he must have been to a posh public school. That beautiful voice didn't seem to go with saying things like "awesome" and "like, totally", or "that sucks". Gerry stole a sideways glance at him. His face was grim, his eyes distant. She shivered briefly, and knew it was not the breeze making her feel chilled.

'My property was searched,' Justin continued, 'but of course there was no chalice there. Yet the men would not give up, and questioned me over and over again. It was as if they thought I was some sort of wizard, that I could magic the chalice away without trace.'

He looked as if the very memory made him restive, as if he

wanted to get up and pace about. However he remained where he was, his eyes now fixed on Gerry's.

'If I can borrow the chalice from the Guardians I can use it to clear my name, and disgrace Gregory. Then he can be on the receiving end of the forces of law. I shall enjoy doing that.'

'But,' Gerry began. She had spotted a big hole in this argument. 'If the chalice that was stolen from your family home' - mansion, or whatever it was, with all these precious things - 'was unique, what good would the Guardians' one be to you?'

It seemed quite reasonable to her, and she was dismayed when Justin became impatient.

'I thought you'd have understood by now. It's the same chalice, in earlier times. It was made about two thousand years ago. By the time of these Guardians it's six or seven hundred years old. That's where you were when you saw them on Chapel Carn Brea. Back in the so-called Dark Ages.'

Gerry felt her throat close, her mind go numb. Time travel. She thought of Dr. Who; of Hermione in Harry Potter manipulating time to get to extra classes. Of the film "Back to the future".

'No,' she whispered, 'It's not possible.'

'Of course it is. You've already done it twice.' Justin sounded exasperated, like a teacher when a usually bright pupil fails to grasp the workings of a maths calculation. 'Think of what you saw when you were there; and what you didn't see. You must know I'm telling the truth.'

The most frightening thing was that she did. She had known before he said it. Gerry didn't need to review the absence of all traces of the twenty-first century. Justin had told her the night before that she already knew where she was but was refusing to believe it. Plus he'd said that her second visit to the hilltop was five days later than the first, though for her it had been the evening of the same day. Time travel would explain that. She thought of Seona assuring her that mind-reading was perfectly reasonable. That had been trifling by comparison with this. Gerry wished with all her heart that she could talk to her great-aunt. Then she caught her breath. If she could travel in time, then perhaps she could go back to when Seona was still alive. And with that thought, she knew she wanted it to be true.

Justin saw it, of course.

'Good girl,' he said. 'So now all I need to do is tell you where to find the chalice. Or have you already worked that out too?'

'No,' Gerry said, then stopped. A terrible suspicion had come to her. The place where men could not go. The place she had been so afraid of.

'They're in the fogou.'

'What's a fogou?' But Gerry was hedging. She'd guessed what Justin meant.

'They are part of Cornish history. A fogou is a very old passage, stone-lined, leading to a circular chamber walled with stone. No-one in this century,' he waved his arm around towards the town, 'knows for certain what they were used for. The commonest theories are that they were used for religious ceremonies or for storage of food. You were standing by the entrance of one of the oldest and best preserved.'

'Where Delenyk's ashes are?' Gerry could hardly frame the words. She looked back at Justin, dread catching her voice away from her.

'That's right.' He was horribly matter-of-fact. 'The Kelegel a'n gammneves is hidden beside them.'

'I can't.' Gerry spoke involuntarily. 'I can't go in there.'

Justin put his hand on her arm in warning. Three girls with bare midriffs and tight, short skirts came up the steps, giggling and talking loudly about whether "the boys" were going to follow them. They stood and waited briefly, supporting each other, then went up the next flight of stairs to sit at a wooden table with fixed benches on each side, on the level above Gerry and Justin. From her bag, one girl produced cans of lager which they all proceeded to rip open. Wholly self-absorbed, they weren't even aware of the couple on the bench.

But for Gerry the spell was broken. She and Justin were no longer alone, and the eerie atmosphere around them was destroyed by the girls' noisy laughs and chatter. The interruption had given Gerry time to recover but not to change her mind.

'Can't you go?' she asked. 'You're good at keeping out of sight.'

Justin sighed. 'I can't go near their sacred chamber. One of the Guardians is always on watch, or nearby, and they have ways of knowing if any man sets foot in the fogou. It has to be you.'

'They'd kill me fast enough if they found me marching out of that passage clutching their precious chalice.' He'd been so impatient earlier that Gerry found herself responding in kind. 'Do you have any suggestions?'

'I'm sure we can work out something between us.' He smiled at her properly for the first time. 'Have you changed your mind about helping me, Gerralda? I warned you it wouldn't be easy.'

It was the first time he'd addressed her by her full name, and hearing him pronounce it made Gerry quiver, even more than his smile and the touch of his hand had done, but she had to resist. Just as surely as she knew that danger awaited her within that stone chamber, Gerry knew that she had to be very careful around this man. She'd never told him her name. He had either overheard

81

her conversation with Kerenza and Wylmet on the hilltop from a distance, or was reading her mind again. Neither was good.

Justin seemed to sense her change of mood, for he stood up. 'I'll let you think about it.' Gerry stood up too. The sky was slowly turning to dusk above the lights of the fair and of the town. Shrieks came from the occupants of the cars on the big wheel, high above the ground. 'I'll catch you later,' Justin said.

There was a scuffle below them, and more loud voices. It appeared that "the boys" had decided to come up after the girls. There were half a dozen of them, shouting, boisterous, holding cans of beer or lager. Gerry glared at them for a moment, then turned back to share a look with Justin. But in that moment while she was looking at the lads, he'd already gone.

"I'll catch you later". Did he mean later this evening when the rockets went up? Or would it be after she went to bed, when Gerry would again find herself in that strange world which was already as real to her as Penzance or Windhaven?

Gerry still had to drive back on an unfamiliar road, so she joined one of the pub queues and got a low alcohol lager. It came in a plastic cup; no pub sold drinks in glasses on this night. She wandered along the front, past the Queens Hotel with its tall lighted windows shining out across the still-crowded pavements. Then she leaned on the sea wall, supporting her drink on the stone top. Lights were coming on in the boats, some close in, others far out in the bay near the horizon, or eastward towards the beach and village of Marazion and the sloping silhouette of St Michael's Mount. On her right, street and house lights had sprung up in Newlyn too: from buildings along the coast road, houses scattered at random up the hillside, and the long line of Chywoone Hill stretching upwards.

Despite the entrancing view spread before her, and her recent meal, Gerry felt hollow inside, her stomach a flat pain below her ribs. He, Justin, wanted her to go into that stone passage and hunt around beside the ashes of a dead woman. A woman who'd been killed ignominiously as a traitor with no funeral rites. Kerenza had said no-one but Baranwen knew where the ashes were, but Gerry had no concerns on that score. She was certain the Jewels of the Rainbow would call to her, or else to the sapphire, which would come to the same thing. She wouldn't need Justin to help her locate them, but getting out of the fogou with them was another matter.

She stared into the gently moving water as it slowly darkened to nearly black. The string of lights slung between the street lights reflected in dancing patterns on the water's surface, as Gerry turned the problem over and over in her mind. At last she came to her decision. She had to try to get into the fogou or she wouldn't be able to live with herself. If Justin wanted the chalice, he must have some scheme to get her away from there safely.

It had grown fully dark and Gerry hadn't noticed. She moved away from the wall, turned round and saw Justin. He'd been standing watching her; she had no idea for how long. She looked at him then nodded slowly.

'I'll go,' she said, and Justin smiled.

'Good girl,' he said. 'Now, come here. I'll teach you something that will help.'

Gerry walked towards him, shivering a little; the temperature had dropped as the darkness grew. Justin put his arm round her then pulled her against him. At that moment there came a whoosh and a bang in the sky from the direction of the harbour. The fireworks were starting at last. Cries of excitement came from the crowd round them. Gerry started; she'd felt as if they were alone despite all the people on the front.

Justin's arm steadied her as she looked upwards. He turned her to face the fireworks, her back held tightly against his chest, then leaned down. She could feel his hair falling forward and brushing the top of her head.

'You need a way of clearing your mind,' he told her. 'You have a talent within you, or I could not have brought you to the Guardians, but you have never learned to use it.'

Gerry could hardly take in what he was saying; she was too aware of being in his arms. She tried to concentrate. Justin put his hand below her chin and tilted her face towards the red and green sparks of a rocket's tail, high above.

'Now, watch the centre of the fireworks as they explode,' he instructed. 'Then hold the memory fast in your mind. Think of nothing else, and fix it there so that you can call it up when you need. Then you will be able to find the way to the Chalice. And it can help you too if you ever need to make a quick getaway.'

Gerry didn't understand what he meant, but resolved to try. Though as well as remembering the pattern of the fireworks, there was a another memory she vowed to keep. The sensation of leaning back against Justin's firm, strong body, his arm holding her close to him. She felt hollow inside again, but this time it was with wanting him. It felt so good to be with him that all her doubts melted. If Justin said the Kelegel would call her and she could travel in time, then he must be right.

Mrs. Angove hadn't exaggerated; the display was spectacular. Gerry had loved fireworks for as long as she could remember. She gazed up at the radiating explosions of red, green, blue and white, crying out at the most dramatic ones: a circle of red within a larger one of green, huge showers of purple and blue like giant dandelion clocks, a succession of small cream circles lapping over each other. And as she looked at each, she tried to do what Justin had said and form an image of it in her memory. It didn't seem difficult. The easiest to focus on were the circles of blue and purple, exploding into huge rings around each other. She could have stayed there watching all night, but suddenly the display ended, amid spontaneous applause and shouts from the watching crowd. And in that same moment, Justin removed his arm and disappeared. Gerry was still pressed in on all sides, but now there was just an emptiness where he had been.

She went off reluctantly to find her car and make her way back to Claudia's house in the dark. She mustn't be downhearted. She was sure she would see Justin again soon. She hoped he wasn't going to expect her to look for the chalice that night. Gerry thought of the knife-wielding Guardians, the owners of the Kelegel. No way would they agree to let her borrow it. She wanted to know what plans Justin had to protect her if she was attacked. She was certain she would be. Something more than just the Chalice was waiting for her in that chamber.

Chapter Seven

But that night Gerry didn't find herself on the hilltop at Chapel Carn Brea. When she went up to her bedroom at Windhaven, she pulled her hoodie over her day clothes and changed into warm leggings and boots. She stood beside the bed and thought about the fogou. Then she closed her eyes and tried to clear her mind as Justin had told her, picturing the centre of the exploding fireworks. She stayed still, waiting to see if anything happened, but could only feel darkness and silence. Wasn't this going to work? She'd got there twice without even knowing, and now she wanted to go and, more to the point, Justin wanted her to. He said he'd brought her there before. She had to trust him. Then she felt ground, not floor, beneath her feet, and the temperature changed.

Gerry opened her eyes, but was dismayed to find she was standing among trees. It was nearly dark underneath them, the thick branches overhead blocking out most of the light. This was all wrong. Gerry wondered at first if she was just having an ordinary dream, but now she'd accepted the fact of time travel she could tell that the air felt different here. Gerry remembered the woods she'd seen from the hilltop, and hoped that was where she was, not too far from Chapel Carn Brea. The trees were in the full, dark green leaf of mid to late summer. Beyond them there was a large clearing, and she could hear sounds coming from there. Gerry moved forward to investigate, while remaining within the cover of the trees. She wouldn't risk showing herself till she had a better idea of where she was – and who else was here.

In front of her, Gerry saw a tall, solid stone wall which curved away on both sides. A wide gate in this wall stood open and she could see stone buildings inside, their walls looking as thick as the outer wall. The buildings were oval, as far as she could judge, with sloping thatched roofs, and reminded her of the ones she'd seen when she looked down towards the foot of Chapel Carn Brea. These houses, if they were houses, each had smoke rising through the roof, and Gerry could smell cooking. This must be another village.

She could hear men and women talking, and children squealing and laughing. A dog barked, and some cattle were lowing, close enough to be within the enclosure too. Then Gerry noticed four men standing further along outside the wall surrounding the houses. They would be invisible to anyone not positioned as she was, and there was something furtive about their movements.

Gerry was curious enough to step nearer. As she did, the four men slipped away from the village and moved off through the trees to the right of the clearing. She wanted to follow them, but in the gloom she was sure she would step on a twig or something and give herself away. Besides, she was waiting for Justin, who seemed to be able to appear out of and vanish into thin air. She moved one foot forward, drawing the fastenings of her hood close about her neck to hide the sapphire, and found herself caught from behind and held fast.

Gerry's heart jumped. She hadn't heard the slightest sound but Justin was there, one hand across her mouth to prevent her crying out, the other arm firm around her as it had been on the promenade in Penzance. The men had already disappeared but she guessed Justin knew where they were going, and that was why he'd brought her here. Justin released Gerry, too soon for her liking; being held by him felt so good. He touched his fingertip fleetingly to her lips to enjoin silence, then set off in the direction the four men had gone. He was back in the tunic and leggings he'd worn on the hillside, and he blended effortlessly into his surroundings. Gerry made her way cautiously after him.

It was darker ahead, though the sky above the trees was not yet approaching dusk. Oak and hazel grew close together here, as if the villagers had made a clearing in the wood for their houses but the trees were trying to encroach back onto their former land.

After a few minutes, when they had to be well out of earshot of the settlement, Justin paused and turned to Gerry.

'I take it you saw the Wasps,' he said.

'Did you say "wasps"?' she asked, puzzled, then realised he meant the four men.

'Yes. The Guardians and their acolytes call themselves the Gwenen, the Bees.'

Gerry didn't ask why, but remembered the wrist marking that she'd thought looked like a bee. Hadn't Wylmet said something about sacred hives?

Justin began to lead the way between the pathless trees again and Gerry followed, wishing they were holding hands. She squashed the thought. 'The difference, of course,' Justin continued, 'is that bees can only sting once, then they die, while wasps can sting with impunity.'

It sounded as if he favoured the Wasps' side. Gerry stopped walking.

'What's this got to do with me, or the Rainbow Chalice?' she asked.

'There's something happening here which you should see,' Justin replied enigmatically. 'Then you can go back to your Bees.'

Gerry wanted to say they weren't "her" Bees, but didn't. What did Justin want her to see in the middle of these seemingly endless trees? They tramped on and on, until at last Justin halted and motioned Gerry to keep still. Ahead of them she could see the four men standing beside a particularly large old oak with a hole in the trunk at about head height. All four had moustaches and beards. They wore long-sleeved tunics, woven in various colours, over leggings and rough boots. Two of the men were supporting a third, heavily-built man who had his arm inside the hole in the tree. As they watched, the man withdrew his hand, clutching a package, and dropped to the ground, to the visible relief of the two who'd been holding him up. On the ground between them was a large, carefully sealed and stoppered leather flagon, which the fourth man was supporting between his knees as he sat on a carpet of leaves and twigs.

The wood was quite still; it seemed the birds had already gone to roost, and only the occasional rustle of some small animal disturbed the silence. Then as the burly man displayed the package to his fellows, their shared tension vanished and they broke into loud exchanges.

'There now, Cathno, I told you no-one would find it here.'

'Open the stopper, Talan, and take the greatest care. It has to look as if no-one has touched it.'

'That can not be done.' The man thus addressed, Talan, was the smallest of the four. He had untidy hair falling forward around his face, hair as pale as the fair woman Gerry had noticed among the otherwise dark-haired Bees. 'Elwyn, what do you say?'

The heavy man who had taken the package from inside the tree trunk came to inspect the flagon. He had a cruel, satisfied look on his large square face.

'They will think the one who brought it wanted to try out the gift. Why think anything else?'

Elwyn began to unwrap the bundle he held, cutting the bindings with a dagger which he took from a sheath in his boot. The outer layer appeared to be sacking. Inside was something small, carefully wrapped in cloth. Elwyn held this gingerly in one hand. It looked like a phial.

The three standing drew around the seated man, who was working to open the sealed top of the flagon while disturbing the wrappings as little as possible. His hands were surprisingly deft; perhaps he was a craftsman.

'Get on with it, Talan,' Elwyn grumbled. 'We must not be away too long, and have someone notice.'

'I do not hurry this,' the man sitting down responded irritably. 'Do you want to spoil all our work, all our planning?'

Cathno had begun to stamp his feet on the ground, but the other man pulled his arm.

'Go home now if you can not keep quiet. Though I would be glad enough of your help to carry it back. Stand still, can you.'

'Leave be, Kenver. I prefer doing things to standing about.'

Kenver gave a knowing laugh.

'We all know what you like doing. Have you heard any more news from your woman?'

Cathno shook his head. 'We do not do much talking,' he answered, leering at the other man. 'But no, no news. This,' he gestured towards the flagon, 'should stir things up.'

'Hush,' Kenver urged, glancing around. `I thought I heard something.'

Gerry was certain the men couldn't see into the deeper shade where she stood, though she wondered how Justin, with his shining hair, could merge so effectively into the shadows. She looked around to check – and found he was gone. Justin had left her there alone.

There came a small sound of triumph from Talan, and looking back at him Gerry saw that he had finally unsealed the container. Elwyn passed him the phial, still holding it in its cloth. Talan took it, opened it cautiously and tipped the contents straight into the flagon. He re-stoppered the phial and tossed it into the undergrowth. Then he began the business of resealing the flagon.

'Be sure to carry it very, very carefully going back,' Talan warned when he finished at last. He looked anxious, but the others were jubilant. Cathno clapped him on the back.

'Make sure that stopper is well in. It's a good two miles there, and all the tracks are rough. Wrap a bit of that cloth or something round the top.'

Gerry was so absorbed in watching that she'd moved forwards without realising she was no longer concealed by the trees. Kenver looked round again, and spotted her. He gave a yell.

'There is a boy over there, spying on us. Catch him!'

Gerry turned to run, but it was already too late. Cathno and Elwyn were on her, pulling her back into the comparative light of the small clearing by the oak tree. Cathno shook her, his hands gripping her arms viciously.

'What are you doing here? What have you seen?' He gave her a clout round the ear that made her head ring. 'Answer me!'

In the gloom they, like the Guardians, had taken her for a

boy because of her clothes. Gerry took her cue from that, cringing away from the blow.

'Sorry, master.' She tried to put a whining note in her voice, and in her very real fear that wasn't hard. Whatever these men were doing, they were dangerous. 'I was trying to follow a fox through the brushwood, then I came out here and saw you.'

Cathno shook her again. 'What did you see?'

Gerry shook her head as if dazed. Terror spurred her imagination.

'I saw you'd got something there to drink so I thought you'd come here to drink it, you men alone, away from the women and their scolding.'

She heard a small snort of amusement from Talan, but Cathno's eyes were dark and hard. Gerry could smell ale on his breath. 'Let me go,' she pleaded, 'my mother will be looking for me.' She jerked her shoulder and elbow upwards as if to ward off another blow.

'Should have thought of that before you went off chasing foxes,' said Elwyn grimly. He was still gripping the dagger he'd used to cut the wrappings on the bundle. The blade was wickedly sharp, and there was murder in his face. 'Hold him still.'

Everything had happened so swiftly Gerry had scarcely had time to grasp the danger she was in, but she saw that Elwyn meant to cut her throat to make sure of her silence. How pointless that would be, to die here because of something she didn't even understand. This could have nothing to do with the Jewels of the Rainbow. Justin had brought her here to see these "Wasps", and he needed her alive to enter the fogou, so he couldn't have meant them to kill her. All this passed through Gerry's mind in seconds, as the thought of Justin triggered a remembered picture.

92

Watch the centre of the fireworks as they explode, he had said, hold the memory in your mind, fix it there. You'll find it useful if you ever need to make a quick getaway. He'd better be right, or she was dead. As Elwyn moved forward and raised his arm Gerry blanked out everything and focussed wholly on the image of blue and purple stars bursting into a giant dandelion clock against the dark sky. She concentrated with every scrap of attention, not daring to leave room even for the expected touch of the knife's point against the bared skin of her throat. Gerry's mind filled with the circle of stars and she was fleetingly aware of the faintest throb from the sapphire and the briefest sense of comfort from Seona's gold chain. Then she came out by the stacked granite stones on the side of the Brea. The impact drove her to her knees but she was there, and safe.

Safe, or at least alive, though very shaky. Gerry looked around. It looked as if she had come back only moments after leaving Kerenza and Wylmet, though for her that had been a whole day earlier. She could see they were still standing where she'd left them, easily spotted, Wylmet shorter and plumper than her friend. Gerry checked her neckline to ensure the chain was securely out of sight. Then she walked, a little unsteadily, back to the two novices, just as the singing came to a halt and there was a general movement towards the table in which the three of them joined.

Morvoren was there, drawing something towards the front of the table. She lifted her hands, and around her the general bustle fell into silence. Her face was golden in the light of the torches, and the copper strands bound into the braids of her long dark hair caught the light and flickered like flame. As did the hilt of the knife she carried at her waist.

'You will all remember,' she announced, 'that in the

spring Meraud went to help in the village when many of their children had sickened with a dangerous fever. With her healing skills she was able to save almost all of them, and in gratitude they gifted us of their best: food, drink, soft fleeces and finest cloth. The food has long since been eaten,' at this, there were some reminiscent smiles and appreciative murmurs, 'but we kept the wine and have chosen to drink it here tonight. Let us all taste this gift and make a pledge to devote ourselves to the recovery of our lost treasure.'

Everything fell into place as Gerry recognised the flagon Morvoren was opening. Abandoning caution, she rushed forward, grabbing Morvoren by the arm as she was about to start pouring the wine into beakers.

'Don't touch it!' Gerry yelled at the top of her voice. 'It's been poisoned!'

There was an outcry all round. Baranwen and Ysella came forward at once, along with a tall, spare woman. She was older than they, and walked with a pronounced limp. There were lines of pain drawn into her face, but her severe expression did not invite sympathy. Beside her was a small and sprightly woman with reddish brown hair, who stepped up to the table and looked at Gerry with surprise and doubt.

'I am Meraud, the healer,' she said. 'This wine was gifted to me, and I chose to share it with all my sisters here, to use for our midsummer vows.'

Ysella moved to stand before Gerry, looking at her with disdain, but without recognition. Gerry realised belatedly that all three Guardians were surrounding her. Ysella and Baranwen hadn't been close to her, though, and Morvoren had been looking only at the sapphire, so perhaps they wouldn't make the connection.

'This woman is not one of us,' Ysella was saying scornfully.

'She has only come here tonight to join in the rites. She seeks to make herself important by crying out.'

'Wait.' Kerenza came to Gerry's side and addressed the older woman with a respect in her voice that she hadn't used to Ysella. 'Hedra, this is Gerralda from Trewellard, who has, as Ysella said, come to join us tonight. I had intended to bring her to you tomorrow. I am certain that she has the Sight, and if she says we should not drink the wine, we ought to believe her.'

'Do you want proof?' It was Wylmet who spoke this time. She looked scared at confronting the most senior members of the Gwenen, but determined. 'Shall I taste the wine and see?'

'No!' Gerry interrupted her, horrified. 'Ysella says that I am lying. Let her try. If she is right she has nothing to fear.'

There was a rustle through the circle of women now closely packed around the Guardians. Gerry doubted that Ysella had made herself loved among the Bees. But Baranwen addressed her peremptorily.

'It is not for you to speak. Wylmet is our youngest sister, and like all here is bound to obedience. Wylmet has offered herself to take this test. If you should be right,' she gave Gerry a dubious glance, 'she will be saving all of us. Every woman of this circle is pledged to sacrifice herself if needed, to protect,' but she didn't complete the sentence. Did she mean to protect the Bees, or the Kelegel?

There was absolute silence when she ceased speaking. The faces in the circle wore varied expressions: horror, doubt, disbelief and fear. Gerry gazed at Wylmet, who now looked scared. Her hands were trembling. Gerry tried to go to her but Morvoren was holding her arms as hard as Cathno had earlier.

'You can't,' Gerry protested. 'Wylmet, you mustn't!'

'Silence!' It was Morvoren who spoke this time. 'Hold your tongue or you will be removed from here.'

Gerry could hardly bear to watch, but she had to. Meraud, her face anxious, poured a little of the wine into a beaker and passed it to Wylmet. Wylmet took the beaker with a quick glance in Gerry's direction. Gerry could only pray that she'd misunderstood, that this was not the flagon she'd seen in Talan's hands but a harmless one, a gift given in gratitude for the saving of the children's lives. But she knew she was not mistaken.

Wylmet took a sip of the wine, then a mouthful. Gerry caught sight of Ysella and wished she could force the wine down her throat instead. Ysella had a greedy look on her face at odds with the concern of her companions.

Nothing happened at first. There was absolute silence in the circle of watching women. Kerenza ran to Wylmet's side, putting an arm round her shoulders. Gerry felt Morvoren stir as if to restrain the novice, but she contented herself with keeping Gerry back. Gerry wished now she'd thought to simply pull the flagon from Morvoren's hands and pour its contents onto the ground. The Bees would have been angry, but it would have been worth it.

Kerenza looked as frightened as Gerry was. She'd caught Wylmet's hands and was speaking to her, trying to be encouraging, asking how she felt. Gerry listened breathlessly, hoping against hope that Wylmet would smile, reassure them that she was fine. So this why Justin had wanted her to see what the Wasps had done, so that she could save the Gwenen from being poisoned. She had failed. If Wylmet died, Gerry would never forgive herself.

The seconds passed, and for perhaps half a minute she was able to hope that the wine was harmless after all. Then Wylmet made a horrible noise, between a gasp and a cry. That sound told Gerry all she needed to know. She felt as if she'd administered the fatal dose herself. Then Wylmet began to vomit violently as her body made a frantic effort to reject the poison.

After that it was soon over. Meraud, in great distress, ran to the convulsed figure, but it was obvious to all that Wylmet was beyond help. Gerry could feel tears running down her face when Wylmet finally lay still. The shock reverberated throughout the hilltop as every woman there realised that it could have been she instead of Wylmet. Morvoren forced Gerry down to her knees, gripping her hair to tilt her head back while Baranwen stood over her, her hand on her knife.

'How did you know?' she demanded. 'Are you in league with whoever did this?' Baranwen was accustomed to self-control, but the outraged fury showed through.

Gerry made herself meet the accusing eyes.

'I was walking under the trees near the village,' she said. 'I don't know how long ago it was.' Gerry had indeed no idea of when, in their time, she'd been there. 'I saw four men creeping off, and I followed them into the forest. They had a flagon which they'd hidden, and a small phial which they handled very carefully. The flagon looked just like this one. They opened it, tipped in the contents of the phial and stoppered it again. Then they saw me and – and I had to escape to save my life. I didn't know then what they were doing but when I saw that just now,' Gerry gestured to the container where it stood on the table, 'then it came to me and I understood.'

She looked down to where Wylmet's body lay. Kerenza was weeping as she knelt by the huddled shape that had been her friend. She cried to Baranwen, 'I told you Gerralda has the Sight. Why would you not believe her?'

Baranwen ignored this. She turned to dismiss the others, telling them that the Midsummer rites could not now be completed. Four women stooped to raise the body of Wylmet and bear her off. The remainder departed in the quiet brush of sandal-shod feet on stones, the rustle of robes and a whisper or two exchanged as they moved down the path on the far side of the hill, taking two or three torches to light their way. Gerry and Kerenza were left with the three Guardians, Meraud the Healer, and Hedra, who from what Kerenza had said earlier must be a teacher or guide.

Morvoren had moved away and Gerry stood up slowly. She was angry now, and bitter that Wylmet had been the one to pay the price of their disbelief; Wylmet who'd welcomed her when she first arrived. Couldn't any of them see that she'd just saved their lives? But perhaps they were all in shock. Hedra supported herself unobtrusively against the table.

'Can you describe these men?' she asked Gerry.

'Not really,' Gerry admitted. 'They wore plain clothes: tunics and leggings. One was fair-haired, small and neat-handed, one heavier than the others. Oh, that won't be any help to you. I don't even know if they came from the village or just happened to be near there. I'm sorry.'

It was very late; soon the sky would be changing to the dim blue-grey of the early midsummer pre-dawn. Gerry felt utterly wretched about Wylmet's end. But for her cry of warning, they would now be carrying another woman's body, or maybe several, down the hill instead. Gerry couldn't tell how that would have affected her. She only knew that as Wylmet had raised the cup to her lips, she'd looked very like Debbie.

Meraud came over and put her hand on Gerry's arm.

'You look very weary, Gerralda. Are you staying here with us tonight?'

Gerry glanced towards where Ysella was standing with

Baranwen. 'No, I can't, but I'd like to come back here. I really want to talk to you and Hedra.'

Meraud urged her to stay, concerned about her travelling alone in the dark, but Gerry assured her she often did it. Then she took leave of Meraud before the others could decide to detain her, and went off as fast as she could down the opposite slope from where the rest of the group had gone. There was a path of sorts, but the invisible undergrowth caught against her boots several times. It was true she was used to travelling alone after dark, but that was by car, or, if not, then in places with street lights. The sky here was partly covered with clouds. The few stars were much brighter than Gerry was used to, even at home in Lochallaig or in present-day Cornwall, but they didn't show her enough of the path. However she only needed to get safely out of sight, which didn't take too long.

Gerry had brought herself here in fear for her life, escaping the Wasps, and travelling a relatively short distance in both miles and time. Could she manage to return to Windhaven which was physically quite near but many hundreds of years in the future? When she fled the Guardians that first time she thought she was only returning to her car; after leaving Justin on the hillside she believed she'd woken from a dream. Now she supposed Justin had sent her back both times. He'd brought her to the village tonight, and he must intend her to return home.

Besides, Gerry had Seona's gold chain, which Justin knew nothing of. She'd felt it respond when she flung herself out of the hands of the Wasps. Kerenza had told her that the Kelegel a'n gammneves was rumoured to enable adepts to move in place and time. Gerry was no adept and had merely a solitary stone, not the whole chalice, but she would have staked her life that Seona had passed whatever power or knowledge she possessed into that chain, to remain dormant until her great-niece should need it. The two combined might be enough for her need.

Suddenly Gerry heard a sharp voice from above, 'Which way did she go?' Ysella had discovered her departure and was after her already. Gerry had no time to waste; she couldn't let Ysella see her disappear. She placed her right hand on the sapphire and her left on the gold chain. She thought hard about Windhaven. Then she summoned the same image of blue and purple stars bursting out into a giant globe and once more threw all her mind into it.

After several unnerving moments of silence and darkness she found herself on the floor of the lounge at Windhaven. She was flat on her face on Claudia's thick, soft rug; luckily she hadn't crashed into any of the furniture. She'd done it; she'd actually succeeded in bringing herself back here. But it was lucky Claudia was in bed. Gerry's immediate exultation was checked by the sobering thought of what could have followed had Claudia been in the room. Justin would know how she could improve her style; he arrived calm and upright, not thudding into the ground, and even in a crowd no-one but Gerry noticed his sudden appearance or vanishing. But she wouldn't ask him. She had no wish to even see Justin, still less try to get the chalice. Gerry had given her word that she'd help him, but she hadn't known this would involve having a knife held to her throat, or watching a friend being poisoned.

Gerry got undressed and into bed automatically, filled with longing for Seona. She could have told her great-aunt about Wylmet, and her terrible guilt. It was the Wasps who'd put the poison into the wine, and Wylmet's death had saved all the others, but that was no comfort to Gerry. Seona would have been understanding but also sensible; would not have cushioned her great-niece, but put things in perspective.

Gerry lay in the dark, one hand on the gold chain, willing

herself to believe she could feel from it some sense of the solace she so desperately needed. She knew she had to work tomorrow, but that didn't seem real. She didn't want to go to sleep; and didn't want to go back in time ever again.

Chapter Eight

Saturday 28th June 2014

Gerry did fall asleep in the end, and woke to find it was nearly nine o'clock. She scrambled through washing and dressing, barely noticing her new luxurious surroundings, and dashed downstairs to the kitchen to grab a cup of instant coffee. There wasn't time for breakfast. She found Claudia there with a freshly made cafetière, and as Gerry rushed in Claudia filled a mug and handed it to her. Then she walked to the conservatory and gestured for Gerry to follow.

'I can't,' Gerry gasped. 'I overslept.'

'I can see that, but don't panic; it'll only take you ten minutes to drive to Penzance,' Claudia told her. 'You won't be late, and I need to talk to you.'

Something in her tone alarmed Gerry. She didn't waste any more time arguing, but followed Claudia to the table and sat down.

'I heard you were at the fireworks with Justin last night,' Claudia began without preamble. Gerry gasped. Was Claudia about to give her notice? She'd only been here one night. Had one of Claudia's friends spotted them, and phoned Claudia to tell her that her ex was out with a young redhead? Then either Gerry's erratic telepathy kicked in or her tardy brain put two and two together and she realised who it must have been. Monica, venting her spite on both of them.

'I'm sorry,' Gerry said. Claudia shook her head.

'No, I'm the one who should be sorry.' Gerry looked at her landlady, wondering if she'd heard right. 'I didn't think he'd start on you so fast,' Claudia went on. 'I thought I'd have time to warn you.'

Gerry stared at her, confused. She wanted to say that she'd only seen Justin because he'd asked her to help him find something, but there was no way she could explain that. Besides, it was only part of the truth. The way his hand brushed her arm was more sexy than a major clinch with anyone else. The excitement of his touch kept coming back to her, despite everything else that had happened. If she wasn't careful she'd become obsessed with him, which was so not a good idea.

Gerry remembered she was holding a mug of coffee, and drank some. Claudia was looking very grim, and Gerry tried to reassure her.

'It's all right,' she said, hoping she sounded convincing. 'I don't want to see Justin again.' And just how did that square up with what she'd just been thinking? She doubted if Claudia believed her. Claudia leaned against the back of her chair and eyed Gerry over the top of her own mug.

'Why do you say that?' she asked, but her tone was curious rather than accusing.

Gerry tried to think how best to explain.

'After the fireworks, I met some people he knows,' she said. Which was true enough. 'They were, well, they were seriously bad news. I think spending time with him would be dangerous.'

She expected Claudia to be surprised or disbelieving, and was shocked when she simply agreed.

'He's dangerous all right,' Claudia agreed, 'though I'm impressed that you realised, given that you told me you were no judge of people. I had my doubts about letting you have the room in the first place, but you did seem to want it very badly. I know Justin only too well, and was afraid this might happen, but I didn't think he'd get hold of you before you even moved in. Did you tell him you don't want to see him any more?'

Gerry shook her head. 'No,' she said, 'but I will if he asks to meet me again.'

Claudia looked at her with kindly pity.

'I'm afraid that won't work,' she said. 'It would only amuse him or, if he's interested, make him more determined. Let me break this to you: once you've met Justin what you think you want doesn't come into the equation. I've never met a woman who could hold out against him. If he wants you, he'll have you. If he doesn't, nothing you do will make any difference. Still,' she added, 'who am I to talk? He's the only man who ever managed to make a fool of me.' She put her mug down. 'I ought to finish packing. I'm seeing a couple of gallery owners in London over the weekend, to promote some of my artists. I'm hoping to be able to arrange a showing there for a couple of them. Ethan, my assistant, can cover for me at the gallery today, and on Monday morning. I should be back by the afternoon, but I could postpone the trip if you're worried about Justin.'

Gerry could see that Claudia meant it, but she'd got herself into this, and would get herself out. She shook her head.

'I'll manage,' she said.

Claudia gave her a searching look and accepted that Gerry

104

meant it. If she still had doubts she didn't voice them, except to reiterate that Gerry could ring her any time if she had problems, of any sort.

'If you have to answer the door, always put the chain on first. And if Justin does try coming up here, call me, whatever time it is. I'll talk to him.'

Gerry promised, then took the mug upstairs to her room to drink while she finished getting ready. It occurred to her that Claudia hadn't asked how she and Justin had met. Gerry couldn't see Claudia believing in the supernatural, so how did she account for his latching onto her new lodger? Perhaps she was used to Justin doing things that would seem impossible for ordinary men. But there wasn't time to worry about that just now.

Gerry had completely forgotten that Mrs. Angove had said there would be processions today as part of the Golowan festival. Penzance was every bit as busy as it had been for the fireworks, and half the main streets were closed to traffic. Gerry had to park in a side street at the far end of the town centre, then fight her way back through packed streets where the Mazey Day parade was in full swing. Schoolchildren in extravagant costumes, bright in the sunlight, were playing assorted instruments, and jazzy pirates in purple and white produced foot-tapping tunes on a variety of instruments. Fragile giant constructions of plywood and tissue paper were being carried down the centre of the road on long sticks, high above the heads of the crowd watching from the pavements. Gerry saw three huge brightly coloured birds, one dressed as a pirate, waving above the parade. One group after another trooped along, the marchers looking round for faces they recognised on the pavements, beaming at the applause. There was a festival atmosphere: people in summer clothes, banners across the street, and long colourful pennants waving from the shops. Gerry spotted a mermaid with two tails, a cow jumping a crescent moon, and a fringed banner right across the road in green and pink announcing 'Golowan'. Excited children were everywhere, some with their faces painted, and even the adults seemed to have left their cares at home. Gerry wished that she could. Her sorrow and guilt over Wylmet were haunting her.

In the end she was quarter of an hour late for work, though in the circumstances that wasn't bad going. The branch was below minimum staffing, but when Gerry came in she found the library all but empty of customers. Ernie, who also worked for the agency, had been asked to cover too; everyone on the permanent team wanted to be at the festival. Hilary, the manager, was working. Gerry knew Debbie had drawn the short straw among the full-timers, so she'd be somewhere around. Ernie had been sent upstairs in case anyone wanted to use the library computers, and Hilary was in her office. Gerry knocked on the office door to say she was in and why she was a bit late. Hilary didn't make an issue of it, as Gerry had never been late before, and simply sent her off to see to the shelving. Gerry found Debbie helping a child stack his books onto the issue machines, and occupied herself sorting the DVDs on the returns trolley while she waited for her friend to be free.

'I don't know why we open today,' Debbie said after the boy had left. 'Hardly anyone's going to come in. Helston library closes for Flora Day. Anyway, how was your first night in your super-duper new home?'

'I didn't sleep well,' Gerry said. 'And then of course I overslept. Great start.'

'Oh, don't worry,' Debbie said. 'It's always hard sleeping in a new place.' If only it were that simple, Gerry thought wryly. 'Oh,' Debbie added, 'Ryan came in earlier and asked if you were working today. I said you'd be in at ten, so I expect he'll be back later.'

Gerry didn't answer. Debbie grinned and went off to the desk to catch up with some reserves while it was quiet. Gerry turned to the shelving. She tried to concentrate on putting the books in order but couldn't have said if she'd put a single one in the right place. Her thoughts kept shuttling between Wylmet, Justin, and Claudia.

Later in the morning Gerry stopped by the desk where Debbie was sitting, to rest an armful of books on it while she took a small handful to put away. Ernie appeared and asked Debbie if she'd look after the desk upstairs while he had a break. Once she'd gone, Ernie gave Gerry an exaggerated wink.

'I saw you with your boyfriend at the fireworks last night,' he said. 'You really looked like you were enjoying yourself.'

Gerry turned pink with embarrassment, grateful Debbie hadn't heard. Ernie sauntered towards the staff room, giving her a smile that was more like a smirk, then suggested Gerry should call Hilary if she got any enquiries she couldn't deal with.

Gerry didn't make any progress with shelving the books. She cursed Ernie, but she should have expected this. She'd grown up in a small village, where everybody knew everyone else's business. Gerry didn't think her overloaded brain could cope with anything else. Then she heard someone say her name and found Ryan at her elbow. He took the books from her arm, sorted them expertly, and moved off to the shelves. Gerry went with him, remembering only then that Debbie has told her Ryan would be back to see her.

'Best look as if you're working,' he said, and passed the books over in shelving order so she could put them back in their places. Then he gave a quick glance round the library. There were only a couple of customers browsing through the DVDs. Having checked that Hilary's office door was shut, Ryan pulled two small pieces of paper out of his pocket.

'I don't know if you like blues, but there's a live jam session at the Mill, down by the station, next Saturday. I've got a mate in one of the bands and I've seen them before, they're pretty good.' He paused for breath, then added 'I was wondering if you'd like to come? Unless blues isn't your thing?'

Gerry pulled herself together.

'I don't know much about blues, but I could give it a try. Only,' she hesitated, trying to think how to phrase this without hurting Ryan's feelings 'could I think about it and tell you on Monday? It's just, I've got quite a lot on at the moment.'

Ryan looked disappointed but returned swiftly to his usual cheerful countenance. 'No problem, you'll be here next week, won't you? Anyway, I ought to go, I'm meeting a friend at the Turk's Head. Don't worry, it's not a woman.' He flashed his irrepressible grin and Gerry couldn't help smiling back. Then he bounced off and disappeared out the front door.

Gerry swore under her breath. This was rubbish timing. She'd come to Penzance badly bruised by her experience with Martin in London, and hadn't meant to go out with anyone. Yet she really did like Ryan. He was fun to be with, he made her laugh, and she'd never heard him say anything unkind. A couple of days ago Gerry would probably have said yes, but now… What would that uncomplicated young man say if he knew she was on a mission to recover something so precious and so dangerous that people ended up battered and in hospital, tortured or poisoned because of it? And that in spite of herself she was couldn't stop thinking about the man who'd involved her in this.

Gerry was still standing by the shelves, going over it all, when Debbie came back to the desk.

'Well?' she said, then added, 'did Ryan come and see you?'

Gerry looked at her blankly, then realised what she was asking.

'Yes,' she said, then explained. 'He asked me to go to some blues session with him next Saturday.'

'And of course you said yes?'

Gerry shook her head.

'I said I'd tell him on Monday.'

Debbie looked so surprised that Gerry knew she had to give some sort of explanation. She was glad Debbie hadn't heard Ernie's teasing, but if Ernie was here on Monday he'd certainly tell everyone. Including Ryan. Gerry didn't like the idea of Ryan feeling hurt, and thinking she'd lied by default. If she'd really had a boyfriend she'd have said so, but she couldn't tell Debbie or Ryan about Justin. She was suddenly glad of Claudia's instant understanding. Then she remembered that Monica had seen her and Justin together too; was it likely she would keep quiet? Gerry looked at the closed office door.

'Even Hilary can't expect us to do much work today,' she said. 'It's good enough of us to be here at all. Well, d'you remember that when we were at the bonfire at Chapel Carn Brea the other day, you kind of asked me if I had a boyfriend in London?'

'Yeah,' said Debbie, immediately on the alert. Gerry hadn't felt like talking about it at the time, but now it didn't seem to matter.

'Well, I was seeing someone in London this summer. He was awesome: looks, experience, the works. Only it turned out he was just using me to fill in while his regular girlfriend was away.

He ditched me when she came back, and of course all his friends knew. I felt like everyone was laughing at me.' Gerry noticed it didn't seem to hurt so much now. 'So I, like, don't trust men.'

'Yeah, but Ryan's not going to do something like that,' Debbie pointed out reasonably. 'He's really nice. I've seen how patient he is with people who can't get the hang of things on the computers. And I know he's not got a girlfriend. He was with a girl who looked like a catwalk model, then she chucked him for someone with money. That was a few months ago. He seems to be recovering now, though. Specially since you started working here.'

Debbie was right, Gerry knew, she and Ryan would be good for each other. Except that the image of Justin's face, the feel of his body hard against her own as they watched the fireworks, kept intruding. Gerry knew Debbie was puzzled, but couldn't say any more.

In the afternoon Hilary sent Gerry upstairs to cover the tea break. The computers for public use were on this floor, as well as the Reference, the Cornish, and the specialist Art collections. Usually whoever was on the desk upstairs did nothing but book people onto the computers, deal with the printer and take money. Today, however, there was only one person on the computers, so Gerry made a beeline for the books on Cornish history. She didn't know what century she was looking for, and her English history wasn't that good, but she guessed it was before the Middle Ages.

When Ernie came back from his break he found her sitting at the desk, deep in a thick volume.

'Can I help you?' he asked in a mock-librarian voice. Gerry was so engrossed she'd all but forgotten where she was. 'Looking at books? What do you think this is, a library?'

Gerry looked up, startled; she'd been too absorbed to hear him come upstairs.

'I'm trying to find out stuff about Cornwall in what they called the Dark Ages,' she explained, 'but there doesn't seem to be much.'

'That's why they're called the Dark Ages, innit?' Ernie replied, taking the book out of her hands. 'They don't know much about it, even in England. You go and have your break.'

Gerry went off, smiling at his separation of Cornwall from England, which she'd first come across when staying at the Angoves' house. Mr. Angove said things like, "We make all this money from tourists then have to pay it back to England in taxes".

Then on her way downstairs Gerry stopped dead. If she'd been time travelling, not dreaming, she didn't have to wait for night time to go and see Hedra and Meraud. She needed to talk to them, but even more than that, she wanted to get into the fogou. Gerry decided that she'd get Justin the Chalice of the Rainbow, then she could be done with him. He could go and sort out his brother, and she could get on with her life. She tried to overlook the trembling she felt when she remembered the feel of his hand touching her, his arm holding her. She ignored the suspicion that when she walked through Penzance she'd be looking out for a glimpse of shining fair hair; or that when she went to sleep she'd be hoping to see him again. Claudia was right; Justin was too dangerous.

It would be best to get to the fogou in the evening of the day after Wylmet's death, and trust the hilltop would be empty. It would be dark in the passage, but hopefully the daylight would reach at least part of the way in.

Once Gerry had worked this out, she could barely wait till the library closed at 4. At the end of the afternoon, Debbie said she was going to the 'Men and maids' Serpent Dance through the streets down to the harbour, then meeting up with a couple of friends at the fair. She asked if Gerry wanted to come, but she made an excuse. It sounded like fun, but she had other things to think of.

Gerry wanted to go back to Windhaven and try to go into the past from there. With Claudia away, it wouldn't matter how or where she landed back in the house. She said a hasty goodbye to Debbie, left the library and set off on the long walk back to her car. The streets were just as busy, and considerably noisier, than they'd been in the morning. Quite a lot of the crowd had spent part of the day in the various pubs in town. Every kind of place that sold food and drink was doing a roaring trade.

Halfway down Market Jew Street, which was the main shopping street and also the centre of the parades, there was a passage between two shops with steps leading up to the street above. Gerry thought this was the easiest way to get back to the side road where she'd parked. She'd almost reached the passage when, in front of her, standing on the pavement like any other festival-goer, she saw the Guardian Baranwen.

Chapter Nine

Saturday 28th June 2014 continued

Gerry tried to move back but was hemmed in by people on every side. Baranwen raised her hand, palm outwards, in a formal gesture.

'I mean you no harm,' she said. 'I have to talk to you. Will you come in here with me?'

There was a coffee and cake shop on the corner next to where they were standing. Gerry decided nothing could happen in such a public place, took Baranwen inside and even got tea for them both. This felt weird. The Guardian wore plain brown today; her fine copper ornaments had been replaced by others which looked like silver but might be Cornish tin. Now that she wore the sapphire Gerry could see how Baranwen would appear to other people: the long brown robe as a loose ankle-length dress, the sandals on her feet subtly changing style. The spiral earrings, serpent ring and bracelet didn't need altering; Gerry could have worn them herself. The long waving hair, loosely pulled back, and the lack of make-up, along with the style of dress, matched the New Age look, common enough in Penzance. But only Gerry could see where Baranwen wore the painted mark of the bee at her throat, and the circle with its crossed lines on the inside of her left wrist.

The high stools at the counter along the windows overlooking the busy pavements were all taken, so the two women went down to the floor below and sat at a table near the foot of the stairs. Gerry carried their tray down, wondering if the Guardian would eat or drink in this century. Once they were seated Baranwen rested her fingers on the handle of her cup but did not lift it.

'We can speak here,' she said. 'I have ensured that no-one will pay any attention to us; no-one will hear what we say.'

Gerry was confused. If Baranwen was so powerful, what did she want with her? Hopefully she was about to find out. Gerry took a mouthful of her tea and waited. Around the two of them the ordinary sounds – cheerful voices, the clinking of cutlery on plates and cups on saucers, the ring of the cash-till at the top of the stairs - faded to insignificance as if an invisible bubble had enclosed them. Baranwen looked straight at where Gerry wore the sapphire concealed by her clothes.

'There are things you have to know,' she said, then let her gaze drop to the table, her eyes unfocussed as if remembering.

'The Jewels of the Rainbow, the Tegennow a'n gammneves,' the Guardian began, 'are not only extremely powerful but also very valuable. Despite this, no-one would ever have committed the blasphemy of even thinking of taking the Kelegel, still less of trying to sell it for gain, for its renown is such that it would have been known anywhere.'

Involuntarily Gerry's hand went to the sapphire, and she shuddered. Baranwen continued without comment.

'Nor would any man, even the most desperate, have considered trying to steal it, separate the jewels, cut them down or melt the gold. None would be so lost as to risk incurring the

114

wrath of the Goddess and the vengeance of the Gwenen. We are called the Bees because we work together for the good of all, but we would take a terrible revenge if we had to.'

'But,' Gerry said, confused, 'someone did take one of the Jewels – the sapphire. So how did that happen? Did they –'

Baranwen interrupted. 'I removed the sapphire myself,' she said. 'I have worked with the Tegennow a'n gammneves for more years than you could imagine. They are in my blood and my bones, and I know if they are threatened. I became aware some months ago that someone was planning to seize the Kelegel. It had to be a man, with considerable power of his own and enough knowledge to harness the powers of the Chalice. He would be wanting to turn the Jewels to ill usage; no-one would steal them for good purpose. And someone that powerful could accomplish terrible evil using our sacred Tegennow. So one night when it was my turn to watch in the chamber I took out the Kelegel and removed the sapphire and hid it. It was like taking out my own eye, but with one Jewel gone the Chalice could not be misused. Then I returned the damaged Chalice to its place in the fogou until I could decide what was best to do.

'It was a sorry plan for whatever happened now the Rainbow Chalice of fame and song was sullied. If it had been taken, and used for ill purpose, then it could never have been restored to its full use and beauty. The taint would have hung over it for ever. If I gave out that it was stolen and then subsequently 'found' it, it would still be diminished, but to a far lesser degree. Either way, an artefact unmatched in our knowledge and history was irreparably discredited. I have cursed that would-be thief every day, but it has made no difference.'

Gerry recalled her first visit to the hillside.

'I thought I heard Morvoren say that someone had,' what

was it, ' "failed in her vigilance",' Gerry said. 'Was that Delenyk?' Delenyk, who Wylmet and Kerenza, had spoken of with admiration and affection.

Baranwen looked at Gerry, her face sombre.

'You must understand,' she said, 'that every girl or woman who comes to the Gwenen is sworn from the start to put the Kelegel above all else, even her own life. Guarding the Kelegel a'n gammneves is the most sacred charge our people know.'

She had said as much last night, when Wylmet had offered to test the wine. Gerry was appalled. How could these women take such an oath?

Baranwen was now gripping the handle of her cup so tightly that Gerry thought it would break. Gerry put her own cup down, rather unsteadily, then changed her mind, raised it to her lips and took a long gulp. 'Please carry on,' she said, and could hear her voice sounding husky. Her throat felt dry and she swallowed the rest of the tea, then replaced the empty cup on the saucer.

'I am the oldest of the Guardians.' It sounded like a punishment. 'I have the greatest knowledge of the Kelegel, have served it for more years than I sometimes care to remember.' Gerry looked at her in surprise. 'Oh, I am far older than I look. Another gift of the Stones to those who serve them,' the Guardian said bitterly. 'Sometimes it is more like a curse.' Gerry could think of no reply, and waited in silence. Her hand slid to Seona's gold chain; the touch was a comfort.

'Any Guardian responsible for the stones,' Baranwen continued, 'and allowing them to be taken from us would suffer death by torment. I believed I could find a way to save Delenyk from this fate, but I failed. I had to order her death, and felt her suffering as if it were my own. Then I concealed the Chalice, hidden from vision and touch and mind, lying by Delenyk's casket whose location I alone knew.'

There was terrible pain in Baranwen's face. Gerry had lost awareness of where they sat, surrounded by ordinary people heedless of the tragic tale being unfolded in their midst.

'I prayed to the Goddess for help,' Baranwen said. 'You must have realised the Tegennow permit the wearer to move among past, present and future.'

Gerry nodded mutely, holding her breath, willing Baranwen on.

'Although the Tegennow were protected from immediate theft, I had to find the man who wanted them. I called on the Tegennow a'n gammneves to aid me. I was waiting for a vision, an image of my enemy, or someone to guide me to him. The next day I showed the violated Chalice to the other Guardians; and then I saw you.'

That had been Gerry's first trip to the past, five days in their time before she had met Kerenza and Wylmet. She found the time shifts confusing, but was more moved by pity for Baranwen's dilemma.

'Please go on,' she said, leaning forward a little, not wanting to miss a word.

'I saw you,' the Guardian said, 'and dressed as you were I took you for a boy from the village, and could not understand how you came to be there when I was seeking an accomplice. Then I saw you were a woman and a stranger, and knew my prayers had been answered.'

The moment was too solemn for Gerry to even think of smiling at the notion of herself as, literally, the answer to a prayer.

'An odd way of showing it,' she pointed out. 'You told Morvoren and Ysella to attack me.'

'No.' Baranwen shook her head. 'I called to them not to kill you. I hoped to speak with you in private, but you ran away, and I had to search for you without knowing when or where you might be.'

'But,' Gerry's head was beginning to hurt, 'you had already given me the sapphire?'

'That had happened in your time, but not in mine.' That just made Gerry even more confused. 'I mean within the sequence of events in your life, not in the time you were moving in. When I saw you on the hill, and wearing the sapphire, I knew I had to find you and give you the stone. You were not from our age, I could tell that. I began to search through time, calling on the Kelegel to guide me, so I could give you the stone.

'I stayed within a few miles of our home, looking in other centuries and seeing many strange things, yet search as I might, I found no trace of the woman I sought. Then I cast myself further into the future than I had ever been, wearing the guise of this age. It is a simple matter of a glamour; you can see through it now, can you not?' Baranwen indicated the outfit she appeared to be wearing.

That was "a simple matter"? To Baranwen, perhaps it was.

'The stone had brought me to you. I stood by the table, blocked you from seeing the stall's real owner, and dropped the stone onto that tray.' She gave a shudder. 'It was blasphemy for one of the Tegennow a'n gammneves to lie amidst such trash. But my plan worked. You came up, careless, just passing idle moments. I knew you at once, and, astonishing yet fitting, you were wearing an object of power.'

118

Gerry stared at her, baffled.

'But that was before I bought the sapphire.'

Baranwen gestured towards Gerry's throat. 'The gold chain you wear; it called out to me.'

Gerry let out a long sigh. 'This chain? My great-aunt Seona gave it to me. I've been thinking about her ever since I bought the stone. She knew things about me that I never guessed. We shared a heritage.'

Baranwen looked at her curiously. 'What do you call your heritage?'

'Celtic.' Gerry believed it now as she never truly had before. 'Our family is from the north-west of Scotland; I don't know what it's called in your time. Everyone else in my family is practical and down-to-earth, but I was different. Seona understood, always took pains to reassure me that the odd things that happened to me were perfectly all right.' She looked at Baranwen, sharing her grief. 'She died over three years ago. I've wanted so terribly to talk to her, these past few days. When she gave me this,' Gerry touched the gold, 'I just thought it was a lovely present. But I'd swear it turned Morvoren's knife, and when I brought myself home from your time, I'm sure it helped. It felt like it was reassuring me.'

Baranwen was nodding. She stretched her hand towards the gold chain, and her fingertips hovered close but did not touch it. 'Your great-aunt was a wise woman, and she was protecting and aiding you. Whatever she knew of wisdom and power she transferred into your gift.'

'She died of cancer,' Gerry said, 'only weeks after giving me this for my 18th birthday, as if she'd been holding on till then. Soon afterwards I went to London. Then I had trouble with a man and came to Cornwall instead.' Gerry fell silent for a moment, then looked up, worried again. 'But how can I help you? You say the stones brought me to you?'

'Yes. You must possess some special gift, some quality. How were you received by the others? Did they accept you?'

'Yes, easily.' Gerry hadn't even wondered about that. 'They were friendly, except for Morvoren and Ysella.' Recalling Ysella's face when Wylmet had drunk the poisoned wine, Gerry hoped helping Baranwen wouldn't mean working with her. 'I thought of Wylmet as a friend. She was the first to make me welcome.'

And Wylmet had reminded her of Debbie.

'You need to put your grief aside, as I have,' Baranwen said. 'You have been chosen by the Tegennow a'n gammneves. You must do this. Or do you want them to be lost to us, to bring evil to the world?'

'No!' Gerry exclaimed. 'Never. I've seen real evil for the first time, when I saw the Gohi put the poison into the wine.'

'The Wasps, Gohi, is that what they call themselves?' Baranwen appeared grimly amused. 'Then remember it if you should feel unsure of your purpose. They had no mercy.'

'No.' Gerry shivered. 'And three people have been half-killed to protect the sapphire. They're in hospital, oh,' she corrected herself, 'being looked after by healers.'

'You do not have to explain your words,' the Guardian said. 'The stones allow us to understand each other. Did you think you would have been able to talk with Kerenza and Meraud if you had not been wearing the sapphire?'

'Oh.' Of course Gerry couldn't speak Dark Ages Cornish. Somehow that hadn't occurred to her, and she felt stupid. She did have a good excuse; so many other strange things had happened that day. 'Anyway I don't even know if those men are still alive. One tried to take the sapphire from me, but one just happened to

be there, and the first was an old man who was kind, and patient.'
Gerry's voice shook as she thought of Mr. Trewartha. 'And they
were all attacked by some unknown thug.'

'There is an unknown person seeking the Jewels of the
Rainbow,' Baranwen said calmly, 'but he did not attack those men.
I did.'

'No!' From beginning to feel like an ally, the Guardian had
swung back to being an enemy again. Horrified, Gerry found
herself on her feet, pushing back her chair. She stared around,
seeking help, but it was as if no-one could see them. Within her
reach people were eating and drinking, talking and laughing; but
they were quite oblivious.

'Sit down,' Baranwen said, and there was something so
compelling in her voice that Gerry did so. Baranwen pushed her
own untouched cup of tea towards her young companion and
Gerry took a long mouthful.

'I don't understand,' she said. Her head was beginning
to throb as if she'd been punched. Baranwen looked as if
her patience was wearing thin, but Gerry was more confused
than ever.

'I will try to explain,' Baranwen said, 'but you may just have
to trust me.' Gerry drank some more tea, wondering if she could
ever trust anyone again.

'I had sought desperately for you, and had found you
at last,' Baranwen said. 'I felt the sapphire respond as you
appeared; if I had any doubts that dispelled them. And then,
after all my endeavours, the first thing you did, before you
were even out of my sight, was to take it straight to a man
who could see at once that it was both old and valuable. I
could not allow that. He may recover; if he does he will not
remember the stone. But make no mistake, if I were as ruthless

as you believe, I would have slain him out of hand. And the other two.'

'How did you know about that? And how did you get to Redruth?' Gerry had actually forgotten Alastair Fletcher.

Baranwen sighed. 'This is not important. I told you already that I am bound to the stones, and know if they are threatened. You put the sapphire in peril, visiting him. I was warned and came there soon after you left. I knew what had happened; the other stones showed me. And given your actions when he tried to seize the sapphire, do you complain of mine?'

'I was desperate,' Gerry said. The memory came suddenly vivid. 'He said he was going to have me arrested. I've never tried to attack anyone before. It felt like I'd turned into a different person, or like someone else was acting through me.'

'Something, not someone,' Baranwen corrected her. 'If you felt so protective of the sapphire after a mere day or two wearing just one stone, then multiply that several thousand-fold before you judge me. Those three men are not dead, even the one who wanted to rob you. I said I do not kill unless forced to. If they recover they will have no memory of you or of the stone you brought with you. I simply made it look like attempted theft, and I inflicted permanent damage on those, things, on the wall in in the shops. I knew they posed a danger to you. Things are simpler in my world.'

Gerry understood what Baranwen meant. Without even knowing what electronics were, the Guardian had destroyed both jewellers' CCTV footage. She had said Gerry had some sort of talent. It seemed unlikely. What "talent" could she possibly believe Gerry possessed that she didn't have herself?

A couple of teenagers at the next table were texting, and giggling over some pictures one had just received on her phone.

Baranwen eyed them with distaste. Both wore sleeveless low-cut tops, and denim shorts over brightly coloured tights. One had vivid orange hair. 'In my age even whores do not dress like that.'

'I don't know if they do here,' Gerry told her, suddenly defensive of her century. 'As you said, this isn't what's important.'

Baranwen bristled, but only said 'You cannot spend too much time with us.' Gerry looked at her, puzzled. 'If you return to your own time at the moment you left, you will be living too many hours and will drain yourself. If you cut out the time from your own world at night, then you will not sleep and will exhaust your body. Now that you understand better what you are doing, you must find a way to strike a balance. But come back tonight, come the day after-' She hesitated.

'The day after Wylmet was poisoned,' Gerry supplied.

Baranwen inclined her head. 'Come in the evening to our home at the foot of the hill.'

'Will that be all right?' Gerry asked, adding, 'Ysella mistrusts me.'

'You mistrust her,' Baranwen replied with the first gleam of humour Gerry had seen in her.

'She reminds me too much of someone I work with,' Gerry sighed. She would have liked to say more, but she assumed it was Baranwen who had appointed Ysella in her role of Guardian.

There was a sudden rise in the noise level at the top of the stairs. A couple of lads had come in the door, and they sounded as if they'd been drinking since lunchtime. The woman at the counter had moved forward to speak to them, and everyone turned to listen.

'Come to us this evening,' Baranwen repeated. Then while all attention was on the commotion upstairs, she simply vanished as Justin had done the evening before.

Gerry finished the contents of the cup in her hand and rose to make a more conventional exit. She would go home, then into the past. Either Justin or Baranwen would direct her to the right place and time; they both wanted her there. To help Justin, she only needed to borrow the Chalice; if she could time it exactly right, perhaps she could get it back to the fogou after Justin had sorted his brother out, before even Baranwen knew it was gone. Then she would help Baranwen locate whoever was trying to steal the Kelegel. Gerry had changed her decision of the night before to never go back in time again. She left the café feeling confident, believing she truly would succeed in her task.

Chapter Ten

Saturday 28th June 2014 continued

Gerry knew that to start by "borrowing" the chalice meant she would see Justin again. And though she'd told herself repeatedly that he wasn't for her, that hadn't stopped her thinking about him. Thinking about him far too much. She turned the corner of the road where her car was, then stopped dead. All the back streets were deserted; everyone in Penzance seemed to be at the festival. But this street was not empty. Justin was standing beside the Volvo, waiting for her.

Gerry's heart began to thump at the sight of him. At once she felt guilty, wondering if he would expect her to have the Kelegel for him already. She walked towards him, relieved to see a look of cool amusement on his face. Gerry realised then that she'd expected impatience or even anger. Her steps slowed down. What could she say to him?

As before, Justin didn't bother with conventional greetings or small talk. When Gerry reached him he simply asked, 'So what happened after I left you?'

Gerry found she couldn't demand to know why he'd abandoned her in the woodland, where she'd been within an inch of being knifed. Instead she began to explain: about watching the Wasps with the flagon and the phial, and how she'd accidentally moved and been seen. As she remembered the terrifying moment when Elwyn had held his blade to her throat, Gerry found she was shaking.

'Then I did what you'd said I could do, made a picture in my mind of the exploding fireworks and found myself back with the Bees. And then,' her voice was quavering as she reached the next, the worst bit, 'then I saw that the Bees were going to drink some wine, and I realised it was the same wine and I shouted out that it was poisoned. I had to stop them drinking it.'

'You stopped them?' Justin asked, so sharply that Gerry started, but she wanted to finish the story.

'Yeah, at least I tried to stop them, but the youngest one, Wylmet, said she'd test the wine, to see if it was all right. I told her not to, but she'd already said she would and they, the Guardians, made her do it. And I had to watch, and she, she collapsed, and it was so horrible.' Gerry couldn't say any more. She began to sob, and before she knew it, Justin's arms were round her, and she was crying against his shoulder.

'So if it hadn't been for you, they might all have died?' he said quietly. The voice came from just above her ear. Gerry couldn't guess his expression, but again the tone wasn't what she expected. It was too calm, too measured.

'Yeah.' Gerry was still sniffing, and managed to make herself stop. She'd heard that men didn't like women crying. 'I couldn't do anything about getting the chalice for you after all that happened. But I'm going to go home now and go to the fogou from there.' Reluctantly Gerry pulled herself out from his arms and looked up, hoping her mascara hadn't smudged. 'I was just on my way back to the house now.'

'Good,' he said. 'I have to say, I was beginning to wonder if I'd picked the wrong woman to help me.'

That was so unfair that it hurt. What the Wasps had done was hardly Gerry's fault. She looked up at him, intending to protest, but again she couldn't. She was afraid to argue in case he got angry and left. She didn't think she could bear that. Gerry wanted to see those dark grey eyes light up with pleasure when she brought him the chalice, to hear words of praise and thanks, not of doubt.

'How can I let you know?' she asked instead, 'I mean let you know when I've got it?'

'I'll know,' Justin said, 'don't worry. I won't be far away. I'll find you.'

Then he put his arms round her again, holding her as close as he had before. Gerry was sure he must feel her heart beating against his body. She wondered if he was going to kiss her, but he didn't. He only said, 'Good luck – not that you need it. I know you can do this. You'll see me soon.'

Gerry's eyes were still closed when Justin let go of her. She opened them slowly. As she had expected, he'd disappeared. It took her a few minutes to come back to earth and remember she was standing next to her car. Gerry unlocked it and got in, but just sat there, thinking about how good it had felt to be in Justin's arms. Then with a jolt she remembered Claudia saying Justin was very persuasive. But she'd been talking about Justin trying to talk his way into the house, not about Gerry trying to help him clear his name. She sighed, started the engine and drove home in a daze.

It was lucky Claudia was away. Gerry decided to make her attempt from the main lounge, and pushed the armchair and the small side tables to the end of the room, off the thick rug which covered most of the wooden floor. The sofa was too long and heavy for her to move, but even so she'd created a good size space.

Gerry shifted a deep blue glass vase and a crystal decanter well out of harm's way. If her return here was as clumsy as last time she didn't want to hurt herself or damage anything of Claudia's.

She drank some water, but was too edgy to eat. The sandwich she'd had at lunchtime would have to keep her going. Recalling Claudia's warnings, Gerry went to bolt the front door. That would keep out an opportunist burglar, though it seemed unlikely any would come to this remote place. As for Justin, he could simply materialise inside the house. At least Claudia didn't know that.

Gerry's preparations, such as they were, were complete, but still she hesitated, more nervous than she'd expected to be. Now that she'd come to the point, her confidence had disappeared again. The first time she'd seen the fogou she'd been sure something terrifying was waiting there for her. Gerry touched the gold chain and wondered what Seona would have made of this. Probably told her to stop dithering and get on with it.

She would aim for halfway down the hillside, not too close to any shrubs and trees. Looking down at her long top and tight jeans, Gerry wondered if she could make them look more like a tunic and leggings. She'd been able to see Baranwen in the café in both her present and past guise. For a moment Gerry's own clothes seemed to flicker and change; was that like a "glamour"? She went to replace her sandals with a pair of low boots because of the stones on the hill. Hopefully the hillside would be dry, with some hours of daylight remaining.

Then, feeling as if she were about to jump off the top diving board, Gerry put one hand on the chain and the other on the sapphire. She closed her eyes, pictured the circle of rocket stars and thought hard about where she wanted to go; where Justin and Baranwen wanted her to go. They would get her there.

And this time the transition was smooth. Gerry found herself standing part of the way down the slope on Chapel Carn Brea. She was glad of the boots, as the heather was rough, and there were stones among the grass and cow parsley. Judging by the sun, it looked like late afternoon. Gerry made her way upwards to the flat top of the Brea.

When she reached it, she found the crown of the hill empty, and it was missing the direction stone, so this definitely was the past. There was no sound but some buzzing insects. Gerry walked down to the huge boulders and moved round them to the low entrance with its granite lintel. The sun lit the first part of the tunnel leading inwards. Once she stepped down into the passageway she'd be out of sight of any passer-by, but wouldn't be able to see if anyone approached the fogou. She had to take the chance. At the worst she should be able to transfer herself out. Gerry held on to that thought as she stepped down onto the earth and stone floor. She had to duck her head to enter, but once inside she found the roof of the tunnel was high enough to stand upright. There was another exit at the far end of the tunnel, which must emerge further down the hill. She could see the square of sunlight clearly. That was another escape route. The walls of the tunnel were made of graded stones, positioned evenly in horizontal rows, each made of larger stones than the row above. The whole curved slightly to the right. As she walked, a foot at a time, she saw that half way between the two exits there was a low square opening on the right. And there was light coming through it; but it was not daylight.

Gerry froze, understanding for the first time the real meaning of the phrase about your heart being in your mouth. She stood motionless, straining her ears, but couldn't hear anything. She went forward step by step, her soft boots making no noise. The light from the opening became warmer, eclipsing the sunlight. It was probably only two or three minutes' walk but felt like an hour. At last she reached the gap and found the source of the light. Within, two torches were burning in blackened metal holders on the walls, one on each side of an empty circular chamber. It was higher than the tunnel but with similar stone walls which sloped inwards slightly as they rose, like a round beehive with a flattened roof. The doorway was formed by a great slab of granite on each side and one across the top. The torches looked as if they would burn for some time yet, so hopefully no-one would be returning to replenish them yet.

Gerry walked to the centre of the chamber. She had no need to wonder where the Chalice was hidden; the sapphire was tugging her towards it. She realised the stone had been pulsing from the moment she'd set foot in the tunnel, but she'd been concentrating too hard on her surroundings and battling her fear to notice it. She could feel the gemstone throbbing against her skin. It drew her to the wall furthest from the doorway. If anyone came in she'd have no way out. Yes, she would. She could transfer back to her own time.

Gerry had to retrieve the chalice with the Rainbow Jewels now. She could never nerve herself up to come back in here again. She stepped forward to the wall of stones, solid and square. The sapphire was telling her what to do. Although all the blocks looked much the same, there was one which, as she looked at it, started to glow with faint gold light round the edges.

Gerry's hands were beginning to shake, and a growing lump was forming at the back of her throat. Her heart was thudding hard against her ribs. She moved towards the hiding place with a mixture of fear and excitement which was almost unbearable. She put both her hands against the stone and it swung smoothly outwards. Within was a large hollow containing a plain wooden casket which must hold the ashes of the Guardian Delenyk. Gerry found her fears had vanished; this was what she was meant to do.

The Kelegel stood on top of the casket. It was smaller than she'd expected, but even inside their hiding place the gold and gemstones caught the light of the torches and took what breath Gerry had left. She reached inside and lifted it out. She held the Jewels of the Rainbow, the Tegennow a'n gammneves, in her hands.

The stone opening closed softly. And as it did, Gerry heard a sound behind her. Gripping her prize she spun round. Forming a loose semicircle around her stood Kenver, Elwyn, Cathno and Talan, each holding a knife. They were gazing hungrily at the chalice in Gerry's hands. She stood stock still. The weapons were directed straight towards her, and Gerry knew that if she moved they would strike. Behind and beside her were stone walls, and the four men stood between her and the exit.

Elwyn walked slowly towards her. There was greed in his face as he looked at the Kelegel but, unexpectedly, awe too. Perhaps that accounted for the hesitation in his movements. He was almost close enough to reach it. Gerry should have been scared, but was not. She was filled again with the fury she'd felt when Alastair Fletcher had tried to seize the sapphire. The Chalice, and the Jewels, were hers, and only hers; no one else was going to touch them.

Gerry folded both hands about the gold, feeling the space on the side where the sapphire had been taken out of its setting. Her hands covered the cup entirely, leaving only the base visible. The words she spoke did not seem to be her own.

'Go back,' she told the four of them. 'You have no business here. The Kelegel is not for you.'

Cathno gave a low laugh, and he too moved forward.

'So you think it's for you?' he asked scornfully. 'Are you going to fight us for it?'

He raised his weapon. Instinctively, Gerry lifted the chalice high above her head. She could feel her sapphire pounding on its gold chain, and between her fingers the other jewels, the garnet, topaz and amethyst, began to pulse in the reflected torchlight. But the rainbow was incomplete. Separated, the Tegennow had no power to work their magic. The assurance which had come to her as she first held them was beginning to fade. Gerry tried to bring up the circle of stars but some force was blocking her mind. There was another power here in the fogou which could thwart her.

Now she began to panic, and they saw it. All four moved to close in. Gerry backed towards the far wall but could go no further. Elwyn stretched his hand towards her, reaching for her raised arm. Then another voice rang out behind him.

'Stand! Hold still. Do not any of you move. How dare you enter this sacred place?'

Baranwen stood in the doorway. She was alone but her presence seemed to fill the chamber. The Wasps appeared dumbfounded; none of them moved or spoke. Gerry slowly lowered her arm, staring at Baranwen. How could she explain to the Guardian what she was doing here?

Then Kenver suddenly gripped his knife and called to his companions, 'Come on, boys, she's only an old woman. We can deal with her.'

He began to rush forward but Baranwen raised her hand and he froze where he stood.

'You forget yourself,' she said, and her voice was like

132

ice. 'You all know that men are not permitted here. Have you forgotten the penalty for your action? Any man entering this spot faces castration. Then, for daring to think you could rob us of our treasure, you would be chained to the walls within sight of the Kelegel. Then you would be left, feasting your eyes on it while slowly starving to death in your own filth.'

Even Elwyn quailed at her words. They were all held mesmerised. Baranwen faced the four with pure contempt on her face. She'd paid no attention to Gerry, even though she was holding the Kelegel. The Guardian addressed only the Wasps.

'There is one condition under which I might consider sparing you. Tell me who sent you here and for now punishment will be withheld. But never forget that I can summon you any time I choose. You are no longer free. I will give you until the morning to give me that information. Otherwise,' she made a sweeping downward gesture whose meaning was obvious. Even Cathno, the most arrogant, looked defeated.

'Now go,' Baranwen finished. 'Return tomorrow and I will decide your fate.'

They left. Gerry watched in amazement as the four men went quietly out, without any trace of their former swagger. Only then did Baranwen turn to her. Her face was still cold. Was she going to tell Gerry that she was to be chained to the walls? She hadn't merely attempted to take the Kelegel. She'd actually done it.

Baranwen did not say anything. She stood still and waited while Gerry slowly walked across the floor to where she stood. As Gerry moved, an idea came to her. She might as well try it; she could hardly make things worse for herself.

'I don't think the Kelegel is safe here any longer,' she said. 'If you hadn't come, the Wasps would have grabbed it from me.

I was going to take it back to my own time and keep it till you've dealt with them. Surely it would be safer there? Could this be,' Gerry added as she had another thought, 'why you gave me the sapphire? So that I could do this?'

It sounded a lame excuse, and Gerry watched in trepidation as the Guardian considered it. There was no way to tell what she was thinking. At least she hadn't turned on Gerry as she'd turned on the Wasps. Baranwen remained in silent thought while Gerry stood there, holding the chalice. Then slowly she smiled.

'Yes,' she said, to Gerry's huge relief. 'Yes, that would be a good idea. You must keep it by you at all times, and never let it out of your sight. I think in any case you will find that you will not be able to part from it.'

Gerry had an incongruous vision of taking a shower, clutching the jewelled chalice in one hand and washing with the other, but the moment was too solemn for laughter. She looked at Baranwen doubtfully.

'Do you really mean that?' she asked. 'You'll trust me with the Kelegel?'

'Have I not just said so?' Baranwen replied. 'Keep it by you for tonight. Tomorrow I will summon the Gohi and we shall see.'

Gerry should have been reassured, but she was puzzling over the Guardian's words to the Wasps.

'You told me this afternoon that someone was planning to take the chalice and use it for evil,' she said. 'So you think that person sent them?'

'Of course,' Baranwen replied. 'I know these men. They are foolish and greedy, but like everyone in this land they have revered the Kelegel since childhood. They would never of themselves have thought to take it. Now they are in fear for their manhood and their very lives. They will tell me what I need and then I can act.'

134

She spoke with complete assurance. Gerry wasn't so certain, but this was Baranwen's domain, not hers. She looked at the Guardian as she stood, confident and powerful, and wondered how old she really was. However Gerry had more pressing concerns.

'Whoever it was,' she suggested, 'must somehow have sensed that I was intending to open the chalice's hiding place. You told me you always know if the Rainbow Jewels are threatened; could this be something similar, do you think?'

'It must be,' she answered. 'Unless anyone knew you were coming here, of course.'

That was a shock; one person certainly had known. But he was hundreds of years in the future, and besides he knew Gerry was going to bring him the Chalice. He had no need to send armed men to take it.

'From the way those four looked at it,' she said instead, 'I think whoever it is might have had trouble getting if from them. Each one wanted it himself.'

'Then they would have fought to the death over it,' said Baranwen grimly, 'and reduced the number of our enemies. It is one kind of protection the Jewels carry. But now you must return to your home. I should have news before long.'

Gerry was dismissed. Holding the jewelled cup, she left the chamber, and followed the tunnel back to the hillside. She hadn't been inside for long in real time but after so much tension it seemed strange to find herself still in ordinary sunlight. Gerry allowed herself a moment to look at the gleaming gold and perfect jewels, trying to angle the cup so the light shone through the colours as Kerenza had described. She tilted the gems this way and that, and would have carried on trying all afternoon, but heard sounds from below. The sun was sinking and the animals were being brought home to the village. She'd stood there longer than she'd realised. Gerry clutched the chalice and thought of Windhaven.

Almost at once she found herself back in the lounge standing effortlessly upright. She'd got there so easily she'd hardly been aware of moving. She looked in wonder at the chalice, which must have done this for her. Yet Kerenza had said that it took long years of training to learn to use it. She went to put it down on the table and felt a shock run up her arm immediately she let go of it. Baranwen had been right.

Gerry thought she'd better have something to eat. She picked up the Kelegel and took it to the kitchen with her, standing the chalice where she could see it. It felt strange, and not wholly comfortable, to be in an empty house with no neighbours in sight. She scrabbled around in her bag for her phone and found two messages waiting. The first was unexpected.

'Gerry, it's Lowenna from Cornish Studies, we'd like to take you up on your offer. We're going to be short-handed on Wednesday and Thursday, so if you fancy it you can have two days here and see how you get on. Can you leave a message on this number and let me know if you're free?'

Gerry was booked to work that Monday and Tuesday at Penzance, but had no other commitments as yet. Any work was welcome, and this might be interesting. Cornish Studies would certainly have more information than the Penzance library did about Cornwall in the Dark Ages. If she made herself useful they might offer her more time there. Was this just coincidence? Gerry looked hard at the chalice sitting innocently on the worktop. Then she left a message on Lowenna's number to say she'd be there, and to ask what the hours were.

The second message was from Debbie, to say she was

136

going to the Quay Fair in the morning. It was a street fair with stalls, food and entertainment along the front at Penzance as the final part of the Golowan festivities. Would Gerry like to go? She could come to Debbie's house mid-morning and they could walk down together from there. Gerry had felt guilty about refusing to go with Debbie after work today, so she sent a text to say she'd be there. She didn't want to talk just now; she needed to think.

There was a large post-it note in Claudia's clear handwriting stuck to the fridge door. It said there was some cold chicken and salad that Gerry could finish off as Claudia would be bringing fresh food back with her on Monday. Gerry found a plate and cutlery, helped herself, and settled down in the conservatory with her meal, with the chalice on the table in front of her. As she ate she tried to decide what to do.

Baranwen's words were worrying her. Justin had known she was going to the fogou. The Wasps had arrived soon after she got there. She couldn't see any logical connection between the two facts. Justin knew about the Wasps; he'd taken her to see them poison the wine so she could save the Bees. She put her plate aside. The food was better than she was used to but she'd eaten automatically, paying it less attention than it doubtless deserved. She wanted advice and without Seona did not know who to turn to. Gerry thought of Hedra, but she couldn't explain to the Bees' teacher not only that she had the chalice but that Baranwen had actually let her take it. Nor could she explain about Justin. Kerenza had said it was rumoured the Guardians could visit other places and times using the Rainbow Jewels, but would Hedra accept the idea of time travel? Anyway, last time she'd been with the Gwenen, Wylmet had died, and some of them might blame her for it, however unreasonable that was.

The mobile rang suddenly, showing 'number unknown'. Gerry's heart began to pound, certain it was Justin. She hadn't given him her number but by now nothing Justin did would surprise her. Gerry looked at the chalice and remembered how she'd stood her ground in front of the Wasps, defying them to take her prize. If it was Justin on the phone he would want the Kelegel, and Gerry had agreed to get it for him. She hadn't known then that by touching the chalice she would be bound to it. That she would want to keep it herself.

Earlier in the day she'd have seized the phone at once, longing to speak to Justin. But now she didn't. The message signal came through, but still Gerry didn't pick it up. She took the gold chain from her neck and removed the sapphire, then placed it in the gap on the side of the cup, holding it in place with the tip of her thumb and forefinger. The stones were positioned at equal distances around the rim of the cup: garnet, topaz, sapphire and amethyst. The overlapping colours of garnet and topaz would make orange, then topaz and sapphire for green and sapphire with amethyst for indigo. Four clear rock crystals were set on the sides, one between each pair of stones, forming a circle. The evening sun was slanting through into the conservatory. Gerry raised the chalice carefully into the sunlight and stood as she had on the hillside, slanting the gems to try to catch the sun through them. It was no use; she couldn't wake the rainbow. Then her phone rang again and this time she took the call, first setting the chalice down on the table, draping Seona's chain across the top, and keeping one hand on the sapphire. The tips of her fingers touched the gold of the cup and the chain. She hoped they would stimulate her imagination.

'Did you get it?'

It was Justin; no-one else would start a call like that. Gerry looked desperately at the stones, and knew what to say.

'Yes, I've got it,' she said, and heard a slight sound, perhaps a sigh. 'But there's a problem,' she added hurriedly. 'It's been damaged, one of the stones has been knocked out of place. I can get that fixed and then you can have it.'

'No, there's no need,' Justin said at once. 'I can do that myself.'

'It's no trouble,' Gerry said, 'and I'd like to do it for you. Then you can have your chalice as it should be. I'll look forward to seeing you.' And she pressed the red button.

She'd actually cut Justin off. The hand that held the phone was shaking. Gerry checked the message he'd left a few minutes ago but found it was silent. She switched the phone off, hoping he wouldn't appear here in front of her now.

He didn't. Gerry picked up the chalice again and held it close. She knew who she had to go to. The only person who could mend the damaged chalice and restore its powers was whoever had made it in the first place. And the Rainbow Jewels could take her to them.

Chapter Eleven

Gerry returned to the lounge. She threaded the sapphire back on the gold chain and fastened the pendant round her neck. Then she stood still, clutching the Kelegel in one hand and the stone in the other. She had to try to communicate with the Jewels of the Rainbow. Concentrating as hard as she could, she thought: *I need to go back to when you were brought and bound together, to the person or people who did that. Please take me there.*

There was a gap of seconds only, then Gerry found herself in the dark. There was neither sight nor sound. She couldn't feel her body, or the chalice, or Seona's chain. The darkness seemed to go on and on. Had she been over-confident? She couldn't feel the rug, nor earth and grass, under her feet. Was she now to be trapped in an inescapable limbo, caught between times? Or were the stones simply searching? She had no way of knowing how long the transfer lasted, but finally it ended and she found herself standing part of the way down the slope at Chapel Carn Brea.

At first Gerry thought she'd simply come back to where she'd been earlier, but saw almost at once that it wasn't the same. Previously she'd seen the roofs of a village near the foot of the hill, far below. Now there was a similar village, but it stood close to the top of the slope where the ground began to flatten out. She was near enough to hear voices, and to smell the smoke of the fires.

Gerry's tunic-like top had a long pocket on one side, secured by a zip. She thrust the chalice into this, safe and out of sight, and pushed the gold chain under the top of the tunic. Then with one hand clasped over the pocket which held the chalice, she walked towards the village.

A man dressed in clothes very like hers was coming up the slope, pushing a wooden hand cart. It was piled high with firewood, and Gerry could see it was wobbling. The right wheel hit a stone on the path and the load almost toppled. She ran forward to help, steadying the nearest bundle. The man was out of breath, but gasped out, 'Thank you, boy.'

So she'd yet again been taken for a boy. Gerry had understood the man, so the sapphire was still translating for her. The carter was making for an open gate in the stone wall which ran round the buildings. Gerry hurried after him, and he turned to look at her, keeping the cart steady with an effort. The man didn't seem surprised or alarmed at the sight of a stranger, but he wanted to get inside and get rid of his load.

'Please,' Gerry said, 'am I in the right place,' how could she ask this? 'I am looking for the Kelegel, the Tegennow a'n gammneves?' The Cornish words came easily.

'Yes, lad,' the man replied, 'we get many visitors coming here, asking. You need only go up the hill there till you see three great stones with an opening below. There you will find Colenso the Wise Woman and her companions.'

Of course that was where they would be. Gerry thanked the man, and he turned with relief to push his tottering cart through the gateposts. A woman in a calf-length gown came towards him, calling out for someone to lend a hand. A small piglet went running out past the cart, pursued by two children who were yelling as they ran. Another woman came to the gate, shouting to the children. They paid no attention but continued to chase the piglet.

Gerry unzipped her tunic pocket, put her hand inside and gripped the chalice for a moment, but didn't take it out. Then she began to walk upward towards the granite boulders. A large water barrel stood close to the entrance with a tin cup and dipper beside it. This would provide a welcome drink for those who had toiled up the hill, and for those within the fogou. The water must be brought up somehow from the village; there was no sign of a well or spring here.

Gerry approached the entrance cautiously, though the man with the cart had said it was common for people to come here seeking aid from those who served the Chalice of the Rainbow. This time a torch was burning in the tunnel to light the way in. Touching the sapphire with one hand and the Kelegel a'n gammneves with the other, Gerry walked forward into the tunnel and along to the circular chamber.

She stopped at the opening and looked inside. The man on the hill had said she would find the Wise Woman and her companions there. Gerry had assumed that the creator, or creators, of the Chalice would be old; that they would have needed years of learning to create an artefact of such power and beauty. She saw three women dressed in green sitting in the chamber, and certainly one was old, but one was young, and the other not yet middle aged. The scene brought to mind something she'd read that afternoon while searching through the books on early Cornish history. One of them had been about the Celts in Cornwall and had included the era she was looking for. It said that their Goddess had three aspects: the Maiden, the Mother and the

142

Wise Woman or Crone. These three women looked like that image brought to life. The eldest, who had grey hair and a clever face, must be the Wise Woman mentioned by the carter. The youngest, the Maiden, had dark hair flowing loose, a clear unlined face and strong, uncompromising features. The third, who must be the Mother, had lines on her face more like laughter lines than age, and a wide mouth meant for smiling and sympathy.

The moment they saw Gerry they all rose to their feet. The older, the Wise Woman, asked Gerry directly, 'Who are you, child, and what are you carrying? It is as if you hold some power to equal our Kelegel, but there is something wrong, very wrong.'

'She looks innocent, although she comes to us dressed in man's clothing,' the young woman, or Maiden, said. 'I cannot sense any intent for deception, or ill will.' She sounded reluctant to admit this.

'No,' the third woman, the Mother, agreed, 'but for all that, Colenso is right. There is something gravely amiss here.'

'Please don't send me away,' Gerry begged, alarmed at this reception where she had looked for welcome and understanding. 'I'm desperate, and I think you are the only people who can help me.' She'd understood what they were saying, so they should be able to understand her too.

'My name is Gerralda,' she began, 'Gerralda Melinda Hamilton.' She felt her full name was called for here. 'I need to ask about the Tegennow a'n gammneves. I was hoping you'd be able to help me.'

They looked at each other, and the eldest spoke again, her voice cold.

'Before we do, we must know who, and what, we would be dealing with. Do not attempt to lie,' she added sternly. 'No-one can lie within this chamber. It is protected against untruth.'

143

'Of course I'll tell you the truth,' Gerry said, annoyed. After all her efforts, and everything she'd been through, they were treating her like a suspect. 'And you're saying you'll believe me?'

She could tell at once that people didn't address these three in that tone, but she'd done it. Gerry wished she'd had a drink from that water barrel outside; her mouth was dry.

'One thing I must tell you before I start,' she said, not sure if she wanted to be resentful or defiant, 'and that is that I'm not from your time. I live in a century hundreds of years from now. You have to believe that or none of what I want to ask will make sense.'

She felt their reaction and expected them to contest the statement, but they did not. She wondered what happened to anyone who tried to deceive these three.

'We will take that on trust, for now.' Colenso, the Wise Woman, spoke for all of them. 'Please tell us about yourself.'

'It'll take some time,' Gerry said, still resentful. 'Do you mind if I get some water?'

'I will bring it.' The youngest of the three, the Maiden, stepped forward. She looked the most sceptical of the three. Gerry thought of her first meeting with Wylmet, and how friendly the young novice had been. This grave young woman had neither Wylmet's impulsiveness nor her light-heartedness. She picked up a beaker from a table behind them, and left the chamber with long strides, her gown brushing her calves and showing supple ankles.

'You feel we are suspicious,' said the woman Colenso, 'but no-one, young or old, has ever come here radiating power as you do. Yet that power is distorted in some way I cannot understand. We have to learn why, but we shall wait until Keyna returns.'

Nothing in this made Gerry feel comfortable. When the young woman Keyna came back and offered her a clay beaker of water, she drank some and felt better. Then she pulled forward a wooden stool, and the three women returned to where they'd been sitting when Gerry arrived.

For the first time Gerry turned away from their faces to look at her surroundings. The stone walls were of course the same, sloping inward and upward in their carefully laid lines. She glanced towards the stone where she'd found Baranwen's Kelegel, and felt a faint tingle of power. Unless she was very much mistaken, the chalice of this century was there too.

There was a lamp on the table as well as torches on the walls, and a colourful rug on the floor. Also on the table were a bronze coloured platter with what looked like dark bread and cheese on it, a lamp, and a pair of rolled up scrolls. The bench behind the table where the three sat was covered with a thick woollen blanket dyed in bright colours. Everything was more comfortable and well-made than she would expect in a thatched village or hillside cave. The woman who Gerry had seen as the Mother noticed her surprise.

'We ask no payment for our help,' she said, 'our services are free to all of good intent. Yet those who are able to give us gifts in gratitude, fine ones if they are wealthy. But we aid the poor also and expect nothing in return.

'Now, Gerralda Melinda Hamilton from another time, you may tell us your tale. I am Rosenwyn; my companions' names you have already been given. We three are the Makers of the Kelegel a'n gammneves, the Chalice of the Rainbow.'

Now that Gerry had been asked to speak, she didn't know where to start. Finally she began, 'I asked the Kelegel to bring me to whoever made it. So it was you who gave the chalice its powers?'

The three looked astounded when Gerry said that she'd asked the Kelegel to bring her here, and exchanged swift glances. It was Colenso who replied.

'That is so. We created it so that any ability which a woman had within her would be enhanced by it: power for healing, for learning and teaching. We studied far and wide, drew wisdom from many sources, and used it for the good of all our people.'

She paused, and Keyna continued. 'We traded for the gold and the crystals with the tin which is found here and is prized near and far. We sought unusually large and flawless stones to fill with light, in colours from the rainbow, which we would then combine with sunlight and water.'

'And you made it,' Gerry asked, 'how long ago?'

'It was completed perhaps three years ago,' Rosenwyn answered. 'Keyna joined us during the time we were trading; her family are traders in tin. We had to wait long months for the ships to return, but return they did at last, bearing what we had asked for.

'We used what is commonly called magic,' Rosenwyn continued, 'acquired from the wisdom of many peoples. But for all our learning, I never thought to see anyone who could move from one time to another. Are you a powerful sorceress?'

'No,' Gerry said at once, taken aback. That was a spooky idea. Then she qualified her reply. 'At least, I don't think I am. But so much has happened to me this week I'm not sure of anything any longer.'

Then she began to tell them her story, shivering at the memories. Even trying to keep to essentials, there was a lot to relate. She found that, as in the café with Baranwen, the concepts made themselves understood. Buying from a stall in a town, and a man who dealt in jewellery, were common ground to start with.

When she got to her first meeting with the Guardians at the top of the hill, she said, 'I told myself they were modern women acting out an old ritual, but I didn't really believe it. There was nothing there from my own time. I'd gone back perhaps twelve, thirteen hundred years, though I would guess it was still about four to six hundred ahead of the time we are in now.'

At this point Gerry picked up the beaker for another drink. They had remained motionless till now, allowing her to talk uninterrupted, but at this Rosenwyn took a pitcher and went to fetch more water, while Keyna checked the lamp. Only Colenso didn't move, but watched Gerry steadily.

'I accept what you say, extraordinary as it may seem,' she said. 'We will hear you out then decide what we should do.'

When the other two were settled again and Gerry had drunk some more of the clean-tasting water, she picked up the story and soon reached Kerenza's depiction of the Kelegel. 'When she described it I felt I wanted to see it, more than I'd ever wanted anything. And then she said it had disappeared, and that if the stones were separated, the power might be gone for ever. That was when I began to wonder seriously about my blue stone.'

She realised she hadn't mentioned Seona, so briefly explained her great-aunt's role in her life. 'Later I began to discover that the chain she gave me had power of its own. But I'm getting ahead.'

The three women had all shivered at the suggestion of the stones being separated, but again hadn't interrupted. Gerry continued with her visit to Redruth and her challenge to Alastair Fletcher which had been wholly out of character. 'It was as if I was turning into another person, or else someone was acting through me. I was given a reason for that later.' Then she told them of Justin and the fireworks. 'He told me the Kelegel was in the fogou, by the ashes of the last Guardian. I had felt afraid of the place when I first saw it, when Kerenza asked me if I had the Sight. That was when I began to understand about Seona.'

Colenso stopped her for the first time. 'Did this man know you had the sapphire?'

Gerry had thought a lot about this. 'I don't think he can have known. I took care to wear clothes that covered it, but he's got a lot of power himself. He seems to be able to travel in place and time, without using anything to help, and he brought me to the Gwenen. To the Bees that is, the women who work for the Guardians.'

Keyna was about to ask a question but Colenso stopped her. 'Please go on, Gerralda. There's more you have to tell us.'

'I think Seona's chain was protecting the sapphire, so that only I was aware of it.' A week before Gerry wouldn't have believed a word of any of this, but she could tell that her audience did. 'And Baranwen, of course.'

She covered her encounter with the Wasps, and Wylmet's death, quickly, and finally came to her meeting with Baranwen in Penzance. 'She told me that she was the one who took the sapphire off the Kelegel.'

'She, the Guardian?' Keyna had spoken, but all three looked equally appalled.

'Yes. She told me that by taking off one of the stones she would prevent whoever was after the Jewels of the Rainbow from getting or using them. She said she'd "served the chalice for more years than I could imagine", that it "bestowed this on its servants", and she "didn't know if it was a gift or a curse".' Gerry stopped for breath; she'd been talking faster as she went along. 'Then she told me it was her who'd attacked both the jewellers' shops to protect the sapphire, and I remembered my own fury when the stone was threatened.'

148

'We did not put that into the Tegennow.' Rosenwyn could no longer restrain herself. 'Nor did we give them the power to enable movement in place and time, which you say they helped Baranwen, and yourself, to do. They have changed, grown perhaps, but I do not feel that these changes are right, or for good.'

'In the years between us and your Baranwen they have become twisted,' Colenso said grimly. 'We made them beautiful, but not to be coveted for their beauty or their value, still less that acts of violence should be committed to protect them. Nor, as Rosenwyn says, to transport their servants and extend their lives. And this least of all, that a woman sworn to their service should deliberately harm them for any reason. This is bitter news.'

Gerry looked at her sadly.

'I'm sorry,' she said. 'I came here for advice, I didn't think –'

'No,' said Keyna, her face hard in the glow of the torchlight, 'you didn't.'

Colenso silenced her with a look. 'It is better that we should know,' she assured Gerry. 'Perhaps we can undo the harm, return the Tegennow to their original purity. You do have them with you?'

'I do. Let me finish my story, though; I'm nearly at the end. I went to the fogou this evening and found the damaged chalice. My sapphire practically pulled me to it. When I took it out I found the Gohi, the Wasps, surrounding me. Then Baranwen arrived, she threatened them and sent them away. And she said I could keep the chalice for now, to stop anyone in her time from getting hold of it and misusing it. I'd promised to give it to Justin, but since I touched it, I wanted to keep it myself. I don't know what to do.'

Gerry stopped. She'd run out of breath again, and out of words. There wasn't anything else she could say.

There was a brief silence then all three Makers began to speak at once. They looked at each other, then Colenso began.

'There are many matters here we need to debate,' she pronounced, 'but one must come first. You have your concerns about Baranwen, but I believe you greatly underestimate her.'

'You have told us more than you realise,' Rosenwyn put in gently. 'Your own fears and suspicions and longings. I will add to what Colenso has suggested. Perhaps Baranwen was right in saying that by splitting the Tegennow,' she shuddered again, 'she has prevented anyone from laying hands on it to misuse its power. But you have only her word for any of her actions.'

'I thought about the other Guardians,' Gerry admitted. 'Morvoren was hostile, but she thought I'd stolen the sapphire, and later that I was involved in poisoning the wine. One of the Bees is having an affair with Cathno of the Gohi, and that might well be Ysella. Still, whoever's passing information to Cathno may have no idea of what she's doing. It could be as simple as when the chalice will next be taken out, or who knows where it is.'

'Even so,' said Colenso with distaste, 'none of these three sound like women we would have picked as Guardians of the Kelegel. Delenyk sounds more like our ideal. You want us to restore the sapphire to its place. I begin to feel that perhaps we would do better to take the power away from the stones for ever, we who first gave it.'

Without even realising, Gerry was on her feet. 'No!' she cried, raising her hand to her throat as if to protect the sapphire.

Rosenwyn shook her head sadly. 'You see? You are under their spell already, after just two days. Baranwen has been close to the Tegennow for who knows how many years; how can we judge whether she has twisted them, or they have twisted her?'

Gerry found she was shaking. 'You really think she is lying?'

'I have no doubt of it,' Rosenwyn said. 'There is something you have not seen, perhaps because you are too close. I believe that Baranwen will use you in some way to destroy her enemy, then present you to the Bees as a scapegoat. This is why she chose you, who have the power to work with the Tegennow. You are to appear bearing the restored chalice, then, denounced and proven as a blasphemous thief, you will share Delenyk's fate. After that the chalice will be safe for Baranwen to keep again, unchallenged.'

Gerry felt her throat closing. She couldn't speak. She'd never dreamed of such an idea, yet it sounded horribly plausible. Her shock must have been obvious to them all.

'Let us now see the Kelegel which you carry,' Colenso said firmly. Gerry stood up dumbly, undid the clasp of Seona's chain, took off the sapphire, and placed it on the table. The light looked poor to her 21st century eyes, even with a good lamp and two torches burning brightly, yet the stone glowed with the blue that had first caught her. Then she unzipped the pocket of her tunic, reached inside and took out the Chalice of the Rainbow. After what she'd heard she felt uncomfortable showing this damaged cup to the Makers, but this was why she'd come here.

Gerry put the chalice on the table beside the sapphire, feeling a sharp wrench as it left her hands. She put Seona's chain back on, gaining some comfort from it, as if Seona herself had put a reassuring arm round her shoulders. The three Makers leaned forwards, all on their feet now, bending over to examine their injured handiwork. Finally Colenso lifted the sapphire gently and held it in its place on the curved side of the Kelegel, between the topaz and the amethyst.

'We can restore this using our own chalice,' she told me, 'but what happens to it cannot be decided in a moment. Look well,' she said to Rosenwyn and Keyna. 'To me, these do not look like our gemstones.'

Gerry raised her head and stared at Colenso, her thoughts in a whirl.

'Do you mean someone has made a copy of them?' But no imitation could carry the power which, even incomplete, had been apparent to the Makers the moment she'd entered the fogou.

Colenso shook her head. 'Oh, no, not in that sense. They are physically the same stones, although there are marks on the gold which I do not recognise. We wrote the names of the stones in the language of the men who brought them, in thanks for their endeavours on our behalf, but that was all.'

Gerry pointed to the capital Bs reversed back to back, with the little lines above and below, which she'd first seen on the gold round the sapphire and which were visible round the other three stones as well. 'All the Gwenen wear this mark at the base of the throat, and this circle with the crossed lines on the inside of their left wrist. But how else are they altered?'

'These are named the Tegennow a'n gammneves,' Keyna said, 'not just because they are made of those colours but because when we summon them to our aid they pour their light out into the sun as a rainbow. We created them to do this.'

'But they are grieving, dulled within themselves,' Colenso pronounced. 'The colours are as lovely, nothing can taint that, but we made them with joy and hope, and that has left them.'

She turned to Gerry, and the others did too.

'We cannot decide this in haste.' Again Colenso spoke for them all. 'We must ponder this, and debate between ourselves.

You should go back to your own world. Leave your Tegennow with us and return tomorrow.'

Gerry let out an involuntary wail. 'I can't go on my own! I need the stones or I'm trapped here.'

Colenso the Wise Woman smiled, her eyes an unexpectedly warm brown under the grey-white of her hair. 'You are wrong, child. The gold chain your great-aunt gave you has done more than you understood. You may be gifted, but you would never have learned unaided how to use the stones so quickly.' She leaned forwards and passed her hands above the worked gold, not quite touching it, as Baranwen had in the café in Penzance. 'This,' she said, 'holds great knowledge within itself. You have only just begun to understand that. With its aid and our intent you may go and return in safety.'

Gerry was stunned. 'You want me to leave the Kelegel with you until tomorrow? To go back without it?'

'Yes indeed. It seems to me that in any case you are safer without it. Do not fear, you will find us again. It was an astonishing feat to have come here as you did, with no guidance. Go home, and come back to us again this time tomorrow.'

Gerry had wanted advice, and been given it, but this wasn't what she'd expected. What she'd hoped, of course, was for them to mend the chalice and say she could keep it. Like they were going to do that.

'Please,' she begged, 'can I see what the Jewels do when they turn into a rainbow?' As soon as she spoke she felt the words sounded childish, but this was what she'd wanted ever since Kerenza had spoken of the Jewels and the crystals changing sunlight into the radiance of a rainbow. She waited without looking at the Makers, and heard them murmuring together. Then Colenso

153

said 'If you wish you can watch while we mend the chalice you brought here. You should be warned, though, that it will bind you even closer to the Tegennow. You can watch, but do not touch them while we work. That is dangerous for anyone, but far more for so you who have worn the sapphire.'

'Do not look so stricken,' Rosenwyn said. 'What happens is that we create the rainbow in the sunlight. If there is none we can use the light of torch, lamp or fire, but true sunlight is always best. We bathe our hands in the rainbow light and then use them for whatever is needed by way of healing or help. In simple cases, for example, we would use the warmer shades for sore limbs, cramps, back-aches and the like but the colder colours to cool burns. This once, however, we will have to put your Kelegel and the sapphire together in the light of our own blue stone, and it will be a very delicate task; we must get the balance exactly right or the joining will be incomplete and irreparable.'

'So you must remain silent, watching but neither moving nor speaking.' That was Keyna. Gerry would have bet that she'd tried to persuade the others to send her away before they began the work.

'I promise,' Gerry said. 'I'll keep still.'

'Then come with us now,' Colenso said. She went to the stone that Gerry had spotted in the wall, put her hand against its side and drew out the original Kelegel. For a moment Gerry felt giddy; it seemed wrong, more than wrong, that the two should be so close to each other. To her they looked the same except for the marks. Whatever the Makers thought was different about Baranwen's chalice wasn't apparent to Gerry.

'You are shaking,' Keyna said, eying Gerry disparagingly. 'When did you last eat?'

'Hours ago,' Gerry admitted. 'I was too worried about trying to get here.'

'That was foolish,' Keyna responded. 'You had better have this.' She put some bread and cheese onto a shallow dish, and poured wine from a second pitcher into another beaker. 'We will wait until you are refreshed.' Before Gerry could thank her, Keyna added, 'We have to give our work all our concentration, and having you shivering next to us could be overly distracting.'

Well, thank you, Gerry thought, but didn't say it. She ate and drank hastily, finding the bread and cheese strong and full of flavour. When she finished, she did feel better. The Makers waited at the exit, talking quietly, till she was ready. Then she followed the Makers through the tunnel and found the light of a summer evening outside.

The four of them were the only people on this part of the hill. All the villagers had returned home to food and fire, children and animals. Colenso raised the Kelegel to the sun, murmuring what sounded like a short prayer. Then she went to the barrel by the tunnel entrance and picked up the dipper that lay on top of a large stone beside it. She used this to fill the tin drinking cup with water. Keyna had brought out the small wooden stool which she stood on a level patch of bare earth. She laid a piece of green cloth over it, then took the Kelegel and placed it on the cloth. Colenso poured water from the cup slowly into the chalice until it was filled, then scattered the remaining water on the ground.

As Gerry stared at the chalice, a wide beam of sunlight enclosed it. In that light, the rock crystals began to form prisms within themselves, gleaming multi-coloured lines, and the gold of the cup blazed brighter than the sun. Gerry stood mesmerised, watching the Jewels of the Rainbow come alive. They glowed, seeming to fill with light from within, and bright shafts of their colours, red, yellow, blue and purple, began to pour upwards. Drops of water from within the chalice rose between the beams. As the sun touched them, the shafts bent towards each other and overlapped, creating orange, green and indigo. A complete rainbow flowed upwards, perhaps four or five metres from the ground at the topmost part of its arc. It curved high above the entrance to the fogou as the far end settled across the granite boulders and came to rest out of sight. The seven colours, pure and vivid, were more dazzling than any natural rainbow. It was all Gerry could do to stay still as she'd promised. She wanted to run to the Jewels and take hold of them, wrap the beams of colour round her. Above all, the rich blue was calling her. Keyna, expecting this, had been watching her. She moved swiftly to Gerry's side and gripped her arms hard, keeping her motionless.

Colenso moved forward and placed her hands into the centre of the blue beam, taking care to avoid the green and indigo on either side. She seemed to be praying again. Then she pulled her hands back and Rosenwyn stepped forwards, carrying the chalice and sapphire which Gerry had brought. She handed them over and Colenso fitted the sapphire into the gap on the side of Baranwen's cup between the two crystals which flanked it. The two loops which had held the stone on Seona's chain slotted into two small dips in the side of the chalice. Colenso raised it and held it in the blue light, whispering words that even the gold chain couldn't interpret. Finally Colenso withdrew the mended chalice from the rainbow, holding it this time by its base. And the sapphire held. The work was successful.

The rainbow went. It didn't return gradually as it had grown, but simply vanished as if it had never been. The cup was simple gold again, with jewels set around it, beautiful still but without the living force which had filled them. Keyna released Gerry and she walked unsteadily towards Colenso to look at the two Chalices which now, except for the markings, looked just the same. Gerry could hardly believe what she had just seen.

'You must not touch it,' came Rosenwyn's warning voice from just behind her. Gerry turned round and looked round at her, and saw that Rosenwyn looked as weary as if she'd been up all night.

'We will give thanks to the Great Mother for aiding us in our work,' Rosenwyn said, 'then rest for a while. You should leave us now.'

They returned to the fogou and Gerry was readying herself to go when sounds came to them from outside. A woman calling out, a child crying, hurrying feet.

'That will be someone seeking our help,' Keyna explained. 'Many come here, have been coming since the fame of the Tegennow a'n gammneves began to spread.'

Rosenwyn went to see who it was. Colenso sat down, looking even more wearied than Rosenwyn.

'When you return to your home,' she said, 'there is something else you should consider in addition to Baranwen's motives. This man you spoke of.'

'Justin,' Gerry said. 'What about him?'

'I think you should be careful what you tell him. There are things he has not told you, that much is plain. You do not know the source of his power, though you have seen that he can do many things with it. Does he belong in your own time?'

'I don't know,' Gerry answered, 'I'd always assumed he did. Why?'

'Colenso is being polite,' Keyna said. 'I would say you are following your heart, not your head, in this. Would you usually take on such a dangerous task for a near stranger?'

157

'He doesn't feel like a stranger,' Gerry said, 'I don't think he ever did.'

'Then what does he feel like?' Keyna persisted.

What Justin actually felt like was the hottest man she'd ever met. Gerry would do anything to help him if it meant seeing him, being with him again. But she couldn't say that to this stern young woman who looked as if she'd never even touched a man. Instead she sighed. What she really wanted was to talk to Seona. She could tell her the truth. Then with a gasp Gerry realised she could do just that.

'What is it, Gerralda?' Keyna asked.

'Seona, my great-aunt who gave me this chain. She died soon after, but now – I could go back to when she was still alive, and ask her advice. She knows me really well and she was always sensible.'

'No!' Colenso spoke so sharply that Gerry jumped. 'That you must never do. Can you not see that if you were to revisit your own past, you could alter what happened in your life and the lives of those about you? If you went to speak with your Seona now you could cause incalculable damage.'

'I don't see how –' Gerry began.

Colenso had risen, and at the sight of her face Gerry was reminded of Baranwen's ruthless speech to the Gohi, sentencing them as a judge might.

'You have travelled in time, but you do not understand it in the least,' the Wise Woman said sternly. 'Suppose you appeared suddenly out of nowhere in front of your elderly great-aunt. She might receive such a shock that she died of it, then she would not live to give you the gold chain, and you would not be here now in front of me. And then you would never have been able to go back and see her and cause her death. A paradox like that could change time and wreck the course of history.'

Gerry couldn't think of anything to say. Rosenwyn returned, and looked at Gerry's stricken expression, then at her two associates.

'There is a poor woman here whose two children have been badly injured in a fall. Climbing trees, I expect,' Rosenwyn added with a quick smile. 'I gave instructions to the man who brought them up here to give them food and drink, and a place to rest after their journey. I said that we would be with her soon, but that we were with another woman in distress who had also travelled far, seeking our help.' She looked at Gerry with compassion. 'For you are in distress, Gerralda.'

Her kindness was too much on top of Colenso's questions about Justin, then her tongue-lashing about time travel. It was an effort not to just burst into tears, but Gerry couldn't let herself do that in front of these three.

'You need to rest and sleep,' Rosenwyn said. 'Did you not say that Baranwen told you not to use too much of your own time in travelling to the past or you would wear yourself out? Go back now and sleep without dreaming. Go with our blessing,' she added.

'May the Goddess go with you.' This from Keyna.

For a moment Gerry wondered if it would be easier just to stay here. If these women were right about Baranwen, she stood in greater danger than she'd ever realised. She wished she could believe they were wrong, but she didn't. But she also reckoned the Guardian could find her even here, and she couldn't be certain the three Makers would choose to defend her from Baranwen. Staying wasn't an option.

Gerry stood up, feeling it would look more dignified, closed her eyes, and touched the gold chain with both hands. She thought of the blue and purple stars, then into her mind came the picture of Seona's face. Her eyes were sea-green like Gerry's own; her hair, once as red as her great-niece's, was now grey-white like Colenso's. Gerry saw the lines on her great-aunt's face which she'd never thought about, but which she could now see were drawn from the illness Seona had been at pains to keep from her family. But over all this was the familiar expression of warm, loving care.

Take me home, Gerry whispered silently. *Take me back to Windhaven.*

The eyes smiled at her, and she was back in the darkness.

Chapter Twelve

Sunday 29ᵗʰ June 2014

Perhaps it was because of the blessing Rosenwyn had given her, but for whatever reason Gerry slept undisturbed for hours. Neither Baranwen nor Justin came into her dreams, and she remained in her bed in the 21st century. When she woke at last, there was only half an hour to go before she was meant to be meeting Debbie. She scrambled around, grabbed a slice of toast, and gulped some coffee while she got ready. One day she might find a few spare minutes to actually appreciate being at Windhaven.

Gerry was late arriving at her friend's house, which was on the Treneere estate on the eastern side of Penzance, but as Debbie had just changed her mind about what to wear, Gerry needn't have worried. While she waited, Debbie's mother gave her a cup of tea and offered a plate of biscuits. Debbie's brother Mike joined them, cheerful though rather bleary-eyed after a late night at the Barn Club with his mates. The place was untidy but welcoming, and Gerry couldn't help contrasting it with Windhaven. Then with an unexpected pang of homesickness, she thought of her home in Lochallaig, which fitted somewhere between this house and Claudia's. In Gerry's schooldays her mother had fought a permanent losing battle; with three teenage boys at home, the house could never be kept tidy.

Debbie interrupted Gerry's thoughts by pelting downstairs in jeans and a t-shirt, her bag dangling from one hand. Debbie looked more casual and a lot more relaxed than she did at work, and it suited her. She'd left her shining brown hair loose for once, and it swung round her shoulders.

'Come on,' she said, 'let's get to the fair before it rains. We can walk down from here.'

'Like I kept you waiting?' Gerry asked as they set off through the streets of near-identical houses, grey and greyish white with their tiny front gardens, bay windows and green wheelie bins.

'Oh, I forgot to say,' Debbie said, as they hurried along, 'Tasha tweeted to say she'll meet us outside the station.'

'Okay.'

Tasha worked at the library, mostly in the children's section. She wore short skirts, black tights and big jewellery, and multi-coloured nails. With her bubbly personality she was the opposite of the stereotyped image of a librarian, and the children loved her. Gerry liked Tasha too, but she was beginning to wonder why she'd agreed to come at all.

The two young women left the estate and came down a steep hill opposite the bay. The blue sea of the day before had been replaced by a dull grey. There was minimal wind and the tide was in, with small waves washing across the surface against the wall on the far side of the last part of the railway line running into Penzance station.

Debbie linked her arm through Gerry's, surprising her friend out of her thoughts. 'Gerry,' she said, 'you're miles away. You don't have to tell me, but just so as you know, after you shot

162

off yesterday afternoon, Ernie said you were probably off to see your boyfriend, and he told me about seeing you at the fireworks with him. Very cosy, he said.'

Gerry groaned. They'd reached the traffic lights opposite the station. She was about to cross without looking when she realised the lights were green. Gerry stopped dead, and as Debbie's arm was still through hers, she stopped too.

'It's like living in a goldfish bowl,' Gerry protested. 'I'm in trouble over that already, but it isn't what you think.'

'No?' Debbie's voice was teasing. 'Has Ryan got a rival? Is this why you wouldn't go out with him?'

Ryan had asked her out only the day before; it seemed like a lifetime ago. And Gerry hadn't said that she wouldn't go, just that she'd tell him on Monday. That was tomorrow, now.

'Damn,' she said, then 'Oh sod it.'

'What's the problem?' Debbie was surprised. 'I thought you grew up in a village; didn't everyone there know what everyone else was doing?'

'Yeah, but remember I spent three years in London. It wasn't quite so bad there.' Gerry leaned back against the wall of the Longboat pub, out of the way of the people hurrying down towards the front. Debbie moved closer.

'I'm all ears. What've you been up to? You've kept this very quiet. I thought you said yesterday you were off men, after what happened in London.'

Gerry sighed. 'Look,' she said. 'You remember when we went to Chapel Carn Brea I said I'd like to go back when there was no one else there? Well, I went on Thursday, and up near the top there was a man. When I got close enough to see him properly, I knew who he was. It was the man we'd seen in the park that afternoon arguing with Claudia.'

Debbie's eyes widened. 'The one you fancied? And did you still fancy him when you saw him close up?'

'Oh yes.'

'So you arranged to meet at the fireworks?'

'Yeah, that's right.' Leaving out the Bees, the Kelegel, the Wasps and the fogou – and the poisoned wine. 'I met him in Penzance and we did watch the fireworks and he had his arms round me and, oh, it felt wonderful. He's the sexiest man I ever met. That was when Ernie saw us, I expect. Then next morning I found that Claudia already knew. Monica had seen us and phoned Claudia straight away to tell her.'

'Shit, what a bitch!' Debbie's usually kindly eyes flashed with anger. 'I thought she'd make trouble, but I never guessed it would be that bad. What did your Claudia say?'

'Well, not what I'd expected,' Gerry told her, remembering. 'I thought she'd throw me out, but she seemed to blame herself, like it was because of her that he'd picked me up?' Gerry moved aside as a family ran along the pavement in front of her to cross the road before the lights changed, then went on, leaning back against the wall again as the family hurried over the crossing. 'Claudia'd already told me that she didn't want Justin – that's his name, obviously - coming to the house, but she seemed more worried that I didn't know what I was getting into. She's right, of course, he's way out of my league. Plus I'm sure he could be dangerous, he's got some seriously dodgy friends. But Claudia said herself that no woman's ever refused him. He's gorgeous, like I said, but he's bad news. I know I shouldn't see him again, but I so want to. It's all a mess.'

'It's like something out of "EastEnders",' Debbie said, awed. 'Claudia and Justin, Claudia and Monica, and you and Justin. You forget about him and go out with Ryan. He's all right.'

'I know, but is it fair to him? I bet he thinks I'm all sweet and innocent.' Gerry looked at Debbie, considering. 'He'd be better off going out with you. I've seen you together, you get on really well, and I know you like him.'

Debbie was nonplussed, and gave the inevitable glance down at her plump form.

'Who's going to look at me when you're around?' she asked.

'Oh, nonsense,' Gerry said, exasperated. 'You're pretty, you are, if only you'd believe it.' They'd had this conversation before. Debbie had a really lovely smile, and Gerry was sure some of the weight that bothered her would fall off if she was in love. 'Besides, you told me about Ryan's last girlfriend. Shows what happens when you just go for looks. Oh, bugger it,' Gerry finished despairingly. She could tell wasn't getting anywhere. 'Let's go and find Tasha.'

Debbie looked at her, then shrugged. 'All right,' she said. 'But I'm not going back to that funfair. The others dragged me onto the big wheel yesterday. Never again. There's other stuff we can do today.'

Gerry didn't care what they did. They had reached the station by now and Tasha was standing there, outside the exit. There was a paved area with a map of West Cornwall forming part of the paving stones. Like the Pied Piper, Tasha had attracted a group of children. Some of them knew her from the library. She was leading them in a kind of dance round the map to different parts of Penwith. When she saw Debbie and Gerry, she sent the children off and came to join the newcomers. Tasha had pink streaks in her hair today, and her short skirt and bare arms made no concession to the grey skies.

'Can't get away from work,' Tasha grumbled, though she didn't sound serious. 'So what kept you?' she asked, and Debbie and Gerry both said 'She did,' at the same time. The three walked along the road past the large car park to the harbour where a couple of dozen small boats were bobbing on the tide, pulling at their ropes. They walked across the swing bridge which separated the wet dock from the dry dock and the harbour office. From here, a whole section of the front had been closed to traffic for the day. Stalls filled both sides of the road and continued on round the corner out of sight. Some were selling hot and cold drinks, pasties and bacon sandwiches. A noodle bar stood, incongruous, next to the counter with the pasties. The fun fair with its music, ghost train, helter-skelter and roundabouts loomed behind the stalls. The coloured lights glowed against the grey sky, and the big wheel with its shrieking passengers towered above it all. There were more stalls beyond the food ones, selling skirts and sunglasses, colourful shawls and wooden toys. Two men stood on the pavement at the side, playing a banjo and an accordion. People crowded on all sides, filling the road and pavements.

Gerry raised her hand to touch Seona's gold chain, suddenly aware that it was sending her a warning. Somewhere among the bustling crowd, the chattering adults and eager children, there was an enemy. She gazed around uneasily. Above their heads the coloured banners with their seaside images rippled in the breeze, shading from red and orange through yellow, green and blue to purple. Gerry thought of the Jewels of the Rainbow as she had last seen them, blazing in these same colours.

Tasha went to look at a stall selling handbags, while Debbie called, 'Don't get lost, Gerry. Come and look at these. You like earrings, don't you?'

Gerry pushed her way over to Debbie. Her friend was standing at a craft stall, sandwiched between a blacksmith's display of wrought iron and a stand of watercolours. For a moment Gerry expected the stallholder to be Baranwen, but it was a young blonde, her hair twisted up to show her dangling earrings and a necklace of large beads. Both were obviously her own work.

Debbie was browsing through a tray of silver bangles with flecks of colour worked into them. 'I like these,' she said, then put down the one she was looking at. 'Damn, I need the loo. And there's bound to be a queue.'

'Should-have-gone-before-you-left,' Gerry told her, like a cross parent on a car journey.

'Fat chance, with you dragging me out the door,' Debbie said. Before Gerry could protest, Debbie added, 'you might as well wait here, I won't be long. It's just along there, opposite the Dolphin.'

After Debbie had left, Gerry found she couldn't concentrate on the jewellery. She grew increasingly concerned, and the sense of warning from the chain remained. Debbie didn't come back. Even allowing for queues – and there was probably a long one – she should have been back by now. She'd probably stopped to look at something, or met a friend. Debbie had grown up in Penzance, and was always bumping into people she knew.

In the end Gerry gave up. If Debbie came back and they missed each other, she could phone. Gerry checked to make sure she hadn't missed any calls already; it wouldn't be easy to hear even her noisy ring tone in this crowd. There were no missed calls, and she was startled to realise she hadn't heard from Justin. She'd told him she would have the mended chalice for him. Gerry still wasn't sure why she hadn't wanted to hand over the chalice last night, when the only reason she'd gone to get it was so she could give it to him. True, once she'd held the Kelegel she hadn't wanted to let it out of her hands; but how could she explain that to Justin?

That would have to wait, though. It was Debbie she was worried about now. She found Tasha trying on hats in front of a mirror. Gerry told her she was going to look for Debbie, and made off through the throng, looking anxiously all round as she walked. The toilets were next to the open space by the harbour, where the Scillonian III was in dock. The big passenger ferry didn't make the crossing to the Isles of Scilly on Sundays.

Opposite the Dolphin pub, a group of women were performing some eastern style dance with lots of arm movements. They wore colourful costumes and sequins and it looked more suited to India or Thailand than a grey waterfront in Cornwall. Gerry scanned the people watching the dancers but Debbie wasn't among them. Nor was she in the queue waiting outside the Ladies'. Gerry waited till the women inside had come out, but Debbie wasn't one of them either. As a last hope she went into the Dolphin. It was packed, but though Gerry went into each room and made her way from end to end of the crowded bars she didn't see her. She hadn't really expected to; Debbie wasn't much of a pub person.

Gerry tried to tell herself Debbie must simply be talking to friends somewhere, but she didn't believe it. Feeling more afraid by the minute she came out of the Dolphin and stood gazing around. Could she have missed her after all? Should she go back to where they'd been standing before, by that stall with the bracelets? Gerry looked at the dancers again, but Debbie was definitely not watching them. On the left was the low granite office of the weighbridge. A side road sloped up beyond it towards Chapel Street. Gerry looked up it just in case, then froze. Debbie was there, by the wall where two roads met. She wasn't alone; a man was standing on each side of her, and one had his hand gripping her wrist. Debbie just looked bewildered, but Gerry was petrified. Whatever she'd been afraid of, it wasn't this. She knew both of them, and they shouldn't have been here. Not in 21st century Penzance, in a rough equivalent of modern clothes. The men holding Debbie were Cathno and Elwyn.

'Debbie!' Gerry shouted at the top of her voice, and ran towards the two Wasps. If they had their knives, as they probably did, she ought to have been more cautious, but she didn't care about anything except getting Debbie away from them.

'Gerry!' Debbie looked round in relief. Elwyn released the grip on her wrist, and both men turned to look at Gerry. She couldn't tell if they'd recognised her or not. Cathno raised his head, slightly on one side as if listening, then the pair disappeared round the other side of the building, towards the dock.

'Are you all right?' Gerry asked.

'Yes, I think so' Debbie said, 'but I'm glad you turned up. That was weird.' Debbie brushed her arm where Elwyn had been holding it, and began to walk back down the road. Gerry kept close to her.

'They must be foreign visitors, they were talking to each other, but I couldn't make out a word they were saying. I tried to speak to them but they didn't seem to understand me either.'

'What happened?' Gerry asked.

'Well, I came up here to go to the loo, and then on the way back I stopped to look at that dancing.' They'd reached the weighbridge and she gestured towards the sequinned dancers, who were having a break.

'Yeah, I saw them too. But how did you end up there?' Gerry jerked her head back towards where she had seen Debbie and the Wasps. As she did so, she felt the first light drops of rain. The perfect weather of the past week had broken.

'I'm trying to tell you, aren't I?' Debbie said. 'I didn't know how long I'd been away, and thought I ought to get back to you before you decided to come and look for me. I crossed the road 'cos there was more space that side. Then suddenly those two men kind of lurched at me. One of them got hold of my arm and started dragging me up the hill.'

'Didn't you shout out?' Gerry asked, appalled.

'No, to be honest, I was too surprised, and it happened so fast. And if I had, who'd have heard me in all this racket?' She was right; there was plenty of shouting among the general din. 'It doesn't make any sense. They weren't trying to rob me, I mean they didn't try to snatch my bag. Unless they wanted to wait till they were away from the crowd. And I don't suppose they wanted sex.'

Gerry was about to reply when her mobile began to ring. It showed 'unknown number' again, and, as she expected, when she answered it there was no-one at the other end. Gerry felt that sinking feeling which was getting too familiar, the cold chill running down the back of the throat and into her stomach.

Debbie furrowed her brows. 'All that stuff made me forget,' she said. 'I saw someone who might have been your Justin, standing outside the Dolphin, talking on his phone. I mean I only saw him at a distance the other day, but I think it was him.'

Gerry's throat had gone dry. It took her three goes to succeed in swallowing.

170

'I'm leaving,' she said, 'but I'll take you back to Tasha first. Will you stay with her, or if not then with someone you know, for the rest of today? Just in case those two come back?'

Debbie wasn't stupid. She stood still and looked at Gerry.

'There's quite a few people I know here, but I'm not going anywhere till you tell me a bit more,' she said. 'Like why you look scared stiff, but you don't seem surprised.'

'I can't tell you,' Gerry said wretchedly. 'Please, Debs, don't ask me. I can't explain.'

'But you do know something, something about those two men?'

'I think I've seen them before, but not round here. Look, will you trust me? Try not to go anywhere on your own, just for a couple of days?'

Debbie opened her eyes very wide. 'But you won't tell me why?'

'I told you, I can't.'

'Then I'm not doing it.'

'You'd be better off not knowing,' Gerry pleaded.

'I don't think so.'

Debbie stood stolidly on the weighbridge, arms folded, and Gerry realised she had to give her some sort of explanation. She went for a very modified version of the facts.

'You know I had Thursday off?' Debbie nodded. 'Well, I bought a coloured stone from a stall on Causewayhead and showed it to a jeweller to see what he thought of it. He said he thought the stone might be real, and valuable.' Not to mention how old it was. 'His shop was trashed that night. Then I showed it to another jeweller and he tried to steal it off me. Seems the stone really belonged on a decorated gold cup, but someone had taken

171

it off. I found the woman who'd made the cup and left the stone with her yesterday, so she could mend it.'

Debbie gave her a strange look. 'And you've fitted in all this along with working, moving house, and seeing Justin?'

Gerry was trying as hard as she could to make this sound reasonable. 'Most of that was in the evenings, and I wasn't working Friday morning. Anyway, like I just said, I don't have the stone any longer, but I think those two men are after it.'

'And you're telling me not to go around on my own?' It was Debbie's turn to look appalled. 'What if they come after you?'

That was a good question, and Gerry didn't have an answer. She gripped her phone. 'I'll just have to call the police. But in the meantime there's a couple of people I want to go and see. They live in the same village, so I hope I can find them both. I think they can help me.' If she couldn't go back to Seona, or to the Makers, then Hedra and Meraud seemed the best bet. 'I'd better go.'

Debbie put a hand on her arm.

'Gerry, I don't know what you've got yourself into, but please be careful. Are you working tomorrow?'

'Yeah, I'm supposed to be.' She was on the rota to work, but that seemed impossibly far ahead. 'I'll see you in the morning.'

'Good luck.' Debbie was more serious than Gerry had ever seen her. Gerry was glad she hadn't told her about Justin wanting the 'gold cup'.

When she'd taken Debbie back to Tasha, Gerry walked up to the Treneere estate to get her car, seeing nothing of the festivities around her. She doubted if she'd notice if all four of the Wasps had appeared in front of her; she was too preoccupied.

Somebody had brought Cathno and Elwyn through all those centuries to this Penzance, and the only person Gerry could think of was Baranwen. She'd seen the Guardian master them in the fogou. What was worrying Gerry most was why Baranwen had brought the Wasps here. What were they planning to do next?

Even if she got to the Bees' village and found Hedra away from the Guardians, Gerry couldn't tell the teacher that she'd touched the Jewels of the Rainbow. She couldn't explain where she really came from, or her suspicions of Baranwen. To Hedra, and all the Bees, Baranwen was their revered superior. But Gerry hoped Hedra could tell her more about the Sight, and then maybe she could use it to help herself. She could really use some sort of help.

Gerry finally reached the car and drove back to Windhaven. She'd just put her bag down when her phone rang. The sound startled her, and it took her a minute to dig it out from her crowded bag.

'Hello, Gerry?' It was Claudia's cool voice. Gerry had expected it to be Justin. 'Are you all right?'

'Sorry,' Gerry gasped, 'the phone made me jump, and it was at the bottom of my bag.' Somehow, it always was.

'Well, as long as that's all,' Claudia said. 'Have you found everything you need?'

Gerry tried to bring her attention back to the present.

'Yes, and thanks for the food, I ate that last night.' She guessed her landlady had really phoned about Justin, so she said, 'I haven't had any visitors.' Then Gerry remembered that the camera on the drive would show Claudia there hadn't been any cars except her Volvo; but Justin didn't need a car to get here. Though of course Claudia couldn't know that. When Justin was seeing her Gerry guessed he'd have driven to the house like anyone else.

Gerry found it hurt to think of Justin and Claudia together here, perhaps in Claudia's bed upstairs. She wanted more than anything to be back in his arms, and wondered again why she'd refused to see him last night.

'I'm glad to hear it, and I hope it stays like that,' Claudia was saying. 'I'll be back tomorrow. I'm seeing people most of today, but I'll keep my phone on vibrate just in case. I know I said this before, but do ring me if you've any problems, anything at all.'

'Okay,' Gerry said, 'and thanks for calling.' She had problems all right, but none that Claudia could help with.

'I'll see you tomorrow evening, then,' Claudia said, and rang off.

Gerry went to her room to change. She decided to wear a long dress to avoid being taken for a man this time. She had one that should do, a reddish-brown wool one, worn with a leather belt. Flat boots and a brown hoodie should be all right. It didn't quite look like what the Gwenen wore, but she'd already said she came from a long way away.

It was the first time she'd tried to travel purely on her own, not guided by Justin, Baranwen or the Makers, and without the Kelegel either. She'd have to trust in what the Makers had said about Seona's chain. She didn't even have the sapphire now, only her own determination. She could still use the image of the firework to help her concentrate, and fix her mind on her goal. It had worked before. Besides, Colenso had said it was astonishing for her to have come to them at all, and Colenso didn't offer praise lightly. She could do this.

Gerry closed her eyes, laid both hands on the chain, called up the ring of purple stars in her mind, then the memory of the Bees' village at the foot of the hill, as she'd seen it from the top of the Brea. She felt herself in dark, empty silence, as she'd been before, and tried not to panic, but just to keep concentrating. Then something touched her nostrils; a whiff of clean scented air, tinged with woodsmoke. Gerry opened her eyes.

She was in Baranwen's time, not Colenso's. The village was back at the foot of the slope, looking very like the one where she'd first seen the Wasps, with a tall, solid granite wall surrounding the whole. Through the opening in the wall, which was wide enough to drive a cart through, Gerry could make out about a dozen buildings within. Each was surrounded by a very thick stone wall with an opening in it. From where she stood, Gerry could see through the nearest opening. Inside it were separate sections giving onto a paved open area in the centre. Smoke rose through the roof spaces. Gerry could hear voices, and, further away, the bleating of sheep.

Then two women came out through the opening in the nearest wall, and saw her. One was Kerenza, the other Gerry didn't know. The latter gave her a warm and friendly smile. Kerenza, to Gerry's dismay, looked hostile. Did she hold her responsible for her friend's death? Hadn't she seen that Gerry had done her best to protect Wylmet?

The other woman approached, then to Gerry's surprise she embraced her. 'I, Nessa, greet you,' she said. 'You are the stranger with the Sight who warned us against drinking the wine yesterday. I mourn Wylmet as we all do, but I know that many more of us could now be lying with her but for your warning. I would be among them – I always enjoyed drinking wine at festivals. Now I feel I could never bear to taste it again.'

As Nessa spoke her voice had risen with emotion, and more women came from the other buildings until Gerry was facing a group of a good dozen of the Gwenen. Except that most wore sandals rather than boots, and had long hair hanging in a loose braid, her costume fitted in well enough. The women wore gowns dyed in reds, greens, yellow or blue, some patterned like Scottish plaids. Most of the Gwenen were dark, a couple with reddish tints to their hair like Meraud, but one was fair, and stood out in the group. Her father had been a Saxon or Dane perhaps, Gerry thought, thinking of her reading at the library the afternoon before.

The fair woman came forward and embraced Gerry as Nessa had done. 'I, Athwenna, owe my life to you,' she said. 'I would have taken wine myself last night had you not cried out. You vanished and we could not thank you.'

Gerry looked around and was comforted to see that most of the Bees really did look grateful. She realised that Seona's chain was translating for her, even without the sapphire.

'It was late,' she explained, 'and I had to return home. I had,' she paused, then continued, 'other duties, and could not come back before now.' That, she thought, must sound reasonable enough.

Then Gerry saw Hedra, the only one of the Bees who was taller than she was. The teacher, with her drawn face and painful limp, was approaching the group. At her side was the light figure of Meraud. She too looked very pleased to see Gerry.

Gerry cast a glance across the group of faces. There was no sign of the Guardians. The Gwenen varied in age, height and build, but all wore the shape of the bee painted at the base of the throat and the crossed circle on the inside of the left wrist.

Meraud had reached Gerry and took both her hands in her own. 'I am glad to see you safe, Gerralda,' she said warmly. 'I did not like to see you leave as you did. Come inside and we can talk.' Hedra had limped over to join them and looked Gerry over curiously.

'Where are the Guardians?' Gerry asked tentatively. Meraud looked surprised that she should ask. 'They are sitting with Wylmet,' she replied. 'Her family has been told, and we will inter her tomorrow.'

'Gerralda comes from somewhere far away, with an uncouth name,' Kerenza put in. 'She said our customs might be strange to her.' Her tone verged on direct rudeness and Hedra looked angry but said nothing, perhaps waiting for a less public moment to take Kerenza to task.

Gerry moved to accept Meraud's invitation and the others went back to whatever they'd each been doing. The healer led her, with Hedra following more slowly, to another of the walled buildings, and took the visitor through the entrance in the wall. This wall was taller than Gerry, and so thick that the entrance through it was almost a passage. It led to a wide paved area, which had a number of buildings or rooms opening off it. A smell wafting from the right suggested that a long covered space at the side housed animals at night. There was another pleasanter smell which Gerry thought was smoked fish or bacon.

Meraud led Gerry across the courtyard to a door with a stone lintel. This took them into the largest of the rooms, which was round and had a thatched roof, sloping up to the highest point where an opening allowed smoke to escape. In the centre was a fire on an open stone hearth. The space furthest from the fire appeared to be divided into units. One was for cooking, and one probably for sleeping; the others Gerry couldn't see well enough to guess. The room was dim after the brightness outside.

Meraud motioned her towards a bench of light wood near the fire, partly covered with a folded woollen blanket. It was patterned in different shades of blue and yellow, cleverly woven. Meraud had gone to the cooking area and returned with a pottery flask and cups, proffering one to Hedra who had seated herself on another bench. Then Meraud came over to Gerry, saw that she was looking at the blanket and smiled sadly.

'Before she became Guardian, Delenyk was a fine weaver,' Meraud said, with the same catch in her voice that Wylmet had when she first mentioned Delenyk. Gerry wished that she'd met Delenyk, but couldn't think of anything comforting to say. But Meraud changed the subject herself, reaching to pat Gerry's hair.

'It's a lovely colour,' she said kindly, 'like the flames in a bonfire on an autumn evening.'

Gerry thanked her, adding that the colour was quite common where her family lived.

'But why did you cut it short?' the healer went on. 'What did your parents say?'

Gerry was stumped at first, but then remembered something that had happened to a girl in her school.

'You're the healer, aren't you?' she said. 'I don't know if you've ever seen this, but it can happen that your hair, where it touches your skin, makes it come out in a rash, red spots or rough patches. The only thing you can do is to cut your hair right back, and use soothing ointments and lotions.'

The healer looked sympathetic. 'No, I've not met that,' she said, 'though I'm familiar with skin rashes caused by plants, bites or stings. I always keep preparations for bee stings ready, of course.'

Meraud had dropped easily into professional mode. She passed Gerry the cup which contained a golden liquid. 'Honey wine,' she explained. 'I distil it myself and it is better than medh for ordinary use.' Gerry took a polite sip and found the wine was milder than the potent spirit Wylmet had given her. 'We each have our own skill here, as well as the duties common to us all,' Meraud went on. 'Pottery, weaving, care of animals. We also exchange services with the people from the village nearby; my healing skills of course are free to all, while they can help us if our homes are damaged in the autumn gales or if there are floods.'

'And you, Gerralda,' Hedra interrupted, her voice rather hoarse as if her throat hurt her as well as her leg. 'What of your own skill? You have the Sight?'

'Perhaps,' Gerry answered. 'When I was a child small things happened to me: I always knew if anyone was coming to the house even if I hadn't been told or they weren't expected.' Examples of emails and tube trains were no use here. 'As I grew older I found I'd often know if someone was thinking about me, or needed to talk to me' she said. 'Sometimes if I was going from one place to another I knew beforehand if there was a problem, like an accident on the road, or a fallen tree.' Gerry tailed off, and took a sip of the honey wine. Hedra regarded her gravely.

'There is both truth and evasion in your words,' she said. 'I do not have the Sight, but I can tell when I am being lied to. You do not lie, but there is much that you are not saying.'

Gerry was sticking to the truth and nothing but the truth, but no way the whole truth. 'You're right, there's things I can't tell you,' she said, 'but I'm not here to harm anyone. Please believe that. I just need to talk to you.'

Hedra nodded, suspending judgement, and Meraud asked, 'What of your family? Do any of them have the Sight?'

Gerry shook her head. 'No-one else has this gift, if it is a gift, and they wouldn't want it' she said. 'Only my great-aunt Seona understood it. She wanted me to accept it as natural. Perhaps in time she could have taught me more, but I left my home and came south. And while I was away Seona died. I wish,' she said with a pain whose strength still shocked her, 'I could talk to her now. She would have helped me accept this.'

'We can help with that,' Hedra said, her voice a little less harsh. 'Is that not why you are here?

'Yes,' Gerry said. 'I remember Wylmet was so excited about it, she thought I could help you search for the missing Kelegel.' She found there was a catch in her voice. 'But it's not only that. I need to know if I can trust a particular person, and I hoped the Sight might help.'

'Then I fear your hope will be disappointed,' Hedra said. Her right hand was absently massaging her knee. 'Do you really know so little of the Sight? The Sight is not something you can call at will; it comes to you of itself. You would have to train for years before you could try to use it to answer a particular question. Even then it often does not work as you expect. Wylmet's hope would have been doomed to disappointment. She was young, and new here, and eager by nature.'

Last night the Makers had greeted her with disapproval instead of the sympathy Gerry had hoped for. To get this reaction now from Hedra was too much, and she wished she hadn't come.

'Then I'd better go,' she said. 'I'm sorry I've wasted your time.' Gerry knew she sounded bitter, but couldn't help it. She rose from the bench, and put the half-empty cup down on the floor beside it.

'Wait, Gerralda,' Meraud pleaded, but before she could say anything else Nessa's voice called from outside.

'Meraud, are you there? Talan's here, he's brought back your bracelet.'

Meraud immediately leapt up, looking delighted. 'Please wait for me,' she called, and sped out the door.

'Well?' asked Hedra, watching Gerry closely. 'Meraud gave Talan a bracelet which was badly damaged; he is skilful at mending such things. Why should that disturb you?'

Gerry turned but didn't see the round room with its bright fire. She was back in the clearing in the woods with Elwyn's dagger at her throat.

'Why are you afraid?' Hedra repeated.

Gerry looked at her, retrieved her cup and swallowed a large gulp of the honey wine. 'Are you sure you don't have the Sight?' she asked ruefully.

'Quite sure,' the teacher said, 'but I've spent years observing people. My twisted leg never affected my eyesight. You were all right till just now. No, not all right, you were too wary of saying anything you thought I shouldn't hear. Then when Nessa called out that Talan had arrived, you changed. Almost you look like a different person.'

Gerry stood up and shook herself like a dog coming out of the sea. She would have to trust Hedra.

'Will Talan come in here?' she asked urgently. 'He mustn't see me.'

'I don't expect he will,' Hedra replied, moving her right knee stiffly and straightening it between both palms. 'There's no reason why he should. Why, whatever does he mean to you?'

'Because,' Gerry had to say it, 'he's one of the men who put the poison in the wine.'

Gerry had expected a violent reaction, a vigorous denial, but Hedra simply looked at her steadily for a long moment.

'Why should you think that?' she asked at last. 'He is one of our friends, and has been for years. There are none there in the village whom we do not know and trust.'

Gerry sat down again, trying to still her agitation. 'You have

181

to believe me,' she said, doing her best to sound calm. 'I saw them, four of them; they were in the woods near their village. I was hiding in the shadows and they didn't see me at first. There was a tree with a hole in it, high up; two of them had to support the one who climbed up and reached into it. There was a little phial inside and Talan tipped the contents into a flagon.' Gerry remembered how carefully the man had carried out the delicate task, despite the impatience of his companions. She could well believe he would do neat work with his hands. She forestalled the next question. 'They were talking to each other so I heard all the names. Then they spotted me watching.' Gerry was looking into Hedra's eyes now, willing her to believe it. 'They were going to kill me because I'd seen them, but I managed to escape. I never went near the place again. Then last night when Meraud brought out the wine, I knew what it must be, and shouted a warning. It was all I could think of doing.' She couldn't sit still any longer and rose, pacing around in agitation. 'If he sees me he'll recognise me.'

Hedra stood up slowly and again fixed Gerry with that grave look. 'You say you know all four names. Will you give me the others? Can you prove any of this?'

'No!' Gerry tried not to shout out in frustration. 'I can't prove anything. You've only my word. But the others were called Cathno, Elwyn and – I'm not sure about the other, Kevin or something.'

'Kenver, that would be,' Hedra acknowledged. 'I know them all, but I would need more than just your word, I am afraid.'

Gerry tried to speak, then stopped, defeated. She couldn't tell Hedra about the Wasps' attempt to steal the Kelegel, so she couldn't explain any more. 'Please,' she begged, 'please don't say anything about this. Not to Meraud, not to the Guardians, not to anyone. I shouldn't have told you.' She felt wretchedly helpless.

'You ask a lot, Gerralda,' Hedra stated. 'You want me to take the word of a stranger against people we have long known and worked with. You say there are things you cannot tell me but you beg me to trust you out of hand. I believe that you mean well, so I will say nothing, at least for now.' Her steady gaze was fixed on Gerry, her eyes looking deep into the younger woman's. Hedra's eyes were a rich brown that should have been warm, but they were clouded with years of pain.

'Thank you,' Gerry said. It was the best she could hope for.

As they looked at each other, Meraud burst back in, waving her hand excitedly. 'Look, it's done!' She practically thrust the bracelet under Gerry's nose. Gerry took it and held it in the light which came from the large opening in the roof above the fire. It was a thick band of silver, engraved along its width with the crossed circles which the Bees wore at their wrists. There was clearly a significance to this symbol, but Gerry wasn't going to ask about it. She didn't want to display any more ignorance; she'd already been made to look a fool.

The piece had been lovingly made, and it gleamed in the glow of the fire. 'He's polished it, too,' Meraud exulted, 'and you can't see the broken bit at all.' Gerry wondered if the healer's enthusiasm was a counter to the grim and painful tasks she must often have to perform. Then Meraud looked at Gerry, and the exuberance left her.

'Gerralda, we all owe you a debt of gratitude. We have offered to help you, but you should not blame us if you expected something that cannot happen. Hedra would not usually instruct anyone who was not sworn to the Gwenen, but I believe she would be prepared to give you advice in your trouble if you will accept that. More than this she cannot do, and even that offer is greater than you appreciate. I can give you a draught that should soothe your cares somewhat. It is hard to watch someone suffer and be able to do so little to help, and it is plain that you are suffering greatly.'

The healer rose and went to another of the sections beyond the circle of wooden poles, returning after a few minutes with a small sealed pottery flask.

'Drink this before you sleep tonight,' she said. 'You will find that it helps. And please, do come back.'

Gerry tried to smile, but it was a poor attempt. She did her best to thank them, but suspected it sounded ungracious. She would have to go home and try the last remaining person she might get answers from. Justin. Not that she knew how to contact him, or was sure she could trust what he said. Still, whether it was a good idea or not, Gerry did very much want to see him. Like an addict with a drug, maybe. She left the village and as soon as she was out of sight, tried to calm herself then transferred back to Claudia's lounge.

She'd been too sure of herself, trying to go home with no chalice and no-one to send her. She was back at Windhaven, clasping Meraud's flask, but the time was wrong; she'd somehow slipped a few hours and it was early evening. Was it even the same day? Suppose she'd missed a few days instead of hours? Gerry checked the date on her phone; it was still Sunday. All the same, she was trembling from the shock of realising what might have happened. She took off her hoodie and put the kettle on to make some tea. While it was boiling she took off her boots and went up to her room to get her slippers. Gerry had just reached the top of the stairs when she heard a sound and stopped dead. Then she screamed. The door opposite her, the one that led into her bathroom, was slowly opening.

Chapter Thirteen

Sunday 29th June 2014 - evening; Monday 30th June 2014 - morning

Sunday 29th June 2014 - evening; Monday 30th June 2014 - morning
Justin was standing in the doorway in a dark shirt which threw the planes of his face into sharp relief.

'You took long enough to decide you wanted to see me,' he said, looking coolly amused.

Gerry spun round, appalled to find him here, but turned too quickly. She was standing at the top of the staircase; her foot slipped from under her and twisted as she fell. She slid on her back straight down the staircase, and the momentum carried her round the curve and down the last steps. She landed at the foot of the stairs with a crash which knocked all the breath out of her.

It seemed a long time before Gerry could begin to breathe again. She tried to get up, and felt a terrible pain somewhere in her back. Very slowly she half sat up, which was as much as she could manage. With great difficulty she shuffled along the floor of the office and through to the lounge. She couldn't believe how much it hurt to move. At last she reached the sofa and pulled herself onto it. Claudia's sofa was large and somehow managed to be comfortable yet supportive. Her back was agony even so, but she was able to look round. Justin had sauntered down the stairs and was now leaning negligently against the doorpost between the lounge and the office. He made no move to help. He hadn't actually pushed her down the stairs, but no way was it pure chance that he'd appeared at precisely that moment.

Gerry knew then why she'd kept the chalice from him. She must have subconsciously known all along that Justin was simply using her, but he'd made her want him so badly that she couldn't see anything else. Even now it was hard to be this near him and try to keep herself immune.

Justin looked down at her with no sign of emotion. 'Have you got it?' he asked, as if nothing had happened since Gerry had seen him in Penzance standing by her car.

Gerry tried to sit more upright, and failed. She leaned back again, trying not to cry out with the pain. 'No,' she said, fervently glad that this was true. 'It's not here.'

Justin strolled forward and stood just in front of her. Gerry remembered that he must know this house very well. He looked down at her, eyebrows slightly raised. The grey eyes were at their darkest and she could tell that despite his calm exterior, Justin was furious.

'Now, I wonder,' he said, 'would you have hidden it somewhere in the house? I could take the place apart, you know. Smash every ornament, rip open every pillow and cushion, empty out the contents of every single container and cut every picture into pieces. Or I could bring my friends in to do the job. That would be a lot quicker, but the place would be left in rather more of a mess.'

And Gerry knew who he meant. She really had been blind.

'Elwyn and the others, your Wasps,' she said slowly. 'It was you who sent them to the fogou yesterday. You knew I was going there. And you knew about the poison.'

'That's right,' Justin said calmly. 'If that wine had done what it was meant to you could have walked out of there with the chalice unopposed.'

'You mean,' Gerry said, 'you'd have killed all the Bees to get the chalice? And you really thought I'd go along with that?' She couldn't believe anyone could be so cold-blooded.

'Why not? Those women mean nothing to me. I'll do anything I have to,' Justin replied. 'And don't think you're going to stop me.' He picked up Gerry's bag, which she'd dropped when she got home from Penzance earlier in the day, and casually tipped all its contents onto the floor. He threw a quick glance over them.

'No, I should know if the Kelegel was here' he said. 'I can't feel its presence anywhere in the house. Still, I may as well check you don't have it on you.'

He leaned forward and put one hand behind Gerry's back, pulling her forward. The pain redoubled, and she couldn't prevent herself crying out.

'I haven't got it,' she said again. 'I told you, it's not here.'

'We'll have to see about that.' Justin bent down, put his other hand under Gerry's ankles, and in one swift movement twisted her round so she was lying full length on the sofa. Immobilised by the agony of breathing, she couldn't move. Even unhurt she wouldn't be able to push him off; he was far too strong. Gerry was completely helpless and Justin knew it. He slipped her boots off, saying mockingly, 'We don't want to mark Claudia's nice furniture, do we?' Then in a leisurely fashion he unfastened the belt round her waist and began to pull her dress up from her ankles to her knees. The dress had no pockets and he knew perfectly well she had no gold or jewels hidden in her underwear. It was deliberate humiliation. When Justin pulled the dress up across her back Gerry cried out in anguish and he paused, looking down at her dispassionately.

'I should think you've broken a rib, falling like that. Maybe two.' There was no sympathy in his expression. When Gerry first met him she could have dreamed of him undressing her like this. Wasn't there a saying: Be careful what you wish for, you might get it. Now fury towards him fought with anger against herself for being caught like this. When she had nothing left on at all, Justin stepped back and looked her up and down.

'You've changed, you know,' he stated. 'When I first met you, you were just another pretty girl. You've begun to grow up, Gerralda. You're turning into a woman. I think it's time you learned a bit more about what that means. Had a proper lesson.'

A calculating look crossed his face, followed by a smile Gerry didn't like at all. Whatever he had in mind, it wouldn't be for her good. Gerry prayed he wasn't going to hurt her. She didn't think she could stand any more pain, even if it meant telling him where the Kelegel a'n gammneves was. While she was reasonably certain the Makers would be a match for Justin, Gerry didn't want them knowing she'd let them down.

Then Gerry found she'd been wrong about Justin's intentions. Sitting down next to her on the wide sofa, he reached over and began slowly to stroke her hands, then her feet, working gradually along her limbs, then quartering her whole body, relentlessly bringing it alive inch by inch. He was a master of the art. Even though Gerry knew now that Justin was truly evil, she couldn't counter what he was doing. His hands kept moving, as up till now she'd so wanted them to. He was slow and very thorough, and it wasn't long before Gerry was gasping, not just in pain but from growing physical pleasure. No man had ever made her feel remotely like this. Justin knew exactly what he was doing. The cool, deliberate fingertips continued, and finally she closed her eyes, giving in to the sensations building inside her body. She no longer knew if she wanted him to stop or not.

And he did stop. He stopped deliberately just when Gerry most needed him to go on, and stood up again, completely unmoved, as easily as if he'd simply sat down to straighten a cushion. Then, dropping her clothes on the floor where Gerry couldn't reach them without further painful movements, Justin stepped away from the sofa, leaving her horribly frustrated.

'Learned something, have you?' he asked, while she struggled back to earth. Gerry cursed herself silently for giving in to him. She cursed him too, for an unprincipled bastard, but not aloud. She would at least deny him that satisfaction.

'What do you really want the Kelegel for?' Gerry asked, pulling a couple of cushions over to cover herself as best she could. 'It can't be that story you told me about your brother.'

'Very good,' he said. 'You're right, it isn't that, not quite. I don't think I'll tell you the real reason yet, though. I'll see you in the morning,' he added. 'Tomorrow you are going to tell me where the Kelegel a'n gammneves is. Believe me, you will wish you had told me today.'

Then he disappeared. Gerry was left shivering, and furious both with Justin and with herself. Her clothes were out of reach. She could hardly face leaving the sofa, let alone getting to the kitchen for something to eat. She could feel herself burning with shame as she relived what had just happened. Then even that was swept away by the memory of Justin's last words.

He hadn't hit her, yet he could have hurt her to breaking point, vulnerable as she was. Justin was twisted enough to prefer leaving her to agonise all night about what he might be planning for tomorrow. Maybe he didn't use violence himself, and would be back in the morning with Cathno and Elwyn. Of course it was he, not Baranwen, who had brought them up through the centuries. Was this what they were here for – to beat Gerry into submission? Would he just stand by and watch them do their work? But that would be Justin's last resort. He'd prefer something more devious.

Gerry found Meraud's flask on the floor near her clothes. Luckily it hadn't broken or come unstoppered when Justin threw her things on the floor. The potion was quite thick and smelled of herbs. Gerry drank the contents then decided to make a cheese sandwich, the simplest food she could. The pain in her back was terrible, and she didn't have any painkillers. Claudia had said to call with any problems, but Claudia's bathroom was up the other set of stairs, and even if there were painkillers there Gerry couldn't face trying to reach it. She hadn't registered with a local doctor, but if it really was a broken rib, she didn't think you could do anything about it.

It was the middle of the evening before she'd succeeded in dressing, eating and getting up to her room. Gerry moved round the bedroom step by step and closed the curtains against the bright evening light. Even if, between pain and worry, she couldn't sleep, she'd be more comfortable, or less uncomfortable, in bed. There was no doubt she was in for a very bad night. The healer hadn't indicated how long her potion might take to work, but by the time Gerry was lying down she did feel a bit calmer. All the same, she spent most of the night going over what a fool she'd been to be taken in so badly by Justin. Yet Claudia, worldly and experienced, had been deceived by him too. This, however, was no comfort to Gerry.

Gerry didn't feel any better in the morning. No consideration on earth would have made her go into work but one. After what had happened at the Quay Fair, she wanted to see Debbie and be sure she was all right. Gerry got up early but everything took far longer than usual. When she finally got out of the house, Gerry was relieved to find that at least she could drive relatively easily. She parked on the front in Penzance as usual, but it was a very slow walk up Morrab Road to the library. In the end she was late when she walked, or rather hobbled, in through the automatic doors.

The first person Gerry saw was Ryan, hurrying upstairs to the computer suite where he gave lessons. His face lit up.

'I thought you weren't coming in!' he exclaimed. 'You're not usually late.' He stopped and his expression changed as she took a couple of steps, then he raced back down the stairs to where she stood.

'Gerry, what's wrong? You look like you can hardly walk!' Vivid concern lit his face, and for a brief moment Gerry indulged the fantasy of having someone decent and caring around her. Then she squashed it.

'I fell downstairs last night, but it's not important. Tell me, is Debs working today?'

Ryan stared in astonishment, and he moved as if to take her arm, but stopped himself.

'You fell downstairs but it's not important?' he asked incredulously.

'No, listen, is Debs here?' Gerry asked. Nothing else mattered.

'No, I haven't seen her. Why?' Ryan asked.

'It doesn't matter.' Gerry wanted to dash into the office, but could only manage a slow shuffle towards the door.

'You shouldn't be here at all!' Ryan protested, this time laying hold of her arm as if to stop her.

'I know,' Gerry agreed, 'but I need to see Hilary.'

Reluctantly Ryan let her go and turned back to go to his waiting customer. 'Let me know if I can do anything,' he called down as he ran back up the stairs. 'And tell Hilary you're going home. What d'you think you're doing, coming here when you're like this?'

Gerry crossed to the office door, trying to regain the breath that this conversation had used up. She spotted Monica at the enquiry desk, and the tall form of Ernie doing some fiction shelving. There was no sign of Debbie, but she just might be upstairs, or in the staff room. Gerry knocked on Hilary's door and went in. The manager looked up from the weekly timesheets, then as Gerry came further into the office she did a double-take, as Ryan had done.

Gerry asked urgently, 'Hilary, is Debs here today?'

Hilary looked surprised, then irritated. 'No, she's not. She should have been here before 9. She hasn't called in sick or to say she'd been held up. I rang her at home about half an hour ago but there was no reply. It's not like Debbie, she's usually so reliable.'

This was what Gerry had feared. Her insides lurched, and her stomach seemed to be sinking within itself. Her mouth was dry as she answered.

'Hilary, I'm sorry, but I don't think I can work today. I slipped on the stairs last night, and I've probably broken a rib. I thought I'd be all right if I took things gently, but it's not possible. Perhaps I should go to the Penzance hospital?'

193

Hilary looked annoyed at losing another member of staff when she was already short-handed, but she could see for herself that Gerry was in considerable pain. Gerry didn't care what her manager thought; she had to get out of there and try Debbie's phone.

'Yes,' Hilary replied at last, 'that would probably be sensible. But can you let me know what they say? You're down for tomorrow as well as today, and if you can't work I'll have to ring the agency and see if they've got anyone else free.' She gave Gerry one of her rare smiles. 'I'd rather have you, you're a good worker, but I can see you're struggling. I know the hospital's just up the road, but can you walk that far?'

'I'll take it slowly,' Gerry said. 'And I'll let you know what they say. No, you'd better get someone else for today and tomorrow. I'm sure I'll be better in a couple more days.' As a casual worker she didn't get sick pay, but money was the last thing on Gerry's mind.

As she left the office, Tasha spotted her and darted over, just missing an elderly couple looking through the returned books on the trolley by the issue machines. Gerry didn't want to stop for anything just now, but Debbie had been with Tash yesterday and she might know something. Gerry hobbled forward a couple of steps.

'I've had an accident,' she explained. 'I'm on my way to the hospital and I only came in to tell Hilary. How did yesterday go after I left? Was Debs all right? Only she's not here, and I wondered if perhaps she wasn't well.'

Gerry tried to sound casual.

Tasha furrowed her brows. 'Well, she did seem a bit quieter than usual, now I come to think of it. Perhaps she felt a bit dodgy but didn't like to say. Silly girl. But never mind Debs, how about

194

you?' She looked really worried. 'You do look bad. Would you like me to come with you to the hospital?'

Gerry managed to force a smile. 'Thanks, that's really kind, but I think Hilary would go ballistic if anyone else goes off.' She was about to head for the exit at last when she saw Monica leave the desk and come over to them.

'Haven't you two got any work to do?' she asked cuttingly. 'If not, I can find you some.'

'Leave it, can't you?' said Tasha, who always stood up to Monica. 'Gerry's been in an accident.'

'Oh – fallen over?' The sneer on her face suggested Gerry had been drinking and that had caused it.

'Broken rib,' Gerry said shortly, and heard Tasha gasp. Gerry didn't owe Monica any explanations. She turned her back on Monica and moved off as fast as she could, which wasn't fast at all, hearing Monica comment loudly that some people always had to be the centre of attention.

'Why don't you break a rib and see how you like it, then?' Tasha snapped back at her, and returned to the children's area.

When Gerry finally reached the lobby she pulled out her phone and called Debbie's mobile. It rang several times, and her heart was hammering as she waited. Just before the voicemail cut in, Debbie answered.

'Gerry?'

'Debs? Where are you?'

'I'm at home.' Her voice sounded small. 'Can you come round here?'

Gerry's mind raced. 'Is there anyone there with you?'

'Yes.'

She'd known it.

'Is it your mum, or your brother?'

'No.'

Of course not, they'd both be at work. Gerry should have gone to the house first, not the library. Why on earth hadn't she? Because she'd hoped against hope that Debbie would be at work, though she realised now she'd never truly expected it.

'Is there more than one person there?' Gerry ventured.

'Yes.' The monosyllables were terrifying.

'Three?'

'Yes.'

In the background Gerry heard a voice that she knew.

'He says he wants you to come round here.'

'I'm on my way,' Gerry said. 'Only it'll take a bit of time. I can't move very fast.'

There was a laugh in the background which turned her cold all over.

'Just get here,' Debbie begged. 'Please, Gerry.'

'I'll be there,' Gerry told her, and rang off.

Gerry wanted to run down to her car, but despite her best efforts she couldn't do it. As she pushed herself down the road, trying not to scream aloud with the pain, Gerry cursed her own stupidity. If she'd gone straight to Debbie's home instead of coming to the library, she could have rescued her friend sooner. Debbie had sounded scared to death.

She reached the car at last, made for Treneere as fast as she dared and pulled up outside Debbie's house. The Volvo couldn't actually screech to a halt but came pretty close to it. Gerry stumbled up the steps when she wanted to race up. She reached the faded brown door and banged loudly. Justin opened it, with that horrible smile on his face. The hallway was untidy and in need of cleaning, and he looked totally out of place there. He stood across the doorway, blocking the entrance.

'Where is she?' Gerry demanded. 'Where's Debbie?'

Justin gestured towards the front room but made no move to let her pass into the house. Gerry, still recovering from the effort of getting from the library to her car, couldn't even try to push him out of the way.

'I thought,' Justin said with slow deliberation, 'that perhaps you'd left the Kelegel a'n gammneves with your friend as it wasn't at Windhaven.'

Gerry looked at him in horror. The idea had never occurred to her. She wouldn't have dreamed of putting Debbie in danger.

'Still,' Justin went on, 'you're here now, so it looks as if coming here wasn't a waste of time after all.'

'You're just evil,' Gerry hissed at him. 'Let me through!'

He moved so she could see into the room, and Gerry felt as if her insides had fallen out. Debbie was sitting on the sofa. She was so frightened that she seemed to have shrunk inwards, and her face was grey. Elwyn lounged on the cushions on her left. Cathno sat on her right, his arm round her shoulders, holding her. His knife lay against her throat. She started when she saw Gerry, and the edge of the blade grazed her skin.

'Gerry,' she cried, 'tell them it's not here! Please, tell them.' She was virtually sobbing, both with terror, and with anger at not being believed. 'I keep saying it but they won't listen.'

Gerry started towards her and at once Elwyn rose to put himself between her and Debbie.

'That gold cup thing you told me about yesterday,' Debbie gasped. 'These men seem to think I've got it here in the house. I've told them and told them they've come to the wrong place

197

but he,' she gestured towards Justin, 'just said we should wait for you.'

Gerry turned towards Justin who was standing in the doorway. Outside it was breezy and cloudy; the sun had gone in and the room was gloomy. Gerry was wearing tights and a long-sleeved smock dress, and where she stood the light from the window was behind her. In silhouette her clothes looked just like the tunic and leggings she'd been wearing when she'd first seen the Wasps, and Elwyn recognised her.

'It's that spying boy, the one who vanished!' He leapt forward but Justin called to him to stop. Elwyn looked mutinous and for a moment Gerry thought he was going to ignore the command, but he thought better of it.

'It's the same person,' Justin said, 'but she's not a boy. This is how some women dress here. We need this one for now; leave her alone.'

Elwyn muttered something Gerry couldn't catch, though she could guess the gist of it. She ignored him and spoke to Justin.

'You can let Debbie go,' she said. 'You've got me here now. That was what you wanted, wasn't it?'

'Oh no. This is only the beginning.' Justin's voice was soft and deadly. 'You are going to take me to the Tegennow.'

'Gerry?' Debbie looked bewildered. 'What language are you talking?'

'Their language,' Gerry said briefly. She hadn't realised they'd changed to the older tongue, but if Debbie couldn't follow, that was better for her. Seona's gold chain was acting as interpreter even without the sapphire.

'So where are the Tegennow?' Justin was not to be deflected.

198

'They're in the past,' Gerry said slowly. 'But not the part of the past that you've been going to. I can get there but I don't know if I could take you too. I could bring them back with me, as long as you let Debbie go first.'

'Do you think I'm that stupid?' Justin was scornful. 'I let her go, and you disappear somewhere? I don't think so. I'm coming with you.' He turned to Cathno. 'You stay here with her.' He indicated Debbie. 'If this one comes back without me, kill them both.'

'What's he saying?' Debbie demanded. 'What's going on?'

'He wants me to take him to the cup,' Gerry said. 'I didn't want to but I don't have any choice now. It's not near here so I don't know how long we'll be. I'm afraid he won't let you come with us.'

Debbie just looked at her friend. 'And what about me?' Hope had sprung in her face, but now it died again. From grey she'd turned to white. 'What if he doesn't get it?'

'He will,' Gerry said bitterly, turning towards her.

'You've been hurt.' Debbie couldn't miss the pain that even this simple movement caused. 'Did he do that to you?'

'Sort of,' Gerry admitted.

'And you wouldn't be giving him this, cup thing, if it wasn't for me?'

'It can't be helped.' Gerry tried to sound reassuring. 'He'd have used some other filthy trick if it hadn't been this. He's rotten through and through. Nothing's too low for him to stoop to.'

Debbie gave a brief, wondering glance at Justin. Gerry remembered the evening at the fireworks, and how much she'd enjoyed being held by Justin. It was still hard to believe that this breath-taking face and body housed such a manipulative schemer, but she reckoned she knew him now.

'Manners,' Justin said. 'Remember I'm listening.' He stepped forward and ran his hand down Gerry's back, feeling the ribs. She cried out, and again Debbie half rose and was checked by Cathno's arm.

'Are you saying,' she pleaded, 'that you two are going to go off and leave me with these men who don't even speak English?'

'Yes,' said Justin before Gerry could answer. 'Well, Cathno anyway. Elwyn's coming with us. You'll be all right as long as Gerralda does what she's told.'

'Gerralda?' Debbie asked in surprise.

'That's my real name,' Gerry said hastily. She'd always been "Gerry" at work. 'Look, if we've got to go, can we just go now and get it over with?'

'Hang on a minute,' Debbie put in, looking uncomfortable. 'If you're disappearing can I at least go to the loo?'

Justin considered this, and Gerry could see he was keeping Debbie waiting on purpose. 'All right,' he said at last, 'but give me your phone first. I'm not having you ringing the police once you're out of sight. You'd be dead before they got into the house anyway.'

By now Gerry had got used to hearing things like this, but Debbie turned even paler as she put her mobile into Justin's outstretched hand.

'And no tricks like climbing out the window,' he added. 'Remember I've got your friend here. She doesn't want you to come to any harm; do you feel the same way?'

'Of course,' Debbie retorted angrily, and went upstairs.

'How touching,' Justin sneered. 'Childhood friends, are you?'

'No, we've known each other less than a month,' Gerry said. 'We're just ordinary, decent people. Something you wouldn't understand.'

His eyes narrowed, but so briefly that she almost missed it. 'Ah, but people like me have a much better time,' he countered smoothly.

'Thank God there aren't many people like you,' Gerry snapped.

'Are you sure you mean that?' He ran his fingertips over her wrist, deliberately recalling what he'd done on Claudia's sofa. She wrenched it from his touch, turning away to hide the red that had flamed into her face.

There was no way she could get Debbie away from here. And Justin had to come back to this house or Debbie would never be released. Gerry wasn't sure she trusted him to let her go even then; but she wasn't telling Debbie that. Things were bad enough for her already, and Gerry ached to think of her friend sitting alone with Cathno, not knowing what was happening or where the others were. The Makers had tried to warn her against Justin as well as Baranwen, but she hadn't wanted to hear.

Justin came to stand behind Gerry's shoulder. 'So tell me,' he breathed in her ear, 'who are the Makers?'

Gerry gasped. Justin had done this before, but she'd forgotten he could pick up what she was thinking. She heard the bathroom door open upstairs and Debbie came down again. She looked resigned rather than scared now. Gerry hoped that would last but was afraid it wasn't likely. As she passed, Debbie murmured, 'How comes none of them have guns?'

'Don't need them,' Justin answered. He turned back to Gerry, took hold of her arm to keep her still and spread his other hand across her back probing to find the broken bone. 'Tell me about the Makers.'

Debbie saw the movement, and the tears of pain and frustration that Gerry couldn't keep back. She reached over and tried to push Justin's hand away.

'Leave Gerry alone, you bastard,' she said. 'Haven't you hurt her enough?'

He answered as if this was a question worthy of serious consideration. 'I don't think so. Not yet.'

'You've got what you wanted,' Debbie retorted. 'Isn't that good enough for you?'

'Debbie, don't!' Gerry cried. She didn't want her to anger Justin. He was quite capable of telling Cathno to hurt Debbie, or worse, once they'd gone.

'You think I was going to let him carry on with whatever he was doing to make you look like that?' Debbie said indignantly.

Justin had done some fast thinking. 'I've begun to think you were planning to keep the Jewels of the Rainbow for yourself. As if you could do that without my knowing.' From Debbie's look of puzzlement Gerry knew he'd dropped back into the older speech. 'You've been holding out on me, Gerralda. So, do you think that you know how to use them?'

'Only a little,' Gerry said, then bit her lip. She hadn't meant to admit to even that much.

'But I do, you see,' Justin said. 'I could do a lot with them. Tell me, where have you put them?'

'I already told you,' Gerry answered. 'Back in the past. The Bees' village, but about five or six hundred years earlier. Look, let's go now.' The sooner they went, the sooner she could get back and free Debbie. 'Only, can we go from the other room? I don't want Debs to see us vanishing into thin air.'

'Yes, that would make things a bit difficult for you, assuming you come back, that is,' he agreed, and turned to Elwyn. 'You're coming with us.'

Gerry looked back at Debbie, who'd sat down again. At least Cathno no longer seemed to feel the need to keep his knife held to her throat all the time. 'I'll get back as soon as I can,' Gerry promised, and the three of them went into the large kitchen at the back of the house. The unwashed breakfast things were still spread around on the table and in the sink, the end of a loaf on the bread board and a slab of butter beside it. Bits of ordinary people's lives.

Justin laid his hand on Gerry's wrist and took hold of Elwyn's arm with his other hand. 'However you do it, you can go there now. I'll bring the rest of us.'

It seemed an odd phrase to use, but Gerry didn't couldn't spare it any attention just then. She had to concentrate, yet try to keep her thoughts from Justin. She didn't want him knowing how to reach the Makers without her. The sooner they went, the sooner she could be back for Debbie. Yet she dreaded what the Makers, especially Keyna, would have to say to her. Could the three of them together stand up to Justin? Would they choose to protect the chalice and condemn Debbie? Or would they give it to him to use for whatever unthinkable scheme he had planned? Whatever happened, things were about to get a lot worse.

Chapter Fourteen

Monday 30th June 2014 - continued

Gerry wanted to touch her chain but with Justin so close she didn't dare. She mustn't let him be aware of its power. It was precious to her, both because it was Seona's gift, and because without the sapphire it was her only link to the past. Gerry closed her eyes and thought of Colenso, Rosenwyn and Keyna. Justin wanted to go there; that should be enough. It had been before. Take me back, she breathed, and as before was plunged into darkness, with no awareness of the chain, or of Justin's fingers laid on her wrist.

After the same scarily long time, they arrived outside the wall surrounding the settlement. Gerry looked round in the faint hope that Justin might have been left behind. That hope was dashed, and more. He hadn't only brought Elwyn but had somehow picked up Talan and Kenver as well. If he planned to use force against the Makers, she could only hope he'd be in for an unpleasant surprise.

A little girl, perhaps four years old, dashed out of the village gate, saw them and immediately turned and ran back inside again. They were used to strangers here, and apparently welcomed them, judging by her last visit, but this group was different. The Wasps carried no visible weapons but their body language suggested a raiding party. Gerry noticed that, as Baranwen had done, Justin had cast a glamour over himself to make his clothes match the setting. The Wasps' clothes and her own fitted well enough.

In one of the nearby houses, a baby began to cry. The sky was clear and there wasn't a breath of wind, unlike the brisk breeze and gathering clouds they'd left at Penzance in the 21st century. Smoke rose up into the air in a straight vertical line.

'Where do we go?' Justin asked. 'Where are the Makers?'

'At the fogou,' Gerry told him shortly, and set off up the path, wishing she'd tried to arrive outside the fogou itself. Beside her, Justin was rigid with expectation. She had no idea how long he'd been working and scheming to get his hands on the Tegennow a'n gammneves; it could have been years and years. Now he was almost there, but for once wasn't in control of the situation, and he was on edge. Gerry wondered briefly how he'd come to know of the chalice, whether he really belonged to the past or the present, and if she would ever know the answers.

She felt utterly wretched. On the one hand there was Debbie, waiting at home, a terrified prisoner; on the other were the Gwenen. What would Hedra, Meraud, Athwenna and the others say if they saw her about to hand over the Jewels they served to a man who must have some terrible plan for them? Her heart was beating hard. Whatever happened, there was no good resolution.

It seemed a long time before they came within sight of the entrance to the tunnel. Gerry noticed the water barrel which Colenso had used as part of the ritual to bring the Jewels alive, and tried to blot out the memories in case Justin was reading her mind again.

Then she saw they were expected. Keyna the Maiden had come out onto the path, and stood waiting. She seemed to expect the Gohi too, for she showed no surprise at their presence.

'We greet you, Gerralda,' she said formally, then turned to Justin. 'Is this the man you spoke of?'

'It is,' Gerry agreed miserably. 'Justin Chancellor, and his, um, assistants, Elwyn, Kenver and Talan.'

Keyna contemplated Justin with that grave dignity which Gerry had observed on first meeting her. Young as the Maiden was, she had an unshakable air of authority.

'If your men carry weapons, they cannot come within our chamber,' Keyna pronounced. 'It is not permitted.'

Justin's mouth tightened. He was not accustomed to being told what to do. 'Then we will talk out here,' he said. 'I have come to take the Tegennow a'n gammneves.'

Keyna's eyebrows rose. 'Indeed? And you expect us to give them to you?'

Justin gave his smooth smile. 'I believe you will, when you hear what Gerralda has to say.'

Before Gerry could say anything, Rosenwyn and Colenso appeared beside Keyna. She assumed they'd heard Justin's words, but they said nothing, only looked at her.

Gerry spoke miserably, unable to even look at the three women facing us. Nor could she look at Justin. She gave the briefest explanation possible.

'Justin has captured my friend. He intends to kill her unless he comes back with the Kelegel. His man is holding her now, waiting for our return.'

Keyna's face became icy. 'It is not "now" to us here,' she said. 'We trusted you, Gerralda, and you have betrayed us. You have brought someone who would seize and misuse our treasure, brought him to our very home. A man who covets the Kelegel for purposes of pure evil. We can all read that within him. And you have done this because of one woman, hundreds of years in the future. Can you even be certain that he will keep his word and release your friend?'

Gerry could not reply. No doubt the hopeless look on her face was answer enough. Rosenwyn the Mother spoke, less harshly than Keyna.

'It is good that you do not wish harm to come to your friend,' she told Gerry. 'But against that you must set, as Keyna has said, the evil that Iestyn would accomplish in your own time. Can you not tell how wicked his intentions are?'

'You didn't see Debbie's face,' Gerry said sadly. It was the only answer she had. 'There was nothing else I could do.'

'There may be several things you could have done,' said Colenso the Wise Woman. 'However changed your world is, are such actions sanctioned there?'

'No, they're not,' Gerry said, 'but Debbie would have been dead before any help could reach us.'

'In any case, you and these men are here now.' Rosenwyn's face was calm but her eyes were suddenly angry. 'Do you believe this man is a fit owner of the Tegennow a'n gammneves? A man who uses such means to gain his ends?'

Gerry hadn't thought it was possible to feel any worse than she already did. Now she found that it was.

'And now he knows how to find us,' Colenso continued remorselessly. 'If we drive him away he will return. Perhaps it will be your daughter, Rosenwyn, whose life is held in the balance next time. No, this must be decided now.'

The Makers stood close together, talking too softly for the others to hear. They stood in the midday sun, the slope of Chapel Carn Brea behind them, the smell of cooking drifting up from the village below. All round lay the view Gerry had first climbed the Brea to see: the wide sweep of land on every side, the grey of granite blocks, the slopes dappled with the green and yellow of gorse and purple of heather, and the blue of the sea round the edges. The Wasps looked impatient for action, but Justin was keeping them in check for now. Gerry would at that moment have happily given her own life if it could have resolved the situation; but it wouldn't.

Then four men appeared, climbing the path from the village and making straight for the Wasps, radiating hostility. Either the little girl below had told her mother that enemies had come to the gate, or Colenso had her own means of sending messages to the settlement. The four stopped just below the group, waiting for a word from the Makers before coming nearer. One carried an axe, hefty enough for cutting trees. The second had a hunting bow ready to hand, and the other two held heavy wooden poles. The weapons were held loosely but they plainly meant to protect their holy women from any threat. The Gohi were stirring restlessly; it would take very little to provoke a full scale, and very bloody, encounter. Keyna had said armed men couldn't enter the fogou, but that wouldn't prevent a fight out here.

Justin alone seemed oblivious to everything around him. His eyes were fixed on Colenso whom he'd recognised as the ultimate authority here. He'd been tense before; now he was so taut that at a touch he would vibrate like a violin string. He hadn't interrupted the reproaches being heaped on Gerry. Now he dropped one syllable into the silence. 'Well?'

Colenso turned towards him. Gerry hadn't realised there were tears of mortification in her eyes; as she looked at the three Makers a rainbow shimmer appeared around them.

'Tell us,' Colenso said, regarding him steadily, 'what will you do if we refuse?'

Justin laughed. It was so unexpected that Gerry started, and took an involuntary step back. Colenso caught the awkwardness of the movement and the sudden gasp of pain.

'Are you hurt, child?'

'Yes,' she admitted. 'Broken rib, I think.'

'His doing?' she asked, nodding to Justin.

'His fault, rather. That's how he works.' Gerry's own words accused her. How, how could she have been so foolish as not to see what would happen if she brought Justin here?

'What would I do?' Justin repeated, as if the exchange had not taken place. 'Anything I have to. You cannot hold me back. I could be in the centre of your village with a thought. If I must I will seize the place, burn down your dwellings, and my men will slay any of your people who survive.'

Gerry caught her breath. She should have thought of it before. She could transfer herself to inside the fogou. Once she was in there the sapphire would call to her. She could take her chalice and return to her own time. Perhaps she could undo some of the harm she'd brought here.

Gerry hadn't allowed for Justin's awareness of her; he had heard the intake of breath and followed her thoughts.

'Don't try it, Gerralda,' he warned. 'This time it would be you I would take prisoner instead of your Debbie; and I think these women might not choose to save you.'

Gerry didn't answer, but suspected he was right.

'Could he do it?' Keyna asked her.

'Yes,' Gerry conceded. 'He can move between places as I did. I believe he would do just what he said.' And how would they respond now it was their own folk who were threatened,

209

not one distant stranger? They reacted as Justin had known they would.

The three withdrew a little way, and conferred between themselves again, but not for long. Finally Colenso came back, her step heavy, her face set. She spoke to Justin alone, ignoring Gerry.

'You leave us little choice,' she said, 'but we require two things of you.'

'You are in no position to bargain,' was the arrogant response. 'But you may name them.'

The look Colenso gave him would have made a charging bull quail. 'You will send your men away. You have our word that you will not be physically attacked, and our word holds good.' The scorn in her voice made Gerry squirm, but Justin was unmoved. 'And we require that you release Gerralda's friend unharmed and unthreatened. Gerralda will doubtless tell us if this has not been done.'

Gerry could see Justin resented being addressed this way, but at the very moment of reaching his goal, he could afford to be magnanimous.

'And if I agree?'

'Then you shall have what you demand.'

An indescribable look flashed across those chiselled features. It somehow combined disbelief, sneering contempt and utter joy. For a moment his reluctance to concede anything warred with his hunger for the Rainbow Chalice. Then he smiled slowly. That smile was the most frightening thing Gerry had seen that day.

'I agree,' he said.

Rosenwyn turned and addressed the four men who stood there. Plainly reluctant but obedient, they lifted their makeshift weapons and returned down the hill. Justin spoke a word to the

Wasps, then they disappeared. Gerry had no idea how he did it. She would have given anything to make Justin vanish too.

Keyna had gone into the fogou. Now she returned carrying a small bundle which she handed to Colenso. The object was wrapped in cloth, and Gerry couldn't feel anything from it. If this was the chalice she'd brought here for the Makers to mend, wouldn't it speak to her? She should at least feel something from the sapphire. Surely they couldn't have some obvious trick in mind, like offering a copy? No, Justin would know it at once. She guessed he was thinking along the same lines, for his brows had drawn together and his face darkened.

'Gerralda, come here!' Colenso called.

Gerry approached slowly, step by painful step.

'Take this,' the Maker ordered, 'place some water in it then hold the Jewels in the sunlight.'

Gerry thought of that glory of colour which had dazzled her yesterday. That couldn't be faked. She put her hand out, took the bundle and opened it. Gold, crystal and gemstones flashed in the sun. At once she recognised the markings on the gold; this was the chalice Baranwen had used, not the earlier one. The sapphire was now fastened securely in place, so perhaps it no longer linked with her.

This was the moment. Gerry could vanish from here with the Kelegel, to somewhere no-one would ever find her: not Justin, or Baranwen, or anyone. And if she did? Justin would torch the village and kill every man, woman and child there. Even to keep the Rainbow Jewels from him, she couldn't do it. Would the Makers want her to? She had no way to ask them.

Gerry moved slowly to the water barrel and picked up the dipper with some difficulty, trying to keep her balance and not drop the chalice despite the pain it cost her. Somehow she managed to tip some water into the cup, aware of the Makers and Justin watching her every move. Gerry didn't know what words Colenso had used to invoke the power of the stones, but she lifted the Kelegel a'n gammneves to the sun, and prisms kindled inside the clear crystals, shining rainbows flashing within them. Then the four precious stones drew the sun into themselves and their shafts of red, yellow, blue and purple flowed upwards. As before, the beams of light joined, drew up droplets from the water within the chalice, overlapped to bring in the other three colours and formed a curve of such splendour that it brought warmth to Gerry even in her despair. Justin, who'd never seen the Rainbow Jewels come alive, watched, spellbound. Then he stepped forwards swiftly and reached for the chalice. The instant he touched it, the glowing shafts vanished. He wrenched the jewelled cup from Gerry's hand and turned on the Makers.

'Trickery!' he snarled. 'What have you done to them?'

Colenso stood her ground, unmoved. 'They were made to be used by women, to enhance knowledge and understanding. Now that you have seen that these are indeed the Tegennow a'n gammneves, we shall have to alter them to respond to yourself also. You cannot expect something that took so many years and so much secret art in the making to be changed at a word. But we will allow you to stay while we work. Come within, but remain with us and do not trouble another soul here.'

She turned and disappeared into the opening, Keyna at her side. Rosenwyn came to Gerry and put a gentle hand on her shoulder, then followed the other two Makers into the tunnel. Justin was close on their heels, and in a moment the hillside was empty. Gerry hadn't been invited in, and wouldn't have wanted to be. Now that the struggle was over and the decision made, she felt drained. From the moment she'd first stood at the top of the hill and heard Kerenza describe the Jewels of the Rainbow, she'd wanted them. Be careful what you ask for, Gerry thought, as she had the evening before in a very different context. Now she had held them, had herself called up their magic. It should have been a moment of wonder and delight, but Justin had ruined even that. She was horribly tired, having hardly slept, and very thirsty, but more than either she was overcome by a weariness of spirit. There seemed no point to anything now.

Well, she wasn't needed here and she still had Seona's chain. She could take herself back to Penzance, to the 21st century. It wouldn't be far enough to free her from her guilt, but there was one useful thing she could do. She clutched her chain and thought desperately about Debbie. In a matter of moments Gerry was outside the house in Treneere, knocking on the door. When there was no reply she rang Debbie's mobile in panic. Had Justin already broken his word, so reluctantly given? Had he given Cathno secret instructions? It was the longest minute of Gerry's life before Debbie answered.

'Gerry?' she said. 'Where are you?'

'I'm outside your front door,' Gerry answered, overcome with relief. 'Are you all right?'

'Yeah, and that man's just gone,' Debbie said. 'It was like he disappeared, one minute he was there, then when I turned round he'd gone. I didn't even hear the door.'

'Oh, thank God,' Gerry said. Or Goddess. 'Debs, will you let me in?'

'Oh, sorry.' That sounded more like her usual voice. 'When I heard the knocking I thought it was him coming back, or the other one. I didn't want to –'

'Debs,' Gerry interrupted her. 'Let. Me. In.'

'Sorry,' Debbie said again, and Gerry heard her footsteps, then the door opened. Debbie was still pale but otherwise looked more like herself. That dreadful sunken look of utter terror had gone.

Gerry shut the door firmly behind her and moved to bolt it, even though it wouldn't keep Justin out. Debbie stopped her.

'Leave it, Mike sometimes comes home for lunch if he's working round here. Come and have a cup of tea. You look terrible,' she added, surveying her friend. 'What happened?'

'Thanks,' Gerry said, not sure which bit of the sentence she was answering. She followed Debbie into the kitchen where she, Justin, and Elwyn had disappeared such a short time before. Debbie pushed the frying pan and several plates to one side, and switched on the kettle. She still looked shaky, but, with Justin and the Wasps gone, was beginning to return to normal.

So,' Debbie said, 'tell me about the cup. I want to know what I went through all that for, and I want the truth this time.'

'You'll have it.' The truth and nothing but the truth, but it couldn't be the whole truth. 'The jewels on the cup, well, it's more like a chalice, they're called the Jewels of the Rainbow.'

'Oh,' Debbie said, her face lighting up. 'Like that jewel in 'Titanic', the Heart of the Ocean, the one she drops into the sea at the end.'

'Debs,' Gerry said, exasperated, 'do you want me to tell you or not?'

'Yes, of course, sorry.' Debbie put two large mugs of tea down on the table and sat down opposite Gerry who took a hasty sip and scalded her tongue.

'You've burned me,' she said. 'And I don't take sugar.'

'You do this time. You look like you're in shock.' Debbie

was already more concerned for Gerry than for herself. 'So, tell me.'

'The chalice – it's the most beautiful thing I've ever seen or ever will.' Gerry had to describe it with no mention of power or magic, but she could feel the longing in her voice. 'Made of gold for the sun and crystal for water, with a garnet, a topaz, a sapphire, and an amethyst, really big ones, with crystals between them. If you hold it in the sun at the right angle, and the gems catch the sunlight then you get beams of light in all the colours of the rainbow.'

'Sounds pricey,' Debbie said, 'and I can see you liked it. But what had all that to do with your pendant?'

Trust Debbie to be down to earth. "Liked" was hardly the word – "enchanted" was closer.

'D'you remember,' Gerry asked after a more cautious mouthful of tea, 'that I told you I bought a blue stone the other day, and showed it to two jewellers? One was attacked, he's still in hospital, and the other one tried to grab it off me for himself.'

'Yeah, I'm not likely to forget it, after what happened this morning, am I?' Debbie said. 'Or that weird stuff yesterday. Sounds like this cup thing is bad news. Like those eastern jewels in stories that have a curse on them. People steal them and then die.'

The reality was even more unlikely, but Gerry could hardly say so. Instead she carried on with her story.

'Well, the woman who sold me the stone was the owner of the chalice. She knew Justin wanted it, so she took the sapphire out 'cos the chalice wouldn't be any good with one of the colours missing. Justin got me to get the chalice for him, only once I'd seen it I wanted it myself. But there was no way Justin was going to let me keep it. I took it back to the woman who'd made it in the first place so she could put the sapphire back on. Justin didn't know where to find her, and I wouldn't tell him. So –' Gerry looked at her helplessly.

'So he came here this morning with his friendly mates.' Debbie considered this, eyeing Gerry over the rim of her solid white mug. 'I can see you're still leaving stuff out, but it's a start. Are we going to report this morning's "incident"?'

'We could say what happened,' Gerry said, 'but there's only our word for it, and I can't tell the police about the chalice. They'd want to know stuff that I can't explain.'

Debbie gave her a searching look. Gerry couldn't tell if she wanted to argue, but she left it for now, changing the subject.

'I suppose those two blokes with the odd clothes were from Eastern Europe, working over here like the daffodil pickers in spring,' Debbie said. 'So he's got this Rainbow thing now? You were back pretty quickly.'

'Yeah, it didn't take very long after all,' Gerry agreed. 'We went to the village where this woman lives. Justin used threats to make her hand over the chalice. And I had to stand and watch.' Gerry was close to tears as she relived that humiliation. She finished her tea to keep them at bay, then stood up.

'Thanks for the tea, Debs,' she said, anxious to get away now she'd seen her friend really was all right. 'Look, I told Hilary I'd go up to the hospital, but there's not a lot of point. They can't do anything for this. I'll just go home and rest.'

'Good idea,' Debbie said, looking her over. 'I'll text you later, see how you are. I'm going in to work. I don't fancy sitting here on my own this afternoon, waiting to see if they come back. Perhaps I'll tell Hilary I couldn't come in this morning 'cos I was held at knife point in my front room by three men who thought

I'd got some precious jewels. I don't suppose she'd believe me, but it would be fun to see her face.' She became serious again. 'You reckon I'll be all right walking into town?'

'Oh yes. You shouldn't have anything to worry about now.' Gerry gave her a hug, but cried out when Debbie hugged her back and caught her ribs.

'Sorry, I'm rubbish at the moment,' Gerry said sadly. 'I'd better go home.'

Debbie waved her off with an encouraging smile, but Gerry had to make a massive effort to smile back. She was beginning to realise how empty was the future lying ahead. She'd been totally absorbed in wanting Justin and wanting the Rainbow Chalice, and now there was nothing left.

Gerry didn't go straight home. What, after all, was there to go home for? She found a place to park on the front, and phoned the Cornwall Centre. Lowenna was with a customer, but Gerry spoke to Graham and agreed to be there on Wednesday and Thursday. She trusted she'd be a bit more mobile by then. She might still be hobbling but at least she could take messages and do bookings. She couldn't feel any enthusiasm at the prospect, but anything was better than sitting at home brooding, and waiting for Justin to turn up again.

Gerry got out of the car and stood on the promenade, leaning on the wall and watching the grey sea. This was close to where she'd stood on the night of the fireworks, trying to decide if she could face going into the fogou. Was everything in Penzance going to be linked to the Tegennow for ever? Already Gerry felt like an addict deprived of their drug. Still, if she went home perhaps she could get some sleep. She turned her back on the breeze-whipped surface of the water and drove along the front to Newlyn and up the back roads to Trewellard.

As Gerry came down the lane to Windhaven she was surprised to see the Audi outside the house, since Claudia had said she wouldn't be back till evening. She would just say hello then go and lie down. She was too listless to want to talk.

In the kitchen Gerry found Claudia surrounded by bags with names she didn't recognise. They looked like the logos of smart London delis and bakers; not the sort of places where Gerry had shopped. She toyed for a moment with the idea of going back to the capital, to get away from the constant reminders of her loss that she'd be surrounded by here. But in the city she would still have the memories, and she'd hated it there. Gerry had wondered why Claudia lived here rather than London, which seemed like her landlady's natural habitat. Maybe it was because of the artists' communities at Newlyn, Lamorna and St Ives. Windhaven was beautiful, of course, and even in Cornwall there weren't many locations which were isolated and with stunning views, but within easy enough reach of village and town.

Claudia heard Gerry coming in and turned round, a bottle of truffle oil in one hand and a tin of cassoulet in the other.

'Oh, aren't you working today?' she asked. 'I didn't expect to see you yet.' She pulled some jars from another bag. The nearest looked like fruits in liqueur. 'I managed to get round all my contacts by yesterday evening,' Claudia went on, 'finishing with a boring but very useful dinner. I loathe London in summer, so I just got up early this morning and came straight back here.'

Gerry decided she might as well have a coffee while she was

in the kitchen and limped over to the sink to fill the kettle. Claudia put down her shopping and stared.

'Gerry, what on earth's the matter?' she asked. 'Have you hurt yourself?'

'Yes,' Gerry admitted. She couldn't be bothered to pretend. 'That's why I'm not at work. I slipped on the stairs last night.'

'But you can hardly walk!' Claudia exclaimed. 'Do you know where you're hurt? Would you like me to take you to the hospital?'

'Thanks, but no,' Gerry said. 'I don't think they can do anything. It'll just take time.'

'But how did it happen?' Claudia was dismayed. 'There's no frayed edges on the stair carpet, and nothing to trip over.'

Gerry wondered whether to tell her or not, but it was too much effort to lie.

'It was Justin,' she said. 'He turned up here unexpectedly, at the exact moment when I was standing on top of the stairs. I missed my step and landed at the foot of the staircase with rather a crash.' She hoped it sounded as if Justin had banged on the front door and made her jump.

At the mention of Justin's name Claudia's face, vivid and concerned a moment before, became a cold mask.

'It's no use getting angry,' Gerry said. 'I didn't ask him here. I know you said you didn't want him in your house.'

Claudia looked at her blankly, then seemed to come back to herself. 'Christ, I'm not angry with you,' she said, 'it's him. He always had a gift for doing things like that, for knowing the exact moment. It was as if he was a mind-reader, like in movies, and a cruel one at that. I did warn you he was dangerous.' She thought briefly. 'He must've left his car in the lay-by up on the road, he certainly didn't drive down to the house or the camera would have picked him up. And he managed to avoid the motion detector when he walked down. If he's done that – I'll have to think about this.'

When Claudia made coffee she used freshly ground coffee in a cafetière, but Gerry had brought instant granules when she moved in. She found the jar, poured hot water into a mug and reached for the milk jug. Luckily Claudia had already got that out, saving Gerry a further painful walk across the kitchen to the fridge. Claudia was flattening the thick empty paper carriers with more force than she needed to. Gerry picked up her mug. She'd intended to take it up to her room, but couldn't help being curious. This might be a chance for her to learn more about Justin.

She did, but it wasn't what she expected.

'Do you know why we split up?' Claudia asked abruptly.

'No,' Gerry said, surprised, then ventured, 'I thought it might be because you were both strong personalities.'

Claudia gave a bitter laugh. 'I wish it had been. No, he started having an affair. Well, that was inevitable, I mean he was never going to be faithful. But he picked the person he knew would provoke me most. I said he had a genius for inflicting pain. It was someone you know too. Monica – Monica Fraser.'

'What?!' Gerry was so startled she splashed hot coffee on her hand, and grabbed a cloth to dab it with. She stared at Claudia. Even after driving 300-odd miles her clothes looked as if she'd just put them on. Her hair shone, her skin and make-up were immaculate and her figure perfect. Gerry thought of Monica's skinny body and plain face, and was bewildered.

Claudia read her confusion and gave a twisted smile. 'Thanks for the implied compliment,' she said, 'but Justin likes variety. That's another reason why he went for you; you're very different from either of us. And that's why Monica was so angry when she saw you with him the other night. She called and told me as a kind of backhanded snipe at both of us.'

Monica. Gerry thought how Monica had sneered at her in the library that morning. Was she really jealous? Debbie had said Monica resented Gerry because of Ryan. This was getting too complicated. A memory nudged at her: Justin looking at her in Penlee Park, then leaving; Monica coming over to her and Debbie. Gerry felt she was missing something important but she was just too tired to try to work it out. Mug in hand, she leaned back against the stripped pine units and the work top of polished granite with grains like tiny lights sparkling under the surface. She wasn't sure she liked the word "different". Gerry was younger than both Claudia and Monica, and far less sophisticated than either. At the fireworks Justin had made her feel, for however short a time, that she was special. It was as easy for him as switching on the kettle was for Gerry, and meant about as much. Gerry nearly asked why Claudia had put up with Justin's affairs, for Monica wouldn't have been the only one, but last night had given her the answer to that. Her body still quivered with the memory, however much her mind revolted at the idea.

'I don't think Justin wants to have an affair with me,' Gerry told Claudia, trying to ignore the recollection of his hands moving so skilfully across her body. She shifted position, trying to find an uninjured part of her back to prop against the edge of the work top behind her. 'Last week I bought a lovely blue stone on Causewayhead. It turned out to be part of a gold chalice set with gemstones, made in Cornwall hundreds of years ago. Justin told me how to get the chalice for him but once I saw it I wanted to keep it myself. He came for it last night, but I didn't have it here. So this morning he got a couple of thugs to hold my best friend at knife point till I agreed to give it to him.'

Claudia had gone completely still as she listened. At last she said, 'So that's what he was doing here? And then he did that to your friend? What a -' she spat out a word Gerry wouldn't have expected her to even know, let alone use. 'But why did he need you to get it for him?'

'It was in a place only women could go to,' Gerry explained. It was unexpectedly comforting sharing this with Claudia, who knew Justin so well.

'I see,' Claudia said thoughtfully. 'Yes, if it was old, valuable, and unique, that would certainly appeal to him, the more so if it was difficult to get hold of. He was always after old things, and the older the better. I don't suppose he paid for it?'

'No. He just took it. With heavy threats.' As Claudia seemed to be in confiding mood Gerry asked on impulse, 'How long have you known Justin? Do you know where he comes from?'

There was a definite pause, so long that Gerry wondered if she'd pushed her luck too far, but then Claudia said slowly, 'I first met him, must have been soon after I moved here, around seven years ago, but we didn't become an item, if you could call it that, until a couple of years back.' She sighed, reminiscing. 'I think he was after me because I was so very definitely not interested in him. I've spent most of my life keeping men at arm's length and I had no intention of making an exception for Justin Chancellor. I was so definite about it that of course it was a challenge for him. I'd have done better to ignore him completely, but by the time I realised that it was far too late. As I told you, he always gets what he wants, and he wanted me for as long as I was keeping him at arm's length. After that – well, then I began to see what he was really like. Which you seem to have learned already. But as to his family and where he grew up, he never said, and he made it impossible to ask.'

Gerry had expected that, though she still wanted to find out. 'There was one other thing,' she added. 'This chalice was so old it had kind of gathered legends round it. Supposed to have magical healing properties and stuff.'

'Like the healing crystals in that funny shop in Penzance?' Claudia asked. 'Now that does surprise me.'

She brushed that aside and returned to her usual brisk self. 'I just want to finish putting these away,' she said, 'then I was going to make a salad. I've got some tinned lobster and there's quite a decent Chablis in the fridge. Would you like some?'

Gerry felt her eyes widen. She'd never expected Claudia to ask her to join her for a meal, but it did sound inviting. She didn't like to admit ignorance and ask what Chablis was. 'I'd love to,' she said.

'Right. You go and sit down next door,' Claudia told her, 'and I'll call you when it's ready.'

'Thanks very much,' Gerry said gratefully. She returned, step by agonising step, to the lounge and sank down cautiously on the armchair. She didn't want to sit on the sofa; it was too full of memories of Justin and his actions. She wanted to swear, but no words seemed strong enough. Gerry leaned back and shut her eyes, wondering how long it would take the Makers to re-programme the Kelegel, or whatever they were doing. And what Justin would do once it was his. She couldn't begin to imagine.

Time passed, with only the sounds from the kitchen to disturb the silence. Gerry had begun to doze, and was on the edge of proper sleep when she was jolted awake by a crash and a shout. She opened her eyes to find Justin himself standing in front of her. He was holding the Kelegel, and there was murder written on his face.

Chapter Fifteen

Gerry shrank back, catching her broken rib against the back of the chair and jerking forward, gasping with pain. Justin came forward and deliberately pushed her back again, holding her there with one hand. He put his other hand against her throat.

'What did you do to it?' he said. His voice was low, and the beautiful tones were distorted with fury. 'What did you do, you bitch?' He took his hand from Gerry's throat long enough to hit her hard round the head, then began pressing her windpipe as if he meant to throttle her. Gerry tried to pull away, but Justin forced her down into the chair with his knee across both of hers so she couldn't move.

Gerry shook her head; trying to speak though the pressure on her throat was almost impossible.

'What are you talking about?' she managed to choke out.

'Don't pretend, you know damn well!' he snarled, still in that horrible voice, and slapped her head again. 'They were all right when I left those women; I tried them there and they worked for me. Then I came back here and they were dead. Look!' He waved the chalice in front of Gerry's face. 'It wasn't anything those three did so it has to be you.'

Where was Claudia – surely she must have heard the noise? Why didn't she come rushing in from the kitchen and pull Justin off her? Gerry tried to fight back, wondering what he was accusing her of, and why she'd assumed he would never hit anyone himself, but get other people to do it for him. Justin released her throat to grip her two hands in one of his. At least that made it easier to speak.

'You've got the chalice,' Gerry said hoarsely. Her throat hurt and made speaking difficult. 'That was what you wanted, wasn't it?'

'Look!' He thrust it almost under her nose, and Gerry gasped. It was the Kelegel, the chalice of gold and gems – and yet it wasn't. The marks of the Bees were there, so were the clear crystals and the four great gemstones, yet she could tell at once it contained no more magic than a cardboard coffee cup.

Justin let go of her, snatched up a vase of flowers from a side table and tipped some of the water into the chalice. He flung the vase down on Claudia's fine rug, drenching it with the remaining water and the scattered stems and leaves. Then he held the Tegennow in the sunlight which came in through the window overlooking the garden.

Nothing happened. Gerry hauled herself gingerly out of the chair and limped to the window to join him. It must have been plain to Justin, even through his fury and frustration, that she was completely mystified. For the first time, Gerry was glad that he could, at least partially, read her mind.

'It's nothing to do with me,' she said shakily, afraid of provoking another attack. 'I haven't been near it since you all went into the fogou.'

'And a lot of mumbo-jumbo that was,' Justin said impatiently. He thrust the chalice into her hands. 'You try it.'

Gerry tried. She held the Kelegel as she had on the hillside. She tried flicking drops of water from the cup into the air in case that did the trick. Justin watched every move, which only made her more nervous. She didn't know the words the Makers had used when they called on the Jewels of the Rainbow, but the Tegennow had shone for her earlier that day without any invocation. Gerry tried to picture those glowing shafts of colour rising from within the water. Still nothing happened. 'Perhaps,' Gerry suggested hesitantly, 'they only work on Chapel Carn Brea?'

Justin had begun to pace round the room, but at that he stopped.

'You'd better be wrong,' he said. 'I can't do what I need to in Cornwall. I have to take the Kelegel home with me.'

'So what do you want them for?' Gerry asked. At least while Justin was talking, he wasn't trying to throttle her. He seemed to have accepted that she really didn't know what was blocking the rainbow, though he still looked murderous. And now she knew one thing; Justin wasn't Cornish. Why, she thought again, didn't Claudia come in?

'She can't hear us,' Justin said, answering the thought. 'I've put a veil of silence on this room. As for what I want -' he stopped. Gerry edged herself onto the arm of her chair. Justin came to a halt and turned towards her.

'I need the Tegennow a'n gammneves,' he said, 'to teach my brother Gregory a lesson.'

This was so unlike what Gerry had imagined that she wondered if she'd heard him properly.

'Your brother?' she asked doubtfully. 'The one you said accused you of stealing the chalice?'

226

She remembered Justin's story, but the Makers had said he wanted the Kelegel for evil purposes. Rescuing a family treasure wasn't evil.

'You said the Kelegel was a family heirloom. But it can't be.' That didn't fit with what she knew about it now.

'Quite right. It's not,' Justin said. He was calming down. 'It disappeared from all records around the time of the Guardian Baranwen, but I'd read enough about it to know it was very powerful and if I could get hold of it, it would serve my needs. It's true that Gregory seized my inheritance. He denounced me as a user of magic and practiser of the black arts. I had to flee for my life.'

That didn't sound right. 'But – surely inheritance and that sort of stuff's a law thing? If he's the younger brother, couldn't you take him to court? Why was your life in danger?'

Justin's reply was to laugh, but it was a bitter laugh.

'The court would have been on Gregory's side,' he said. 'In our time, unlike yours, people understand that magic is real, but most people hate and fear it. Or claim to. But many of them go secretly to those who employ it. They go to gain what they want – power, money, lust – and still publicly declaim against any known practitioners.'

That answered another question.

'You fit very well into this time,' Gerry told him. 'I was never sure if you were born here or not.'

He laughed that harsh laugh again.

'Oh, this century suits me in a lot of ways. After all the things I've got used to here, and the scope it gives me, I don't know if I'd want to stay in my old life all the time. But I've spent ten years trying to get the Chalice and I'm not going to give up now when I've actually got it in my hands. Gregory is not going to enjoy what should be mine for much longer.'

'But why,' Gerry persisted, 'do you need the Kelegel at all? You can do so much?' She thought how casually he had referred to putting a veil of silence on the room to keep Claudia unaware of him. How he travelled easily between different times, different places, and had taken, or brought, her to him. How he had known, from wherever he was, when Gerry wanted to see him.

'That last one's easy.' Justin interrupted her thoughts as he had before. 'I forged a link between us when I decided I could use you. It only relates to the Rainbow Jewels – I'm not interested in your problems at work or your boyfriends.'

And that was "easy"?

'I want to punish Gregory properly,' he went on, 'and despite the pious front he puts on, he will have protected himself from me by powerful sorcery. He inherited, as I did, the potential to use magic, but was always too lazy to learn how. He will have used part of the wealth that should be mine to pay for the help of the best man he can have, and it would afford me immense satisfaction to lay that bare before the family, and all the gentry too. But the man he would use is skilled in all the arts, and I have to augment my own powers to overcome him. Only the Tegennow a'n gammneves could aid me in this. I have learned of nothing else powerful enough.'

'But surely,' Gerry protested, 'the Jewels of the Rainbow were made to bring good to the whole community. They couldn't be used for something like this.'

'Ah, but they can,' said Justin with complete confidence. He sat down on the arm of the leather sofa, with the smile Gerry had learned to fear on his face. 'They may have been made for good in the first place, but they have passed decades in the care of the Guardian Baranwen. She has other ideas about the Tegennow. I have followed them, traced their history as far as her time. The

Tegennow a'n gammneves were made to interact with the woman who was using them. I can see that Baranwen has moulded them to her own ambition – and they have responded. Your Makers have seen it too, in the chalice you took back to them, and they don't like it one bit, but it's done and they can't change it. It's their own fault, of course. They expected the Jewels would be looked after by pure and selfless women, but there's only a limited supply of saints. Now Baranwen has laid the groundwork, I could adapt the Chalice to my own use with very little trouble. All I have to do now is overcome this last stumbling block. Then I can take my revenge on Gregory. Slowly.'

He was speaking as calmly now as if he were planning a dinner party, and Gerry shuddered. She didn't want to know what he intended to do to his treacherous brother. It wouldn't be as straightforward as a beating, or even plain murder. Gerry thought of the Makers who had created the Kelegel for the good of all their people, and wondered how they could have brought themselves to adapt it for Justin, even to save their village. Perhaps it couldn't be used for real evil, and all they had done was enable him to bring a rainbow from the cup. Now when he tried to use the Chalice towards his ends, it refused to obey. And the same had proved true for Gerry when she tried to do his bidding.

Again she might as well have spoken aloud.

'That,' Justin said evenly, 'is what you are going to find out for me.'

'But,' Gerry asked, 'you don't mean you were planning on going back from here to your own time and changing what's already happened then, do you? You can't do that.'

Justin looked genuinely surprised.

'Why ever not? He's my brother; it's my inheritance.'

'But you mustn't,' Gerry begged, getting up and going to

him in her agitation, forgetting the pain of her rib. Her heart was thumping. 'You don't understand. If you'd found the Kelegel in your own time you could have done what you liked and that would be between you and Gregory. But if you go back from here now and change the past, I mean what's in the past from here, your brother will have lived and died, he might have married and had children, they'll have children on and on. If you go back and change that, it could change history, there'll be people who will never be born, so life now could be completely different.'

'Of course I know that,' Justin answered. Gerry couldn't believe he sounded so unconcerned. 'I understand more about this than you do.'

'But you can't!' She was almost in tears, she wanted to shake him, it must be he really didn't understand. 'You could alter what's going to happen so this Penzance you're in might not exist as it is, then you would never get the Kelegel and what you did to change the past couldn't have happened, oh, and it all kind of explodes. I don't know how I can make you see it. It could be like the end of the world.'

'I told you, of course I understand. But it might not be like that. Anyway I'm prepared to risk it. I can always stay back in my own time if I have to. The Kelegel can protect me from any future consequences.'

'You,' Gerry asked in disbelief, 'are going to risk the future of the world so that you can get your own back on your brother?'

'Yes. And you are going to help me.'

Gerry couldn't think of a word to say. She just stood there, still not really believing what Justin had said. Outside, the clouds were clearing, and the sun shone on the grass and hedges. She found herself staring through the window, her mind numb, at a large fuchsia bush with pale yellow leaves, the hanging crimson flowers too many to count. A blackbird flew across the lawn and hopped around the recently dug flowerbed, hoping to find a worm. Everything was silent and peaceful. Then Gerry heard Claudia open the kitchen door and come into the lounge. The sound block that Justin had created didn't stop her just walking in.

'Gerry? Lunch is ready, if you're –' then she stopped dead. Gerry swung round, aware of how close she was standing to Justin, of how it must look. Claudia, though, didn't seem to even notice Gerry. She was staring at Justin, looking every bit as furious as he had been when he burst in with the Kelegel.

Get out of my house,' she said, every syllable loaded with controlled anger. 'Get out or I'll have you arrested for trespass.'

Justin smiled again. If Gerry knew that smile, she was sure Claudia must too.

'I wouldn't try it if I were you,' Justin said. 'You know I could make you look extremely foolish. I've done nothing legally wrong. Remember, you gave me a key to your house.' He put a casual hand on Gerry's shoulder. 'Do you mind so much that I've come to see your lodger? I would simply make you look like a jealous and hysterical woman.'

Claudia continued to watch him with absolute loathing in her face. Gerry knew how much Claudia would hate such a scene; and Justin was so capable of doing exactly that. She hoped Claudia did believe that she and Justin weren't having sex.

'What do you want here?' Claudia demanded. 'You gave me back that key. How did you get in?'

Justin ignored both questions and turned to Gerry.

Deliberately he took her hand and pressed it gently, like a lover saying goodbye.

'Think about what I told you,' he said. 'I'll give you till tomorrow to decide what you want to do. But think hard. I need that explanation, and I'm not going to be kept waiting this time.'

Then he left. He walked out of the door that led to the hallway and the front door, and a minute later the two women heard the door shut. It was the first time Gerry had ever seen Justin leave anywhere by conventional means, and it confirmed what she'd guessed. Claudia had no idea he could appear out of and vanish into thin air. But then, how could she?

Claudia began to swear, but stopped after a minute or two. Her range of obscenities startled Gerry, it was so at odds with her groomed appearance.

'Sod the man,' Claudia said at last. 'I hate getting angry, and he knows that too. No-one's ever been able to get under my skin the way he can. Or make me swear like that. I'm sorry.'

Gerry wanted to tell Claudia she needn't apologise, but her landlady was still speaking.

'I need a drink,' she went on, 'I'm too wound up to eat till I've calmed down a bit. I'll have to have all the locks changed, every single door. He only had a key to the front door and I got that back off him, but obviously he's had it copied, and I don't trust him not to have copied the others too somehow. That'll teach me not to bolt that door when I got back today. And he must have left his car on the road again so he didn't set off the camera. It's like whatever I do he finds a way round it.'

Then Claudia looked at Gerry properly.

'What did he do to you?' she asked. 'You look like – I don't even know how to describe it. Like you've had the most terrible shock.'

By now Gerry was used to finding the most likely bits of the truth.

'I was just dozing in here, more than half asleep,' she explained. 'I woke up to find him standing here, and he was really angry. You know I told you about that gold cup he wanted me to get for him?'

Claudia nodded.

'Yes – you said he'd got hold of your friend and threatened her.'

'That's right,' Gerry agreed. 'Well, it seems that the cup I got was like a copy, a few hundred years later than the original, and it wasn't what he wanted. The one he's after is about two thousand years old. I was sitting in this chair and he pushed me, pushed me against the back of it, right where I broke my rib.'

Claudia drew in a sharp breath, then called Justin a few more names.

'I'm sorry,' she said at last. 'I knew he could be cruel, but he never did anything quite that bad to me. I shouldn't have let you in for this. You know, I actually had someone else in mind for your room, but you seemed to want it very badly, so I agreed. I feel like it's my fault. Have you had any painkillers, or can I get you some? You must be in agony.'

Gerry was, but somehow it was less important than other things. Something that had been niggling at her had finally fallen into place.

'Claudia,' she asked, 'didn't you say Justin had been seeing Monica, who I work with?'

'Yes, and she's welcome to him,' Claudia replied. 'I don't suppose he's treated her much better than either of us.'

'No,' Gerry said. 'Claudia, I've only just understood. Justin made Monica come and introduce us. She must have pointed me out to him in the library some time, said I was looking for a place to live.' Well, no, he'd have picked that up from Monica's mind or Gerry's own, but she couldn't tell Claudia that. 'When you walked away from him in the park – he looked at me. He knew who I was. Then he went off, and a few minutes later Monica appeared. She came into the park from the other side of Penlee House, that's the way he went when he left. He went to see her and made her do that, and I bet she hated it. And hated both of us into the bargain.' It made a lot of sense. 'Then he could flirt with me and make you angry, and Monica too, and get me to look for the Chalice and score points off all of us.' Gerry had never dreamed anyone could be so manipulative; but she'd never met anyone like Justin.

Claudia was gazing down, lost in thought, and finally nodded, accepting Gerry's conclusion. Then she spotted the water soaking the rug.

'He's ruined it,' she said bitterly. 'That was hand-made Persian wool. My parents gave it to me as my moving-in present when I came to live here.' At least Claudia didn't blame Gerry for the damage. She left the room briefly and came back carrying a couple of large, thick towels and a long plastic bin liner. She spread one towel over half the rug.

'Can you stand on this one for a minute?' she asked. 'Though it's probably too late to do any good.' She picked up the crushed flowers and dropped them into the bin, then laid the other towel over the rest of the rug. She stood the chair on top of it, and pulled some heavy art books from a shelf. 'Thanks - you can move now.' She spread out the bin liner on top of the towel where Gerry had been standing, then arranged the books across the top of the liner so they could weigh it down while keeping dry themselves. 'Perhaps the towels will soak up some of the water. Let's go and get that wine. You must need it as much as I do.'

At that moment Claudia saw the Kelegel. It was still standing on the window sill where Gerry had put it down when she'd failed to raise the rainbow. Claudia picked it up, turned it in the sunlight. The gold was gleaming, the gems shone in the sun, and the crystals looked ready to change into prisms as they had done before. Claudia turned to Gerry in astonishment, her mouth slightly open.

'This is what you were talking about?' she asked. 'The one you said was a copy? I've never seen anything like it.' She turned it over. 'How old did you say it was? I suppose those aren't diamonds?'

'It goes back to the Dark Ages,' Gerry said, 'though they can't have been that dark if they could make something like that. And no, they're not diamonds, they're rock crystals, and the red one's a garnet, not a ruby. But the blue's a sapphire and the gold's real.'

'There's no hallmark,' Claudia frowned, turning it over. 'Still, I suppose it's too old for that. And he just left it here? What are you going to do with it?'

'Give it back to the woman it belongs to,' Gerry said, though she wasn't sure if that would mean Colenso or Baranwen. 'Later.' She leaned on the back of the chair; her rib was really hurting again.

Claudia put down the Kelegel and came over to her.

'Come on, we'll go through to the conservatory,' she said. 'Can you walk all right, or do you want a hand? I forgot you were hurt, there just seems to be so much going on.' She gave a half smile. 'I can see that having you as a lodger is going to be interesting.'

Gerry picked up the chalice, remembering Baranwen's warning about keeping it with her at all times. Claudia led her through to the conservatory where the table was laid. There was wine in two fine long-stemmed glasses, salad in a wooden bowl, cutlery of Scandinavian simplicity and plates in duck-egg blue. A bottle of water stood beside a basket holding poppy-seed knot rolls. Gerry put the chalice on the floor at her feet. She picked up a roll and broke it. It was freshly baked and soft. She'd made a poor breakfast as getting around the kitchen had been so hard that morning, and so much had happened since that it felt more like a week ago than a few hours. She reached for the butter and put some on her plate.

Roll in hand, Gerry gazed out towards the horizon. Her mind was so battered that she'd simply stopped thinking. The clouds were drifting away and the sea turning blue as the sky changed. Just where the coast road disappeared from view one building gleamed white, catching the light. The land beside it sloped up to the right, and the cloud shadows ran up the slope as they moved. It was a view no-one could get tired of.

Gerry tried some of the lobster and salad, and drank her glass of wine. She was sure it was all very good, but it was wasted on her; she'd have been just as happy with a tuna sandwich, and couldn't tell an expensive bottle from a supermarket basic. Claudia talked easily about some of the people she'd seen in London, so Gerry only had to make the right noises. She wondered if Claudia was trying to set her at her ease, or talking to take her mind off her own anger.

'Oh, I meant to tell you,' Claudia said, laying down her fork and turning to look at Gerry. 'You know I mentioned the dinner party I went to on Sunday? Well, the man who gave it, he's got an original work by Richard Hamilton in his dining room. He's no relation of yours, I suppose?'

'I wish,' Gerry said with feeling, pulled temporarily out of her brooding. 'One of my tutors in London was really keen on his stuff and asked the same thing, but no. At least not that I could find out. So, no chance of turning up an early canvas in the family attic, I'm afraid. Pity, my share would pay off my student loan, and more.' Gerry pushed her chair back and stood up, picking up the Kelegel. 'Thanks ever so much,' she said, 'that was lovely. I think I'm just going to go up to my room and rest. Unless you want a hand with the dishes?'

'No, that's all right,' Claudia said, standing up too and walking into the kitchen. 'You do look done in. I'm going to leave this lot and clear up later. I ought to go down to the gallery first and bring Ethan, that's my deputy, up to speed with what I've been doing. So it'll all be quiet for you.'

Once Gerry was upstairs in her room she sat on the bed and placed the chalice in front of her. The sun came in at the windows behind her back, and in the warm light the Kelegel looked as beautiful as always. But neither gold, gems or crystals held any hint of the magic they'd once possessed. She had to go and confront the Makers, and had no doubt that they'd be expecting her. This deadened thing, which mocked her with its echo of the jewels she had rescued, used and been enchanted by, would not take her back to them. But if the Makers were right, Seona's chain would. Gerry leaned back against the wardrobe, held the chain and closed her eyes. *Take me back to the Makers,* she begged. *Take me back to Colenso and Rosenwyn and Keyna.*

And nothing happened.

Gerry panicked. She put her hand on the chain, and the other on the sapphire on the Kelegel that was and was not her

Kelegel. She sought the circle of blue and purple stars. She totally had to talk to the Makers. She tried to call up Seona's face, but the features blurred. She could only see Justin's face, his fury when he couldn't use the Tegennow. Gerry closed her eyes in despair and lay down on the bed. She should try to calm her mind, but that seemed impossible.

Perhaps it was because of the wine - Gerry wasn't used to drinking at lunchtime - but the next thing she knew she could hear noises downstairs. It must be burglars, she thought in confusion, then looked at the time and saw a good two hours had passed. She'd fallen asleep, and now Claudia was already back. That was a nuisance but couldn't be helped. The sleep seemed to have cleared Gerry's head a bit and she felt better. She decided to try once more, and repeated the same ritual: chain, jewels and stars. The next moment she was at the entrance to the fogou, and Keyna stood there.

She was waiting for Gerry. Her greeting was cool, but she led Gerry through the tunnel to the inside chamber. Colenso and Rosenwyn were standing there waiting; both looked grave. Gerry felt more nervous than she used to before exams. How much would she have to explain?

Gerry held out the Chalice which she'd carried with her, gripped in one hand. 'I believe this is what you gave to Justin?'

There was a collective intake of breath, then Colenso said, 'And how do you come by it? Did he just give it to you?'

Gerry found she was trembling. 'Justin came to the house and accused me of, well, of doing whatever it was that stopped him using the chalice. Then he began to strangle me. I never saw anyone so angry in my life.' Gerry was shaking even at the memory. Then she saw Colenso and Rosenwyn exchange a look. 'You knew he might do that? And if he'd

238

killed me?' She stared at the three of them. 'Was that what you wanted?'

They were all on their feet, and there was nothing close enough for Gerry to lean on. The table and bench were on the other side of the chamber. 'Look, do you mind if I sit down?' she asked. 'I still feel half-dead.' Colenso nodded, and Gerry went over to sit on the bench, but with the three Makers still standing she felt at a disadvantage. She'd been wrong-footed again. She'd come here hoping for explanations and support, but instead felt as if she were on trial.

'How is your friend?' Keyna asked suddenly. 'The one whose life was held to ransom?'

'Oh,' Gerry closed her eyes briefly. She was ashamed to realise she hadn't even thought of Debbie since she'd gone home. 'Debbie's sound. She'll be all right.'

'And you?'

Gerry opened her eyes again and looked at the Maiden. 'I was hoping you could answer some questions. Like why the Jewels would work here for Justin, but not in my time.'

Gerry noticed now that all three Makers were in formal green robes, similar to the Bees' ceremonial ones, and had torcs about their necks. Rosenwyn wore a ring with a flat onyx stone. Carved onto it was the crossed circle which the Gwenen had painted onto their wrists. They had made no move as yet to take the Kelegel from her. Colenso and Rosenwyn were motionless, watching Gerry. Keyna moved restlessly about the chamber.

'Did he tell you what he wanted the Chalice for?' the Maiden asked.

Gerry nodded. She still felt drained, despite the couple of hours' sleep. She hadn't expected to be cross-examined.

239

'He did not tell us, but it was not difficult to read his intentions' Colenso said. Of course, she'd be able to see through Justin as easily as he could see into Gerry's mind when he chose. 'And knowing that, you still come to ask us to help him?'

Well, no, that wasn't what Gerry wanted. She just wanted to know why the chalice wouldn't work in the twenty-first century. But being treated as if she were as evil as Justin was getting annoying.

'But you,' she protested, 'you gave Justin the Tegennow to take into my century. Isn't that just as bad?'

'Of course it is not.' It was Rosenwyn's turn. She looked both angry and sorrowful. 'You do not understand time, for all that you have travelled within it. Baranwen's Kelegel could come to life here because this was where it first came from. It could not live in your day where it has not yet been.'

'We prepared the Tegennow a'n gammneves for Iestyn,' Keyna spoke the name with distaste, 'and allowed him to hold them here. He could not see into our plans as we could see into his. We all knew full well that the Jewels' power would cease to function when they went beyond their own time. Thus he could accomplish nothing with them. His purposes and his plots, whatever evil he had planned, were foiled.'

Of course. Rosenwyn had said Gerry had told them more than she realised; that must have applied to what she'd said about Justin too. With their knowledge of character, and worldly wisdom, the Makers would must have realised Justin would find some way to force Gerry to take him back to them. Gerry wondered if the tongue-lashing they'd given her in front of him had been purely for effect, or genuine. Probably both.

'So, you mean – he'll not be able to use them at all?' Did

they expect Gerry to go back and tell Justin that? And she couldn't hide. Anywhere. He would find her whatever she did.

Gerry touched Seona's chain, wishing again that she could talk to her great-aunt. Still holding the chain with one hand, she realised that the chalice in her other hand felt alive again. The Jewels of the Rainbow were back in their own place. 'So what happens to this one?'

'This one must go back to Baranwen,' Colenso replied. 'But first, we have one final task.' She took the chalice in both hands. 'From now until the time when Baranwen separates the Jewels, the Tegennow will remain gifted with power. They will live through the centuries within the care of the Guardians. Then you will retrieve the Kelegel from its hiding place and bring it to us to repair. What we must do now is ensure that from the time they are reunited they hold no more of the powers that corrupted Baranwen, and harmed you also. Maybe other women too that we will never learn of.'

'I don't understand,' Gerry said, completely confused now. 'You said we mustn't change things in time.'

'This is different,' said Rosenwyn, 'because for us, here, what we go to is a time that has not yet taken place. You wanted to go back to your younger self to visit your aunt; that would have altered your own past. If you do not appreciate the difference I cannot explain it any more.'

Gerry's brain was refusing to take this in.

'Let me get this right,' she said. 'You are planning to take away the power from the chalice that Baranwen concealed? The power for, what was it, "healing and knowledge" as well as for moving in place and time?'

'And for conferring unnaturally long life,' Colenso confirmed. 'We cannot remove one without the other. No-one will ever be able to re-create what we did; the knowledge we worked from will be lost by then. The Tegennow have given me some glimpses into the future. I should have recognised that as a warning in itself; we did not bestow that on them.'

To Gerry that sounded a bit like an apology. She found her mouth was open. 'Are you telling me,' she asked in disbelief, 'that you're planning to go to a particular date 600-odd years from now? You're all going from here into another time?'

'We are within the fogou where it happened,' Rosenwyn explained. 'It is not a day or a year that we go to but a resonance. To the events of that day when you find the Jewels, when the Gohi attempt to seize them and Baranwen outmatches them. The violence of these acts should speak to us through the very stones in the walls. You will guide us.'

Still dazed, Gerry rose to her feet, supported by Keyna. These three, the Makers, were to become the destroyers of what they had worked for so long to create. 'I can't cope with this,' she said. 'I'm done in.' She trusted they would understand what that meant.

'I can give you a brew which will lessen the pain you are feeling. We keep some of it ready always. Many people who come here need some of this.' Rosenwyn went to the table, took a cover from a beaker and handed it to Gerry. The contents smelled of herbs, and something else she couldn't identify. She tried a little of it. Something in the drink lifted her spirits at once, though it might be a while before the pain-killing element kicked in.

Colenso waited till Gerry had finished the beaker, then motioned for her to rise. 'We will start from outside,' she said. 'I would like you to recreate exactly what you did that day; how you made your way inside and found the hidden casket. Take us through it, step by step.'

They all went out and stood by the stone lintel that marked the entrance to the fogou. Then for no apparent reason Gerry was swept by a wave of fear. It was like the first time she'd seen that entrance in the torchlight of a midsummer night, when she'd been certain that danger for her lay within, and Kerenza had asked if she had the Sight. Later, she'd taken that flash of terror to be a forewarning of the moment when she'd been surrounded by the Wasps, weapons in their hands all directed at her. This feeling was far stronger, and it scared her to her bones. Gerry stopped so suddenly that Keyna all but fell over her.

'We mustn't go in there,' Gerry said urgently. 'Something terrible will happen; I can feel it.'

The Makers looked at her in surprise. Rosenwyn, her eyebrows raised, took her arm.

'Nonsense,' she said firmly. 'All we want you to do is to take us in, and show us the very stone where the casket was concealed, if you can. If not, then at least which wall and at what height. That is all we need. How can that harm you?'

Gerry's legs were shaking, and she thought she was going to be sick. Even the sunlit sky looked dark.

'I can't go in there,' she repeated, but Keyna took one arm and Rosenwyn the other and between them they took her, still trying desperately but in vain to hold back, under the stone lintel and into the passageway. There was enough light from outside to see as far as the entrance to the round chamber. A torch burned in a holder on the curved wall within. Gerry knew the place wasn't going to collapse about their ears, for it was still standing, scarcely altered, several hundred years from this point. Yet a blackness was filling her head, and her heart was thudding horribly.

Gerry was marched along the tunnel, and into the chamber. Her arms were freed, and she stood in the centre of the empty space. Looking around, she remembered that the Wasps had stood between her and the way out, so she wanted the wall furthest from the entrance. And she had reached easily into the gap behind the stone, so it was about elbow height. Gerry moved towards the sloping stones, then turned to look at the three robed figures watching her intently. They flickered momentarily and took the shapes of the Wasps, then returned to themselves. Gerry turned back to the curved wall, recalling how the sapphire had pulled her towards where the Tegennow lay concealed. She took a hesitant step across the floor of packed earth, then another, more confident. She was sure she had the place now.

All at once the chamber was plunged into darkness. For two, maybe three heartbeats Gerry thought the torch had gone out, but it was a different sort of darkness. A familiar, endless space between place and time. A darkness where she hung, unable to feel or hear or see. Then she crashed onto the same floor, but lit by the light of two torches instead of one, burning with strong, steady flames. The Makers appeared beside her: Rosenwyn bewildered and even Keyna shaken, but Colenso still calm.

The three Makers had all managed to remain standing, but they were staring at something behind her. Before Gerry could turn she was dragged to her feet and someone laid an arm across her throat. Gerry twisted her head just enough to see Kerenza, whose other arm was pinning both of Gerry's. The pressure on her bruised throat and back was cruel. She stood very still. Kerenza's attitude towards her had changed overnight with Wylmet's death, although Gerry had done her best to save the young novice. In her anger and grief Kerenza had found it easier to blame Gerry than to see the truth, which was that the Guardians had decreed it. Gerry looked in front of her again and saw that Morvoren and Ysella were holding Keyna and Rosenwyn. Both Makers had their arms pinioned as her own were, and each Guardian had her knife held ready in her free hand.

In the centre of the tableau Baranwen stood confronting Colenso. Gerry had never before this day seen anyone as furious as Justin had been when he accused her of taking the power from the Tegennow, but even that had been pale beside this. Baranwen was so consumed with rage that it seemed to pulse through her veins instead of blood.

'Did you think,' she hissed, each word charged with emotion, 'that I would let you harm the Tegennow a'n gammneves? I told the girl there that I always know when they are threatened. I was drawn through the ages to her time when a rogue wished to steal just one of the stones. And now,' she turned her rage on Gerry, 'you who craved the Tegennow for yourself, you are conniving with these women to destroy them for ever? But I will not allow it!'

Her voice rose with the last words and she whirled round, raising her arms. Gripped in her hands, the bronze blades catching the light of the torches and turning as red as blood, was a double headed axe.

Chapter Sixteen

Rosenwyn cried out, 'Mother Goddess, a Labrys! How in Her name did you come by that?' She was staring, transfixed, at the double blade with its wickedly sharp crescent moon ends gleaming in the torchlight, not as a weapon to be feared, but as an object of mystery. Baranwen ignored her. She had eyes only for Colenso. Colenso lifted both her hands, palms outwards, and faced Baranwen, quite unafraid. 'Look at you,' she said, and her own eyes were flashing with anger now. 'Look around you. If anything was needed to confirm that our decision was right, you have done it. You,' she swept her arm across, including the others in her condemnation, 'how dare you call yourselves Guardians of the Kelegel a'n gammneves? Axe and daggers, blades and threats and violence, in the name of the Jewels of the Rainbow? You should be ashamed to look us in the face.'

Before Baranwen could answer, Keyna jerked her arm upwards and sent Morvoren's knife spinning across the earthen floor. She had always seemed sensible and severe; now she too blazed with passion. She broke free of Morvoren in the seconds that the Guardian wavered over whether to hold on to her captive or rescue her weapon, and ranged herself defiantly alongside Colenso, confronting Baranwen directly.

'You are no fit Guardian,' Keyna pronounced with utter contempt. 'What of the oath you took – or have you changed it to suit your own purposes? The oath to guard and protect the Tegennow, to use them for understanding and for aid; to keep them in trust and to hand them on, pure and untainted, to the next to hold your sacred office. Well? Even this misguided young woman here,' she waved a hand in Gerry's direction, 'would make a better Guardian than you. She at least values honesty and loyalty.'

Baranwen glared at them both. She had not loosened her grip on the wooden handle and looked ready to strike the two Makers down with the axe. 'Then tell me,' she snarled, 'women of peace and knowledge, what would you do when armed men with criminal intent come to seize and misuse the Kammneves? Words will not avail you against daggers and poison and treachery.'

'Treachery?' Rosenwyn was as angry as the others. She was struggling against Ysella's grasp but the younger woman was too strong for her. Unable to physically stand beside her two associates she nonetheless added her voice to theirs. 'You who can call us here across time; who could hunt out Gerralda through the ages beyond your own to give her the sapphire you had cut from the Rainbow Jewels? You should have cut your own hand off first! And you claim you could find no other means to counter these threats to the Gammneves?'

Ysella with a violent movement lifted her hand to silence Rosenwyn, but Baranwen shook her head.

'No, let us hear these words of wisdom,' she said, sarcasm dripping from every syllable.

Colenso interrupted, putting one hand on Keyna's arm to check the indignant outburst trembling on her lips. 'Let

247

us not fight among ourselves like drunken men in a brawl, or curs scrapping in the yard,' she said. 'But I think, Baranwen, it is time your fellow Guardians learned the truth about their forerunner Delenyk, and your schemes against Gerralda. If you do not tell them, I will.' She stood straight and still, and spoke in a commanding voice that rang through the small chamber and reverberated off the curved slopes of the stone walls. 'I accuse you, Baranwen of the Gwenen and Guardian of the Tegennow a'n gammneves, of plotting to take the Kelegel for yourself and depriving the people you were sworn to serve, for your own traitorous purposes. I accuse you of deliberately causing the death of Delenyk, the most loyal of your followers, and of lying to all the Gwenen. I accuse you of planning to throw all the blame onto Gerralda Melinda Hamilton after she had unwittingly served your purposes and removed the threat of the man Justin Chancellor. And I –'

'No!' The great two-headed blade had swung down in an arc before Colenso had completed her account of Baranwen's crimes. It flashed faster than the eye could follow, but Keyna had been watching the Guardian narrowly, anticipating just such a move, and flung Colenso aside in the seconds that the axe whistled down. Keyna pushed the older woman forward and herself aside in one movement, but wasn't quite quick enough; the edge of the blade caught her hand and blood began pouring from it. Gerry couldn't see the extent of the damage and didn't want to. She tried to move towards Keyna, but Kerenza tightened her grip, making Gerry cry out.

'Please,' Gerry begged, 'I'm hurt already and I'm not going anywhere. You could let me go.'

'You deserve it,' was all the answer Kerenza gave, her tone bitter.

'You're wrong, you must know you are,' Gerry pleaded. 'You saw me trying to prevent Wylmet from drinking that wine; you were there!'

'You told us you knew the men who had brought it to Meraud, and you knew what was in it,' Kerenza snarled. 'Now you're here with these scum who admit openly they want to destroy the Jewels of the Rainbow. And you want me to let you go?'

Gerry gave up and looked back towards Baranwen. She kept her eyes away from Keyna, afraid the Maiden might have lost some fingers. If only she could take her to West Cornwall Hospital they could help perhaps, but Gerry reckoned she'd be lucky to get out of here at all, let alone do any more 'time damage'. Colenso had scrambled back to her feet and had her arm round Keyna, who had twisted part of her sleeve round her hand. Blood was dripping steadily from it.

Gerry expected Baranwen to strike again while Colenso was still off balance but Morvoren, of all people, prevented her. As Baranwen raised the haft again Morvoren caught at her right arm, a dangerous thing to do with the blood-stained blades waving precariously above her. The unforgiving Guardian who had always obeyed her leader without question was struggling with Baranwen, attempting to wrest the Labrys from her, heedless of any risk to herself. She was shouting, 'Is it true, is this true? That you wanted the Gammneves for yourself? And Delenyk, was she really innocent? You caused her death?' The Guardian looked appalled at her own words.

And at the mention of Delenyk, Kerenza released Gerry as if she'd forgotten her existence, and flew to help Morvoren. Gerry didn't even think of joining them; there were too many flailing limbs and the vicious axe was swinging to and fro as they struggled. She watched in fascinated horror as Morvoren and Kerenza fought to overpower Baranwen. Too blinded with anger to be logical, they were hindering each other as much as helping. Ysella kept back, and contented herself with preventing Rosenwyn from joining the melee. Gerry moved forward as unobtrusively as she could, hoping perhaps to help Keyna. Rosenwyn spotted her and cried out sharply, 'Gerralda, trip her up!'

In the swaying confusion of arms and legs Gerry could hardly be sure which was whose, but she edged behind them. The three were too absorbed to notice her. Morvoren and Kerenza were attacking Baranwen from the front. Trying to gauge the best moment, Gerry launched herself forward, gripping the side of Baranwen's girdle with one hand for support and hooking her foot round the Guardian's ankle. Baranwen slipped and the other two came down on top of her as she crashed onto the floor. They missed Gerry by inches, and she landed on her knees beside them. The axe went spinning through the air and came close to decapitating Ysella, who'd stayed well clear of the struggle. One of the twin blades collided with the wall, gouging out a chunk of stone before landing on the ground with a crash. Rosenwyn pulled herself free of Ysella's slackened grip and crouched beside the Labrys.

'Bind her hands,' Colenso called. 'Use your girdles.'

Morvoren and Kerenza knelt on top of Baranwen who was still furiously trying to fight them off. The blade had caught the edge of Ysella's shoulder as it flew, slicing through the fabric of her robe but only scratching the skin. That, Gerry reckoned, was better than she deserved. Ysella looked at the thin trickle of blood, promptly decided which side she was on, and next minute was lending her strength to Morvoren and Kerenza. Between the three of them they managed to subdue Baranwen, and tied her hands securely behind her back. Breathless from the struggle but still growling with anger, Kerenza sat on Baranwen's legs for good measure. Gerry stumbled backwards to the wall of the chamber and leaned gratefully against the curved stone. The flames of the torches had been flickering and guttering in the air currents caused by all the activity, but were beginning to steady again. Gerry's heart was pounding from the tension and fear of the past few minutes.

Colenso called Ysella to her, and indicated Keyna's injuries. 'Send your healer to this place at once,' she ordered. 'Tell her we have a woman who has a deep cut on her hand and should not move; the healer will need to tend her here. Then gather all your community and bring them up to us; we will await you outside. I must address all the Gwenen together, but we need the healer first.'

Ysella didn't move. Instead, she gave Colenso a challenging look.

'Do I take instructions from you?' She came just short of tossing her head.

'If you ever respected the Tegennow a'n gammneves, then you should,' was the answer. 'I created them.'

'I'll go,' Kerenza volunteered. 'I can run faster.' Colenso acknowledged the offer, but shook her head.

'It must be one of your Guardians,' she explained, and added to Ysella, 'tell them nothing of what has happened here. I will do that.'

Ysella, conceding nothing, nonetheless did go, departing with her usual swaggering walk.

Gerry looked at Colenso. 'Will she do it?' she queried.

'Oh yes,' said the Wise Woman. 'She just does not want to look as if she has given in. That one would never take kindly to being told what to do, especially not by a stranger. That was why it mattered that she should be the one to bring the Gwenen. If they see that she has accepted my authority, however reluctantly, it will add weight to what I must tell them.' She turned to the others. 'Let us leave this place.'

Gerry was glad to get outside, into the light of a summer evening, fresh with a breeze off the sea which was blowing the light clouds about. Two birds tried to fly seawards but the gusts sent them back. Gerry's hair blew across her face and she tried to tuck it back behind her ears. She heard voices behind her as Kerenza and Morvoren emerged from the passageway, leading Baranwen between them, holding her arms. Gerry expected the Guardian to attempt to break away, to fight again or try to run, but instead she was silent and unresisting. Maybe it was because both her fellow Guardians had turned against her. Delenyk had been loved and respected by all the Gwenen, and that had been Baranwen's undoing. Gerry wished she could have met her. She toyed with the idea of going back by a couple of years so that she could see Delenyk, but knew she would have tried to find a way to avert the Guardian's doom. The Makers had been right to warn her; there was so much of the past she would want to rewrite.

Gerry leaned back against a large sloping rock. She would have preferred to sit down on the grass, but the prospect of struggling to her feet again when the others arrived seemed too hard. Colenso was tending Keyna, while Rosenwyn had brought the Labrys out into the evening light and laid it on the ground. She knelt beside it, studying it in detail. Gerry was mildly curious, as there was obviously a history to this strange weapon, but didn't have the energy to go and ask.

She guessed that once out of sight Ysella would take to her heels and arrive at the gates in a rush. She would enjoy summoning

252

everyone up here and not saying why. From where she stood Gerry could see right across the coast to the curve of the Lizard beyond Mounts Bay. St Michael's Mount was just visible, looking out of proportion without the familiar castle on top. The sun was laying cool shadows across the grass. The light was golden, the waves across the bay were silver-grey, ruffled in the breeze. Two small butterflies, their wings the blue of the lower bowl of the sky, darted between the gorse and the heather.

As Gerry watched them she heard swift, light footsteps, and Meraud came hurrying up the path, holding a bundle hastily wrapped in a cloth. She gave Gerry a quick smile of greeting, but went straight to Keyna, all professional concern.

'My name is Meraud, and I am the healer among the Gwenen,' she introduced herself. 'May I see your injury?' She unwrapped the sleeve which Keyna had used to try to staunch the bleeding, and exclaimed at the severity of the wound, but didn't waste time asking how it had happened. Instead she set down her bundle, opened it and took out clean cloths and a pot of ointment. Feeling squeamish again, Gerry looked away and saw the first of the Bees approaching. They were puzzled, some put out at being called away from their evening tasks, but all curious about the summons. They stood in a huddle, murmuring together and looking with wonder at the strangers. Gerry saw faces she recognised: Athwenna, who smiled at her as Meraud had done, and the young woman with the braided fair hair. Nessa, that was her name. Last of all came Hedra the teacher, using a stick to help her climb, and Ysella, looking round the assembled group and obviously pleased with herself. Gerry looked at Baranwen; Kerenza and Morvoren were standing each side of the Guardian in a seemingly casual attitude. None of the Bees could see that they were holding Baranwen with her arms bound behind her back.

Colenso stepped forward and raised her hand for silence. Rosenwyn rested the great axe reverently on the ground again and came to stand by Colenso's side. Keyna joined them, a neat temporary bandage on her hand. Meraud went to the Bees, her lively face alight with interest. None of them had the remotest idea of what they were about to hear.

Gerry wished she could take a picture to capture that scene. An image of the slope of the hillside, with the sun just starting to dip, the reddening light catching the faces of the Gwenen and the tops of the granite stones, and throwing the lengthening shadows of the Makers and of the Guardians, silent near the entrance to the fogou, across the uneven ground before them.

Colenso held the attention of every woman present as she addressed them all. 'My name is Colenso and I have much to tell you, some of which you will have trouble believing, and some of which you will not want to believe. Nonetheless it is all true, and your disbelief will not make it any the less so.'

She told them first of the making of the Rainbow Chalice: how those who fashioned it had searched far and wide for the knowledge that enabled them to create the wondrous artefact. She had not as yet identified herself and her companions as the Makers. Then she took the Kelegel from inside her robe and held it up in the afternoon sun. By some power, even without water inside it, the colours began to rise from the gemstones. Then the full arc of the rainbow reached out and upwards, and curved right across the top of the hill, descending on the far side. The Gwenen surged forwards as one, crying out with joy at the sight. Rosenwyn moved to intercept them.

'Wait,' she ordered. 'There is more to tell. Much more. Colenso has told you how the Kelegel was first made. What she has not yet said is that it was we who made it.'

The reaction was predictable: shocked exclamations and disbelief. These were voiced by a short, plump woman with greying hair who stood at the edge of the group.

'Begging your pardon, but that can't be true. You'd have to be hundreds of years old. Everyone knows we have had the Kelegel for centuries, in the keeping of the Guardians.'

Keyna, slender and lithe and obviously not beyond her mid-twenties, responded. 'Do I look that old? Yet I was born several hundred years before this time. Colenso,' she inclined her head to her right, 'has told you how the Chalice was made using much secret wisdom. When we worked on them – yes, we three – the gems acquired more powers than we had ever intended, or knew of. Meaning only to invest them with healing and learning skills, we were working with forces we did not fully understand. It was not until Gerralda came to us that we learned that the Tegennow allowed their Guardian to move within time and place.'

All eyes swivelled to where Gerry was supporting herself against the rocks. It was unnerving. She straightened up and turned to Kerenza.

'You told me, the first time I came here at Midsummer,' she said. 'You said it was rumoured the Guardians could go to other places and times.'

Then she addressed Hedra and Meraud. 'I'm sorry about avoiding your questions but I couldn't give you answers then,' she said. 'I did come from Trewellard but it might not even exist here yet. I come from a time in the future, where many women wear their hair cut short and dress in what would seem to you like men's clothes.'

Gerry indicated her smock and leggings. Morvoren gave a cry.

'I knew I had seen you before,' she exclaimed. 'You are the man/woman who came to us when the sapphire had been taken, wearing the stone itself, and escaped us.'

She looked ready to release Baranwen and seize Gerry instead, but Colenso halted her with a commanding gesture.

'You will get answers to all your questions, I promise you,' she said. 'Gerralda is guiltless of what you believe.'

A babble of voices had broken out, both at Gerry's words and at Morvoren's. Gerry looked helplessly at the Makers, then back at the Guardians. Morvoren and Ysella were both watching her with deep suspicion. Colenso allowed the outburst to continue for a little, then called for silence. She got it despite some reluctance.

'I told you I would speak of things you would not want to believe,' the Wise Woman said. 'I will leave the question of time for now, and speak of things closer to you, above all of the lure of the Tegennow a'n gammneves.'

Colenso trod with extreme caution over the next part; she didn't want a riot on her hands. She spoke of the beauty, power and intrinsic value of the gold and jewels and of how they could be coveted by men or women hoping to use the power themselves or sell them for profit. This they could all understand. Then she said that one man and his allies had plotted to steal the chalice. 'This man had powers of his own, and could have worked much evil if he used the Tegennow to augment them. It was he who sent the poisoned wine, through the aid of men he had corrupted or bribed from among your neighbours. He hoped to wipe out most of you, and so make his task of stealing the stones easier.'

Colenso paused, gauging the mood of her audience. There was a shocked silence but no disbelief at this. The sun had slipped a little lower, and the air was beginning to cool. The breeze ruffled the grass, stirred the garments and hair of the listeners. Gerry noticed Kerenza absently tugging at the skirts of her robe which, without her girdle, were catching under her sandals. Ysella must have hitched up her skirts to run to the village. Gerry noticed that Ysella had taken the opportunity to pick up another girdle for herself before returning. How typical that was. Yet she couldn't deny that in lending Kerenza her aid at the last Ysella had helped to subdue Baranwen.

A flock of small birds swept past, chirping loudly. They were on their way to roost in the belt of trees Gerry could see some distance away across the fields. These must be the trees where she had first seen the Wasps take the poison from its hiding place in the tree trunk. Colenso waited till the noisy birds had passed, then continued.

'Baranwen was aware of this threat to your treasure,' she said. 'Your Guardian took measures to combat it. She looked for an ally and at first sought fruitlessly. At last she found Gerralda Melinda Hamilton, a woman from a far different age but sensitive to the power of the Jewels and possessed of gifts of her own.'

Gerry scarcely recognised herself in this description. She looked sideways at the Bees. Many glances were now being cast at Baranwen, some of the Gwenen plainly wondering why their chief Guardian was allowing this stranger, even if she had created the Kelegel, to tell the story for her.

'Baranwen decided that the best way to protect the Tegennow was to separate them. It would deter any thief who was only after money, for the whole Rainbow would be worth incomparably more than any separate parts. And it would wreck the plotting of the man Iestyn, for the Tegennow must be complete to be of any use to him.'

As the only person other than the Makers who knew the

257

story behind what she was telling, Gerry was fascinated by how Colenso was directing the narrative. No word of blame had been apportioned yet, but that could not last. There was some surreptitious murmuring among her hearers but no-one wanted to miss a word. The rainbow arc held steady and Gerry watched it with longing. Of all those watching only she knew how soon it might be quenched for ever. Colenso passed the Kelegel to Keyna who raised the Jewels aloft. The colours swept out to circle the hilltop, then returned to a simple line beaming from the chalice in Keyna's hand down to the ground. As the circle disappeared there was a collective sigh.

Colenso's manner changed subtly, and Gerry found her hands were clenched as she listened. 'The Tegennow exercise a compulsion over all who come near them,' Colenso said. 'Think how diminished you have all felt in the time since you last saw them. Gerralda guarded them for a short time only, yet was all but enslaved.'

These words came at Gerry out of the blue, and struck her like a blow. She was about to protest when she recalled the fascination the Chalice had held for her since Kerenza first described it; and how empty and grey the world had been since she had given it to the Makers.

Once again she found herself the object of curious glances, but that was not to last. A shiver went through Gerry as Colenso's voice turned cold. 'There was another power the Kelegel conferred which we did not knowingly put into it,' she said, 'the power to extend life. Is there anyone here who can remember a time before Baranwen was Guardian? Or whose parents can remember such a time?'

Now there was a definite shift of mood. Faces became uncomfortable, puzzled. Gerry looked at the woman who had spoken before, the oldest of the Bees. The woman was shaking her head.

Colenso was turning into a judge before their eyes. Gerry wondered if she was the only person who could see it. 'Then think on this,' Colenso pronounced. 'Year after year Baranwen is Guardian of the Tegennow a'n gammneves. She uses them, reveres them, and gradually becomes enchanted by them, literally so. She is under their spell. Most of you never handle the Kelegel; even the other Guardians only do so rarely. Baranwen however is working with them, as well as using them on sacred occasions and at festivals; and seeking them out when she has no other duties, just to hold and admire them. She has become entrapped.'

It seemed to Gerry that the clear evening air was becoming thicker around them all. It was like watching a hypnotist to whose persuasions she was for some reason immune. For the first time she looked directly at Baranwen. The Guardian's face was rigid, but whether in shock, fear or anger Gerry could not tell. She must know what was coming. Morvoren and Kerenza were now gripping Baranwen's arms in full view but to the Bees it would look more as if they were supporting than restraining her.

The remorseless voice went on. 'This we could comprehend, deplore yet pity.' There were nods of agreement, while confusion, distress and a reluctant sympathy were mixed through the Gwenen, but heads went up at the unspoken 'but' in the last words, and uneasy looks were exchanged.

Rosenwyn and Keyna were still as statues now, not distracting in any way from the speaker. Tension was building that would soon come to crackling point like dry lightning before a storm.

'But there is one thing we cannot forgive.' Colenso turned slightly, with a brief glance towards the fogou where Delenyk's ashes lay, then continued.

'One woman close to Baranwen was becoming afraid,' she pronounced. 'She had seen her leader drawn again and again to the Gammneves. She was close enough perhaps to fear the look in Baranwen's eyes when she handled or relinquished the chalice. At the last she must have voiced her concern, and so sealed her doom.'

No-one had understood yet. Gerry could feel her heart banging against her rib cage, her hurts forgotten. She retreated as far back as she could. An invisible line had been drawn around the Gwenen and the Guardians, and it was being tightened. Gerry wanted to stay outside it.

'It was not perhaps Baranwen's fault,' Colenso said, 'that she fell victim to the Jewels. Then when she found they were at risk she used every resource at her disposal to protect them.'

Now Colenso looked directly at Baranwen, and every eye followed hers.

'It is here that we cross from the understandable if regrettable, to the unforgivable.' She raised her voice a little. 'Baranwen is gifted with many qualities: leadership, intelligence, resourcefulness, ingenuity; and she has abused them shamefully. With these abilities and the additional powers gained from the Tegennow, it is hard to believe she could not have found another means of protecting them than by separating them.' Colenso glanced around to make sure that she held the undivided attention of every woman present. 'I believe she had a dual purpose there: to make them unusable by anyone else, but also to fix the blame for her own actions on another woman. She gave the sapphire to Gerralda then brought her to your Guardians, openly wearing the jewel without knowing what it was. She would have been slain for theft and blasphemy had she not escaped. Baranwen could have branded her as the thief and no-one would ever have doubted it. Then she, Baranwen, could

260

have kept the Kelegel for her own exclusive use, as she had begun to crave. You would all have believed it lost for ever.'

Gerry remembered Baranwen in the coffee bar in Penzance, saying that she'd hoped to save Delenyk from her fate; but Colenso was right. Baranwen had spun a web of lies. Like Delenyk and Wylmet, Gerry was to have been sacrificed to the Guardian's lust for the stones.

'Gerralda told us that Baranwen would respond to anything that menaced the Kelegel,' Colenso explained, 'so I announced that I intended to disempower it for ever. The result was as I expected. Baranwen drew the three of us here at once, meaning to put an end to the dreadful threat we posed to her.'

So that was why the Wise Woman had done it, Gerry thought, horrified. Did that mean that Colenso didn't really plan to destroy the chalice? That saying so had simply been a device to bring the Makers to confront Baranwen? The Bees, as one, were appalled at the mere suggestion that the Kelegel could be destroyed. Nessa had tears running down her face.

Hedra had worked her way painfully to the front of the Bees, and turned to the Guardians. Ysella had rejoined them, affirming her rank, though she left Morvoren and Kerenza to restrain Baranwen.

Like Colenso, Hedra could command silence. 'Is this true, Baranwen?' she asked, addressing the Guardian and unknowingly echoing Morvoren in the fogou. 'You have not denied it. Or are you waiting until the end of these accusations to justify yourself? If you truly wished to keep the Jewels of the Rainbow for your own, that would be the most terrible wrong you could commit.'

'No, it would not.' Colenso had reached her moment at last. 'The most terrible wrong your Guardian has committed was the betrayal of a loyal and steadfast woman, one held in esteem by all. I speak of her fellow Guardian, Delenyk. Do you deny it, Baranwen?' For the first time since leaving the fogou she now addressed Baranwen face to face. 'Delenyk suspected your purpose, and you brought her to torture and a shameful death to protect yourself and your infamous desires. Yes, you needed to remove the Tegennow from the place where they were known to be kept, both to conceal them from their enemies and to make them accessible to yourself alone. That could have been remedied even now had you chosen to return them of your own free will, though you would have had to relinquish your position and remove far from temptation. But for Delenyk's fate no-one here will ever forgive you.'

Hedra began to speak again, but her voice was lost in the cries that broke out. Gerry thought they would attack Baranwen physically, but perhaps a lifetime's habit of respect held them back. At last the noise died down and Hedra was able to ask the Guardians, 'What do you say, all of you? Is this a tale dreamed up by these strangers who claim to have come from the past, but could equally be plausible liars? And Gerralda's actions have been strange in many respects. Who is speaking the truth?'

There was only silence. Ysella and Morvoren exchanged looks but did not respond. They were waiting for Baranwen to answer; perhaps hoping she would find some words of explanation, but not really believing it. No-one had truly thought Delenyk capable of neglecting her duties, despite the apparent evidence against her. Baranwen had been too desperate to anticipate that; or perhaps too desperate to care.

Keyna raised the Rainbow Jewels again and the invisible line Gerry had already sensed sprang into visible reality. The beams of spectrum light leaped forward and formed a circle like a boundary around the Gwenen, then crossed and looped to hold the Guardians as well. Colenso spoke out with great grief but implacable decision.

'We made the Tegennow a'n gammneves in joy and in hope,' she said, 'to serve and to aid, bringing knowledge and wisdom. Now we learn they have been corrupted and caused envy, violence, betrayal and death. This is more bitter for us than you could comprehend. The Guardians, who should be models of selflessness, now carry weapons and show many weaknesses: self-aggrandisement, love of power and, worse than anything, no understanding of the purity of purpose that we bred into the stones. They threaten and contrive...' Colenso paused, her voice cracking with emotion, then went on. 'You think the stones shine with colour and the radiance of light? These are dulled, poor imitations of what they once were. They would have dazzled you.'

Colenso was an aging, grey-haired woman of modest height and unremarkable appearance, but as she spoke she appeared to tower over all present. 'We will put an end to this travesty; the Rainbow Jewels will lose their gifts and you will never see them again. You should all return to the homes and families you left, to the lives you would have led had you not been chosen for the honour of serving the Tegennow a'n gammneves. You have this distinction - you are the last ever to hold that office.'

Had they forgotten Gerry? She doubted it, but she posed no threat to them now. When, and she now knew it was when, not if, they quenched the power of the Rainbow for the last time, the Makers would be thrown back to their own time, where their own chalice waited. That one would live through the centuries from their day until it reached this point and was destroyed. And she, Gerry, would be sent forward to the twenty-first century, to remain there for the rest of her life.

No visible lines of light held her, but Gerry found she couldn't move, any more than the others who stood on that slope below the crown of the hill, tied by the rainbow light they'd waited with such longing to see again. When the restraining forces were lifted, would the Gwenen converge on Baranwen in fury? Or would the loss of their life's purpose leave them too defeated to seek vengeance against the woman who'd single-handedly caused this ruin? Gerry didn't know. Like Nessa, she found tears starting in her eyes and running down her face. She wanted to cry out, to plead and protest, but couldn't do it.

Gerry couldn't, but Baranwen could. Held back from movement, from launching a final attack or flinging herself at the knees of the Makers to beg them not to proceed, her face was twisted in anguish. She let out a terrible cry, 'No, no, no-o-o-o-o!' The sound seemed ripped from within her, and echoed on and on, bouncing back from the rocks. Gerry found herself pitying the Guardian despite all that she'd done. Everything Baranwen had schemed and fought for, betrayed her vows and effectively killed for, was about to be taken from her. The woman whose power could bring the Makers to her out of their own time, who'd ruthlessly attacked the jewellers and twice tried to entrap Gerry herself, was helpless now. Gerry had guarded the gems for such a short time yet felt desolate at their loss. All the rest of her life looked empty, pointless and dreary. For Baranwen it must be a thousand, ten thousand times worse. Perhaps she'd already been punished in the most effective way. Leaving her alive to suffer the deprivation through however many years remained to her would be the cruellest sentence the Makers could impose.

Baranwen made a final effort to reach the Makers, using every vestige of power she possessed, but the rainbow lines held her back and she couldn't do it. 'Please - please!!' It came out as a howl, hardly human. Then she fell to her knees, wailing in utter despair.

Colenso threw out her arm towards Keyna, and the young woman came to her. Rosenwyn stood on Keyna's other side. The Makers raised their hands, all three joining to hold the Kelegel aloft. Gerry saw their lips moving but couldn't hear the words. Then the circles and lines of light, the red, orange, yellow, green, blue, indigo and violet, closed in on themselves and faded to nothing. Colenso raised her hand. The chalice disappeared.

There seemed to be no transition at all. Gerry found herself standing in her bedroom, shaking with sobs. And in her hands she held the Kelegel.

There was no mistaking the truth. All its glorious powers were lost.

Chapter Seventeen

Monday 30th June 2014, late afternoon – Tuesday 1st July 2014, morning

Gerry could hear Claudia moving around downstairs; so she must have come back more or less when she'd left. She'd lived so many hours today that she could understand what Baranwen had meant about overstretching oneself; but Gerry didn't want to think about Baranwen. She couldn't bear to look at the chalice, and shoved it into a drawer underneath her winter sweaters. Right at the back where she couldn't come across it accidentally.

All Gerry wanted to do was lie down and sleep for a week, but there was something she needed to do first. She went to her bathroom and splashed water on her face, then picked up her phone and rang the library. When she got through at last, by a lucky chance it was Debbie who answered.

'Hi, how are you?' she asked. 'Are you ok?'

'I've been asleep most of the afternoon,' Gerry said. 'You got in all right, then?'

'Oh yeah.' Debbie sounded amused. 'I told Hilary I'd had a bad stomach upset, so bad I couldn't leave the bathroom long enough to phone in. She believed me. It seemed easier.'

'Good,' Gerry said, but she needed to get on with what she'd called for. 'Debs, is Ryan in this afternoon?'

'Yeah, he's upstairs. D'you want to speak to him?'

'Please.' Gerry listened to the tone for over a minute, then heard Ryan's voice.

'Hello, this is Ryan. Can I help you?' He sounded unusually business-like, probably assuming it was someone wanting to book a lesson.

'Ryan, it's Gerry,' she said. 'About that gig. I really don't think I'm up to going out much for a while. I just need to take things easy for a couple of weeks.' Gerry trusted he wouldn't find out she was going to work at Cornish Studies on Wednesday and Thursday.

'Oh.' That was all but he sounded disappointed. Gerry tried to think of something else to say to him, but her mind was blank. Ryan was silent for a minute, then said, 'Okay then, I'd better get back to my client. Thanks for letting me know, and look after yourself.'

Gerry rang off, and was glad to find she felt genuinely relieved rather than regretful. Ryan was as decent a man as anyone could wish for, but her contact with Justin had left her too scarred to get involved with anyone for now. For all she knew, Justin had marked her for ever.

She went slowly downstairs to find Claudia drying the last of the lunch things with a linen tea towel. Claudia looked up as Gerry came in.

'Oh, Gerry, were you asleep?' she asked. Gerry couldn't guess what she looked like; dead to the world, probably. 'I didn't wake you up, did I?'

'No,' Gerry lied. That had been a long time ago for her. 'I've been dreaming,' she said, 'and I feel as if I'm still half asleep. I think the best thing is for me to just rest.'

Claudia offered her herb tea, but Gerry settled for an ordinary supermarket tea bag from her section of the cupboard. She sat in the kitchen and drank it, while Claudia took her own cup of tea and went off to do some paperwork in the office. Gerry stared at the garden, trying not to think. Outside the window there was a bottle brush with its comical bright red brushes, a hydrangea with unusually deep crimson heads, and a fuchsia covered with red and purple flowers. A trio of sparrows flew in and out of the honeysuckle which tumbled over the hedge.

Gerry tried to concentrate on the flowers, but couldn't keep her mind blank; thoughts kept intruding. Where was Justin now? He must know the Kelegel was destroyed; there was no point now in him coming and threatening her again. She had the answer he'd asked for; the Chalice could never have functioned ahead of its own time, in Justin's own day or in Gerry's. If only he'd known; all his plans and plotting had been for nothing. And now the Jewels of the Rainbow could never be used again. Gerry remembered holding them in the sun only hours – and centuries – ago, as the gemstones came alive between her hands, as the beams of light picked up the water within the cup and poured out their beauty. Gerry buried her head in her hands. What was left for her now?

When she got herself upstairs, Gerry fell asleep on her bed, and only woke later for long enough to make sardines on toast and get undressed. She was beyond exhausted from the overlong day and everything that had happened. She slept all night, without dreaming as far as she could tell. Certainly she stayed in her room and in the twenty-first century. When she woke in the morning, Gerry felt more awake, but no less wretched. She washed, dressed and went downstairs. She ought to do some shopping today.

Claudia had mentioned a village shop, and whatever they supplied would do. Food didn't seem important at all.

Gerry found Claudia dressed for work in pale blue slacks and a fine navy blouse, her make up applied perfectly as always. She was eating what looked like muesli from a blue and white bowl at the table in the conservatory. Claudia looked up as Gerry came in.

'Morning, Gerry,' she said. 'Did you sleep all right?'

'Yes, thanks.' Gerry headed for the kettle, looking out through the conservatory windows. It was a grey morning, threatening rain, but the sparrows were chattering again. 'Lucky my back didn't keep me awake.'

'Good,' Claudia replied. 'You look as if you're walking a bit more easily this morning.'

'Mmm.' Gerry picked up the kettle, but before she turned on the tap to fill it she heard the jingle for the Radio Cornwall news. The announcer's voice rang out clearly in the quiet kitchen.

"The body of a man was found on a beach early this morning, at the foot of the cliffs near Cape Cornwall. He was discovered by a local resident walking his dogs. The man's identity has not yet been disclosed. The police are asking for anyone who may have seen the incident to please contact them."

Claudia had turned to listen too, seeing Gerry's attention caught.

'Probably drunk, like those boys up at Newquay,' she said dismissively. 'They go walking on top of the cliffs at night after drinking pints and pints of lager.'

The news went on to the subject of parking charges, but Gerry had stopped listening. She was just wondering if she had the energy to make herself coffee when she heard the sound of a

269

car coming much too fast down the lane. Claudia got up, surprised, and came over to look out the kitchen window.

'That's not the postman,' she said, 'he doesn't drive like that. Who on earth is it?'

A small red car came racing into view. It stopped with a jolt, the tyres sending the gravel flying as the driver slammed the brakes on, then the car door banged. An unexpectedly familiar woman leapt out and hurtled across to the courtyard. Then there came a loud crash on the front door. Claudia looked at Gerry in astonishment.

'That's Monica Fraser,' she said. 'What does she think she's doing, coming up here? I've never invited her.' Claudia went to the door which led outside from the kitchen, facing the front door across the courtyard. As Claudia opened the door, Monica turned, then exploded into the kitchen, pushing straight past Claudia as she stood on the step, and glaring at both women.

'I've just come from the police,' she announced, not bothering with ordinary greetings. 'They wanted me to identify a body they found on the beach this morning.'

'Oh,' Gerry said, as Claudia seemed too outraged to speak. Poor Claudia – first Justin appearing in her house, and now Monica shoving herself in too. 'That must be the one we heard about on the news. Was it someone you knew, then?'

Monica made a strange sound, half a sob, half a cry of anger. 'Someone you knew too,' she said savagely. 'It was Justin. I had to go and look at,' she stopped, and sounded as if she was trying not to choke. 'It was the most awful thing you could imagine. He'd fallen and landed among a load of sharp rocks, there was blood everywhere, and his face, it was so damaged you couldn't tell it was him. It looked just like someone had hit him, and kept on hitting. All I could really be sure of was his clothes and of course his phone. Even his hands were all scratched and scraped.' Gerry had an unasked-for but vivid image of Justin's sensitive, capable hands. He had always kept them immaculate. The picture Monica was painting made her feel sick. 'And they may think it was an accident,' Monica snarled, 'but I know it wasn't.'

Gerry could feel her heart thumping. He can't be dead, she thought, he can time travel. Then she realised that was stupid. If someone had bashed him on the head, he couldn't have escaped like she had from the Wasps. Was she relieved or devastated? Gerry truly didn't know. Probably both.

Whatever she might be feeling, Claudia managed to keep her expression unmoved.

'Could I ask why the police contacted you?' she asked coolly.

'Probably found my number as the most frequent on his phone, or the last one he called, or whatever it is they do,' Monica snapped. 'I didn't ask them. I had other things to think about.'

'Really?' Claudia deliberately raised one eyebrow, a trick Gerry had never managed to achieve. 'And you say it wasn't an accident? Why would you think that?'

'Of course it wasn't.' Monica slammed her hand down on the glossy granite work surface, making the knives in the knife block rattle. 'He never fell over on the rocks on the beach, he wouldn't have been that badly hurt. He'd landed on them from the cliff top. And Justin wouldn't go for a walk on top of a cliff. Someone got him there and pushed him off; or bashed his head in first and then took him there and shoved him over. Trying to make it look like an accident. And it was down to someone who really hated him, hated him enough to keep on battering him, long after they could have stopped.'

271

Claudia remained deadly calm. 'I'd rather you didn't damage my kitchen,' she said. 'And is this the police's conclusion, or yours?'

'I don't know what they think, but I know what I know,' Monica snapped back at her. 'You just couldn't bear it that he chose me over you. You're behind this, I know it.'

'Hang on a moment.' Gerry decided to interrupt. 'When did you say this happened?'

'Last night, I suppose, though he wasn't found till this morning.' Monica turned her glare onto Gerry instead of Claudia. 'And you can stay out of this – it's nothing to do with you.'

'There's no need to be so rude,' Claudia said. 'And for your information, I was here all evening and all night. Gerry saw me, she can confirm it.'

'That's not much of an alibi.' Gerry had never guessed the superior, sneering Monica could lose control like this. Her voice was rising and she looked as if any minute now she would stamp her foot. 'You've got so much money you could pay someone to do your dirty work for you. Of course I'm not suggesting you pushed him off the cliff yourself. But did you know he warned me that you'd threatened him?'

Claudia looked scornful. 'That's absurd,' she said. 'I never did anything of the sort. I should say you've been watching too many gangster movies. No-one pays people to kill someone in real life.'

Monica was glaring at Claudia. Could the woman really believe what she'd just suggested? Gerry agreed with Claudia; it was a ludicrous idea. If Justin really had said that, he'd just been stirring up trouble.

'I know it was you,' Monica repeated. 'They'll find the evidence in the end.'

272

'Hardly,' Claudia told her, 'as it doesn't exist. I think you'd better go. I'd prefer it if you didn't come to my home uninvited. And I really don't recommend you go around throwing wild accusations. It will only make you look pathetic. It wouldn't have lasted, you know. Justin's affairs never did.'

So even Claudia could be bitchy if pushed far enough. With a last, venomous 'You won't get away with it, I'll see to that,' Monica slammed out of the house and back into her car, banging the door again and skidding into the turn onto the lane.

Claudia's tightly held calm vanished. She closed her eyes for a moment, reaching to support herself against the edge of the nearest surface.

'That must have been a shock for you,' Gerry said, looking at her anxiously. 'Can I do anything?'

'Yes please.' Claudia indicated a table at the far corner of the kitchen, with some bottles and glasses on it. 'Would you get me a brandy? I think I need it.'

Gerry went as fast as she could to the table, located the decanter and poured some into the nearest glass. It was probably top quality brandy and should be served in a special kind of glass, but right now Gerry doubted if Claudia would care if she gave it to her in a plastic tooth mug. She returned to find her landlady sitting at the table and looking pale. Claudia took the glass and drank off half of what Gerry had brought in one swallow, which wasn't like her at all. Then she put the glass down carefully in front of her and turned to Gerry.

'Thank you,' she said. 'Yes, that was a shock. Especially her description of the body. Okay, that was a gruesome experience for her, but she really enjoyed giving us both all those details. Monica's a thoroughly nasty woman. She's probably right, though, about it not being an accident. I expect one of Justin's shady deals caught up with him at last. His money could have come from anything, even drug dealing, and I know he mixed with some scary people. He always did sail close to the wind, acted like he could get away with anything, like he was immortal. It's hard to believe he's dead.'

Gerry found her hands were shaking, as Monica's news began to sink in properly. 'Would you rather be on your own?' she asked. She wondered if she herself would prefer to be alone to think, or to have company.

'Not yet, though thanks for asking.' Claudia picked up the glass, then put it down again and looked at Gerry who stood hovering, uncertain what to do or say.

'Can I do anything else?' Gerry asked in the end, though she couldn't imagine what.

'No, thanks.' Claudia was frowning. 'It's funny, it's like I wasn't surprised. I think that's how I managed not to break down in front of her. Perhaps I've always expected something like this to happen, the way he lived, the risks he took. And I suppose there were enough times when Justin was here that I wished I could see him lying dead at my feet. He enjoyed making me hate him.'

But you still wanted him – like I did. Gerry was so close to Claudia that the other woman's thoughts spilled into her own, unasked. Claudia sitting in her office at the gallery, trying to plan her next promotion but unable to stop thinking about Justin. Remembering his touch, the way his hands slid over her... Gerry tried to block it, but didn't know how to.

Then suddenly Claudia broke out in a changed voice. 'Oh God, it can't be true. Justin isn't –'

It came out more as a cry, or a wail, than a spoken

sentence. Then to Gerry's dismay Claudia, the elegant, the unmovable, buried her head in her arms and began to howl with shattering grief.

Chapter Eighteen

From 'The Cornishman', Thursday 10th July 2014:
Astonishing find at local site:

The Royal Cornwall Museum in Truro has received the donation of an item discovered at Chapel Carn Brea near St Just. A young woman who lives locally, exploring the rocky area near the top of the hill, found what now appears to be a chalice dating back to the Dark Ages in Penwith. She brought it in under the Portable Antiquities Scheme, which is generally used for finds made by people with metal detectors. Readers, please note – the Finds Liaison Officer would be pleased to see your own discoveries, especially those of archaeological interest.

However because this chalice appears to be made of genuine gold and gemstones, it comes under the Treasure Act so there are formalities to complete before it can be displayed for the public to admire. The Museum Curator is delighted with the chalice, which also bears an inscription which has not yet been deciphered. 'It will add considerably to our knowledge of the craftsmanship of the era,' she told our reporter, 'as well as being a truly beautiful object in its own right.'

The donor has asked to remain anonymous.
See picture of the chalice, left.

Chapter Nineteen

Tuesday 1ˢᵗ July 2014 – Monday 8ᵗʰ September 2014

After Monica's news, Gerry had spent the rest of Tuesday in a state of shock, and when Claudia came back from work neither of them seemed able to talk. Claudia looked as shattered as Gerry felt. Debbie rang in the evening to see how she was. Gerry didn't want to speak to anyone, but she owed Debbie for what Justin had put her through. She said she was feeling a bit better, which neither of them believed. Then Debbie said that Ernie hadn't been working on Monday but had been in on Tuesday and told everyone in the staff room about seeing Gerry at the fireworks on Friday night with her "boyfriend".

'Was Ryan there?' Gerry asked with a sinking feeling, guessing the answer before she spoke.

'Yeah. He went sort of quiet.'

Gerry knew Debbie liked Ryan, and wished things could have been different, but there was too much else in her head to think about Ryan now.

'I shan't be seeing Justin again,' she told Debbie, and felt several questions hovering at the other end of the phone. However her friend didn't ask them, and Gerry couldn't bring herself to explain.

After a pause, Debbie said, 'Monica didn't come in till mid-morning today. I've never known her do that. And she was in the weirdest kind of mood. Went into Hilary's office and shut the door, and when she came out at last, if it was anyone else I'd've said she'd been crying. Then a bit later the art librarian came in. You mightn't know him, he spends most of his time upstairs or else at St Ives. Anyway I was on the desk upstairs when Monica came up and started talking to him. You know she likes to think she's in with the art crowd. I was sorting out the printer up there as usual, and did my best to listen in. I got bits of it, and it sounds like Monica's seriously got it in for your Claudia. She was having a real rant about people who think they can get away with anything.'

Debbie stopped, and waited for a reply. Gerry couldn't think what to say to her. She knew she was being mean. Debbie had befriended and made her welcome when Gerry first came Cornwall, and she deserved better than for Gerry to shut her out now. But she literally couldn't think of a word to say.

'Gerry? Are you there?'

'Yeah, sorry.' And Gerry dried up again.

Gerry hadn't realised it would all be so complicated. She rang the Royal Cornwall Museum on the Tuesday afternoon to say she'd found a very old cup and could she bring it in to show them? The first day she was free was the Friday, and she was given an appointment with the Finds Liaison Officer. She'd expected to simply hand over the Kelegel for the museum to put on display, and was totally thrown when the woman looked at the chalice and explained that finds of gold and silver had to be reported to the Coroner under the Treasure Act.

Gerry was soon wishing she'd just put the chalice in a

Jiffy bag and posted it to the museum with an anonymous note. She finally managed to convince the officer. First, that she really had found it behind a loose stone in the fogou; and got the impression that fiddling about with ancient monuments was not approved of. Second, that she totally didn't want her name or picture in the papers or on a tag beside the display case or anything. Third, that she hadn't ever planned to sell the Kelegel. All she wanted was for the museum to have it. The museum people could deal with the Coroner and anything else involved in getting the chalice authenticated and catalogued and whatever.

Of course they couldn't know Gerry's real reasons. The three days she'd kept the Chalice of the Rainbow in her bedroom had been non-stop torment. Every minute she wanted to go and get the chalice out of the drawer, yet looking at it made her feel ten times worse. She could have wrapped it up and buried it in the garden, but Gerry could see herself lying awake all night trying to stop herself from getting a trowel and digging it out again. Besides, some burrowing animal might damage it. Yet despite all that, she simply had to know where the chalice was at any time. If the Museum took it, that would be sorted.

When at last she walked out of the solid stone building of the Royal Cornwall Museum without the Kelegel a'n gammneves, down the steps and along the path into the bustle of central Truro, Gerry expected to feel lighter, but instead she seemed to be carrying a weight inside her. Outside the windows of the museum café, a bus had just pulled in. People were getting out: purposeful shoppers, giggling students, a mother with a pushchair. Gerry looked at them all and wondered what it would be like to live an ordinary life. The Jewels of the Rainbow were out of her hands now, Justin was dead, and life held nothing but a dull emptiness.

Gerry didn't go back to Penzance library. She worked at Cornish Studies on the Wednesday and Thursday as she'd agreed. On Thursday it turned out that Chris, who she was covering for, had got glandular fever and would probably be off for a few weeks. Lowenna asked Gerry if she'd like to fill in, and she was only too glad to agree. It would mean three or four days' work a week, which would keep her in food and petrol. She didn't need much else, and it was a good excuse not to return to Penzance library. She didn't think she could face working with Monica. And she couldn't go back to the old casual friendship with Debbie; or with Ryan. No, Cornish Studies was a godsend. Gerry would have enjoyed working there if it had been a month earlier. Right now she couldn't enjoy anything. Graham tried to flirt with her, but Gerry was too numb to respond even if she'd been interested, which she wasn't. She felt a pang whenever she remembered laughing with Ryan in the staff room at Penzance. Gerry wasn't sure she would ever laugh again.

She and Claudia were polite to each other, but Claudia had withdrawn into an invisible shell, and shut her out. Gerry couldn't complain; she'd done the same to Debbie.

The empty weeks went by. The school holidays started and Penzance and the nearby villages – Newlyn, Mousehole, Marazion - were solid with visitors. Sightseers, surfers and families were everywhere; there were queues in the shops, the cafés, the petrol stations. People spilled off the pavements onto the streets in town, making driving dangerous. The pubs and the beaches were heaving with bodies. At Windhaven the bottlebrush was long gone, along with the foxgloves, agapanthus and honeysuckle. Only the fuchsia and hydrangea were still covered in flowers. The birds became quieter, and the nights began to draw in. Claudia turned the heat on for an hour in the evenings, saying the house was prone to damp because of the salt wind and the porous granite walls. Gerry should have gone home to Scotland to visit her family, but kept making excuses. She couldn't face being asked any questions.

Summer became autumn, and the leaves on the trees on the Penzance bypass began to change to red, gold and brown. The visitors returned home and the children went back to school. It looked as if Gerry's daily routine was set to go on, monotonous but safe, for ever.

Until the morning when Seona's letter arrived.

Words and phrases in Cornish used in the book

Bre/Brea	Hill
Fogou	Underground passage and chamber, stone lined, pronounced 'Foogoo'
Gohi	Wasps
Gwenen	Bees
Kammneves	Rainbow
Kelegel	Chalice
Kelegel a'n gammneves	Chalice of the rainbow
Medh	Mead
Tegennow	Jewels
Tegennow a'n gammneves	Jewels of the rainbow

n.b. Kammneves/gammneves is singular - Rainbow; Tegennow is plural – Jewels

Character list

In the present:
West Cornwall

Gerry (Gerralda) Hamilton	Library worker and unwitting time traveller
Claudia Mainwaring	Gerry's landlady
Justin Chancellor	Claudia's former lover
Gregory Chancellor	Justin's brother
Mr. and Mr.s Angove	B & B owners
Francis Trewartha	A jeweller
Alastair Fletcher	Another jeweller
Simon	Mr. Fletcher's assistant
Ethan	Deputy in Claudia's gallery
Peter	Claudia's gardener
Mike	Debbie's brother

Penzance library

Hilary	Library manager
Debbie	Gerry's friend
Monica Fraser	Not a friend
Ryan Luscombe	Gives computer lessons
Ernie	Agency staff member
Tasha	Works with children

Cornish Studies library

Graham	A librarian
Lowenna	Assistant manager

Elsewhere:

Seona	Gerry's great-aunt in Scotland (deceased)
Martin	Gerry's former boyfriend in London

In the past:

Bees/Gwenen:

Baranwen	Guardian
Morvoren	Guardian
Ysella	Guardian
Delenyk	Guardian (deceased)
Hedra	Teacher
Meraud	Healer
Kerenza	Novice
Wylmet	Novice
Nessa	Beekeeper
Athwenna	Potter

Wasps/Gohi:

Cathno	Villager
Elwyn	Villager
Kenve	Villager
Talan	Craftsman

Makers:

Colenso	Wise woman
Rosenwyn	Mother
Keyna	Maiden

Author's note

In this book I have put a fogou (stone chamber) at the top of Chapel Carn Brea; the one described is actually at Carn Euny, a few miles away. I have also put a couple of fictional villages nearby. The courtyard houses depicted were only found in the west of Penwith, at the far end of Cornwall, and date from the Iron Age, continuing into the Romano-British period. Remains of the foundations of some of these can be seen at Chysauster, Carn Euny, and Mulfra. The Midsummer's Eve bonfire is lit every year on June 23rd at Chapel Carn Brea.

The story is set in 2014, when part of the seafront at Penzance was still damaged from the winter storms. Smock tops and leggings were a popular fashion. The Penzance public library was still a two storey building in Morrab Road before its move in 2016 to the lower ground floor in St John's Hall. The Cornish Studies library was in Alma Place in Redruth. Both libraries are described here as they were in 2014. None of the fictional staff are based on anyone I've met working there.

Likewise there are art galleries in Chapel Street and jewellers' shops in Penzance and Redruth, but none of the owners resemble the ones in this book. There is often a stall at the top of Causewayhead but I've never yet spotted a glowing blue stone on sale there. Also the job agency referred to, though still functioning at the time of writing, no longer supplies staff to the council's libraries department.

Acknowledgements:

I owe heartfelt thanks to Kate Mole, Laura Hodgson, Louise Toft and Liz Allmark for all their enthusiasm and encouragement, which gave me the confidence to get this book into print., starting with Kate's 'You bet I want to read more!'. Plus extra thanks to Laura for converting my few lines of pencil into the cover I'd always hoped for.

I'm grateful to Daphne Chamberlain for support in the earliest days; and to Mark Leyland for useful advice about writing. Then to Inez de Miranda and Steve Blake for critiquing and support; and Teresa Benison for her creative writing classes. Also to Diane Johnstone and Sarah Westcott for professional critiquing, then Sarah Ash, Deb Adams, and the late John Nash, for valuable practical suggestions. Plus Steph Haxton for recommending TJ Ink.

Finally thanks are due to David, who thought he'd retired from the world of design and print but voluntarily returned to it to help with the technical stuff which is quite incomprehensible to me; and to Hannah at TJ INK for her patience in answering my endless lists of questions.

'Chalice of the Rainbow' is the first book in the Jewels of the Rainbow trilogy

The second one is 'Guardian of the Stones'